THE HAIRDRESSER'S SON

Gerbrand Bakker was born in 1962. He studied Dutch language and literature and worked as a subtitler for nature films before becoming a gardener. Bakker won the 2010 International IMPAC Dublin Literary Award for his novel *The Twin* (Vintage, 2009) and the 2013 Independent Foreign Fiction Prize for his novel *The Detour* (Vintage, 2013).

David Colmer was born in Adelaide in 1960. Since moving to Amsterdam in the early 1990s, he has published a wide range of translations of Dutch literature. He is also a published author of fiction. Colmer has won many awards for his translations, most notably the 2010 International IMPAC Dublin Literary Award and the 2013 Independent Foreign Fiction Prize, both with novelist Gerbrand Bakker. In 2009, he was awarded the biennial NSW Premier's Translation Prize for his body of work.

T0322904

THE HAIRDRESSER'S SON

Gerbrand Bakker

Translated by David Colmer

SCRIBE

Melbourne | London | Minneapolis

Scribe Publications
18–20 Edward St, Brunswick, Victoria 3056, Australia
2 John St, Clerkenwell, London, WC1N 2ES, United Kingdom
3754 Pleasant Ave, Suite 100, Minneapolis, Minnesota 55409, USA

First published in the Netherlands by Uitgeverij Cossee as
De kapperszoon in 2022

Published by Scribe 2024

Typeset in Adobe Caslon Pro by the publishers

Printed and bound in the UK by CPI Group (UK) Ltd,
Croydon CR0 4YY

Scribe is committed to the sustainable use of natural resources and
the use of paper products made responsibly from those resources.

The publishers are grateful for the
support of the Dutch Foundation
for Literature

N **ederlands**
letterenfonds
dutch foundation
for literature

978 1 922585 81 3 (Australian edition)
978 1 914484 72 8 (UK edition)
978 1 761385 69 8 (ebook)

Catalogue records for this book are available from
the National Library of Australia and the British Library.

scribepublications.com.au
scribepublications.co.uk
scribepublications.com

I'm a bear called Jeremy,
I can do most anything,
I can play and I can sing,
Little tunes like Do Re Mi.

When he heard me sing,
The King of Birds said to me,
'Here's for you dear thing,
A whistle that goes tweet-tweet
Tweet-tweet tweet-tweet tweet-tweet, tweet.'

I'm a Bear called Jeremy,
I can do most anything,
I can play and I can sing,
Yes my name is Jeremy!

(Theme song from the children's TV series
Jeremy the Bear)

PART I

1.

Igor is swimming. Or rather, swimming's not the right word. He doesn't have a clue about breaststroke or crawl, by the looks of it nobody's ever been able to teach him how to swim. He's moving through the warm, shallow water. He's sloping forward and seems to keep realising how much easier walking was before he got in the pool. His bends his legs, forgets to close his mouth, and gulps chlorinated water. He splutters and burps. Every now and then he shouts something. The woman in the bright-orange swimming costume shouts back at him. 'Igor! Don't shout!' The other woman, the one in the floral costume, hushes him and says, 'Close your mouth, Igor. If you go under water, you have to close your mouth.' The two women make sure nobody drowns.

There are others. Some of them can swim, they're even doing laps. One is wearing goggles. At the end of each lap, she pulls them off, blows on them in an attempt to dry them, then puts them on again. She swims to and fro imperturbably, everyone gets out of her way. Everyone except Igor. Igor grabs her by the legs, pulls her close and tries to take the goggles, maybe thinking he'll be able to swim then too. 'Igor!' the strict woman yells. 'Stop grabbing Melissa the whole time! Leave her alone!' The sun is shining on the other side of the enormous windows, it's almost as light inside as out. It could be summer, it could be winter. Igor doesn't know. Later, when he goes out on the street, he'll feel how hot or cold it is. He can't tell the seasons from whether the trees are bare or in leaf. Igor is the biggest of the bunch. A strong, well-built youth, almost a man. Nothing shows on the outside. If he crossed your path on Kalverstraat, you'd think, Wow, what a good-looking guy. His trunks are light blue, his hair is black, his skin is olive. Two boys who could be brothers hit him on the head with bendy frankfurter-shaped flotation devices. One copies the other, like twins. Sometimes Igor reacts, mostly not. 'Buaahh,' he says.

2.

'Henny! You know who Henny is! Do you ever listen when I'm talking to you? I don't think so, not really. You've never listened, always done your own thing. Is it because you never had a father? Just your mother to bring you up? You know I go swimming every week with those disabled people. I've been doing it for years. Not that it pays very well, but that's not why I do it. You know I do that, right? And I don't do it by myself. I couldn't. There's too many for that, and before you know it one of them's drowned. I said swimming just then, but that's not it, of course. They can't swim at all. They splash around a little, walk back and forth, grab a floaty and drift around. You know that pool, don't you? You go to that centre yourself at least twice a week. It's one-twenty deep. And don't think you can't drown in one metre twenty! That's why we're always there, *always*, with two of us, me and Henny. And now Henny's disappeared all of a sudden. Well, disappeared, *disappeared*. I know she's off on a Canary Island with her new boyfriend, one of those tax-dodging builders with gold chains and a wiry body and a bald head and a broken tooth he doesn't get fixed on purpose. From one day to the next she stopped coming,

5

and now she's sent me a message on WhatsApp saying it could be a while before she's back again. "Ko and I have got it so good here," she says. Not a word about our swimming sessions, not the slightest excuse. Every day a fabulous swim in the pool and a couple of rosés before dinner, she says. Are you still there? Simon? Did you hear what I said? With a photo of two glasses of rosé underneath it. The builder drinks rosé too. That's one photo he won't be sending his mates. They can't swim in the sea yet, it's still too cold for that. And they have such fabulous nights, but that's something I don't even want to think about. I hope she's bought a new swimming costume at least, because that floral thing she wears is a complete travesty, but that doesn't matter here because there's only me and the mentally handicapped to see it. Oh, sorry, *the mentally handicapped.* I'm not supposed to say that anymore. I'm a bit confused about what I am supposed to call them these days, but it's just the two of us now. Anyway, are you listening? I need you. You have to help me. I can't do the swimming session by myself. Before you know it, one of them will have drowned. And I know how often you've got that sign hung up on the door saying you're closed anyway. More often than not. Yes, I know all about that, a little birdy told me, and I also know it doesn't say closed and open, but I'm not going to start talking French on the phone. Why do you do that? Why don't you cut hair all day? You have to earn a living, don't you? I'd actually be happier if you didn't have time to help me out. I'd rather see you working day in, day out. What does your grandfather think about it? Well? Doesn't it break his heart to walk past and see that closed sign all the time? The poor man. You owe it to him to cut hair. You hear me? But you don't and you won't and that's why I'm asking. You have to help me, you hear? Otherwise it'll be your fault if one of those mentally handicapped people drowns. You hear me? You can't let me down! And they haven't had swimming for a whole fortnight already because there's always a kind of spring break in March and then, when they're allowed back in the pool, they always go wild.'

3.

CHEZ JEAN. That's what it says on the big window. Simon's grandfather is called Jan, that's why. Grandpa Jan did men *and* women, unlike Simon, at least mostly. Simon steers clear of setting and perming. He cuts and shaves. Nowadays shaving generally means trimming beards. And he does it in a barber's shop that still looks exactly like the hairdressing salon did in the 1970s, when his grandfather changed the name from BARBIER JAN to CHEZ JEAN because two bistros with French names and wickerwork wine bottles dangling from the ceiling had opened round the corner. Leather chairs with headrests, armrests, and chrome legs. Walls hung with old advertising signs. There's even a collection of Boldoot bottles on a shelf, and birch hair tonic (*'Säfte der Birken, Kräfte die wirken'*), and there's a cabinet with a sign saying FRICTION. Friction means 'scalp massage with a scent of your choice', and the bottles of friction lotion are in the cabinet. Old-fashioned scents for an old-fashioned custom, but Simon still does it, and there are enough people who want it, or better, have started wanting it again. It's a question of what you offer. After a long search, he found a supplier in France.

The sign in the door window doesn't say CLOSED and OPEN, but FERMÉ and OUVERT.

His grandfather comes once a month for a cut and shave. When he comes, he always has a whole block of time to himself because Simon likes to give him his full attention. Jan has left him everything, if you can say left when someone's not dead yet. Jan is eighty-eight and still has a magnificent head of hair. Simon makes sure that — besides his eyebrows and lashes — there are no hairs on his face, carefully removing them from his nostrils and ears. Jan always looks very smart, and claims he has to beat the elderly ladies at the old folks' home off with a stick. 'Twenty years younger!' he says. Simon doesn't believe him, but that doesn't matter. The rest of the month Jan looks after himself, doing a good job of shaving and never leaving any stubble behind in the folds of those difficult, wobbly dewlaps. His clothes are clean, and he always makes a point of choosing the same scent if Simon offers him a scalp massage at the end. Muguet, it's called, quite feminine, but on him it works. Jan used to do frictions too, and loves the way Simon's picked it up again. 'Make sure you charge a good bit extra for it,' he says. 'Nobody else does this anymore.' Simon charges a good bit extra — once in the hope that it would keep him from getting too busy — but everyone's glad to pay.

There are two floors above the shop. That's where Simon lives. All paid off and all his. The first thing he did was knock down the non-load-bearing wall between the kitchen and the living room. He did it himself with a sledgehammer. After that he gradually made the grand-parental home his own. There's no need for him to keep the sign turned to OUVERT the whole day long. He suspects he wouldn't be there if his father was still alive. If he hadn't boarded the wrong plane on 27 March 1977. The wrong plane that crashed on the wrong island. Like Henny, he'd gone on holiday without any advance warning. Alone. At least that's what Simon's mother thinks. Simon hadn't been born yet. It's possible his father didn't even know he was on the way. Simon was born on 4 September 1977, and he was predestined to cut hair — especially with that dead father. Fine by him.

4.

Three times a week he closes the shop door behind him at six thirty in the morning to ride his bike to the swimming pool, then swims from seven to eight. One hour nonstop. It's never busy in the pool and it's always quiet, nobody goes there for company or to catch up on the latest news. The sound of water splashing against the sides, maybe a distant radio. Everyone's there to swim laps, sometimes with grim determination. He keeps to himself. It's only when showering afterwards that he nods to people he recognises, the ones who are always there. They nod back. Of course there are some he likes to look at. They don't know he's a barber, nobody thinks of looking him up for a haircut or a shave. He doesn't know what the others do either, except for the lifeguard. He's a lifeguard.

(His bedroom is decorated with posters of swimmers. Aleksandr Popov, Matt Biondi, Mark Spitz. He brought them with him from the house he was born in. Spitz is from way before his time, but he thought he was a hunk and only later realised how much he looked like a seventies porn star. Almost nobody else comes into his bedroom, which is why he brought the posters from his boyhood bedroom with him and hung them up in it.)

He now swims for his own enjoyment, but once he trained every day of the week in this same swimming pool. He swam competitively, winning now and then, but somehow, as time passed, it turned out he wasn't cut out to be a winner. He won despite himself, not when he wanted to or needed to. That's no help if you want to become the Dutch champion or dream of the kinds of times Popov swam. Popov was actually stabbed in the stomach by an Azerbaijani just after the 1996 Olympic Games. They got into an argument at the Azerbaijani's market stall in Moscow. He almost died. A knife in that belly, the most beautiful belly ever in men's swimming. It took Simon years before he was able to swim the way he does now. For years he cursed it and couldn't understand what he was doing in a chlorinated pool if there was no point to it. Now he can do it, swimming for its own sake, and he's glad he never gave it up.

He doesn't actually have much hair himself. Once a fortnight he puts a half-guard on the clippers and eleven minutes later he's done. It's tricky, a lot trickier than cutting someone else's hair. With someone else you have the mirror and the real head. He only has the head in the mirror.

5.

'I saw this movie once,' says the young guy in the chair. 'The kind of movie people die in.'

Simon never actually says anything in reply. He always just lets them chat away. Very occasionally he'll go 'Hm' or 'Gosh'. He cuts and shaves, he massages scalps. He's not employed here as a therapist.

'There was this guy who got to make a last call to his wife. "I love you," he said. "I love you so much." I don't believe that at all. If I knew I was going to die, and not in a couple of months, right, but in a minute, or half a minute, I definitely wouldn't be calling my girlfriend to tell her I love her. That'd be the last thing on your mind.'

'Hm,' says Simon. He pulls the young guy's head back a little. He's not here for his hair, but for his beard. One of those hipster beards. Apparently these guys can't look after them themselves, and apparently they have enough money to pay someone to do it for them. There's nobody else, he can take his time trimming the beard. No one breathing down his neck. This guy smells really good. That's the barber's prerogative: you've got them captive in your chair, they're at your mercy. He runs his fingers over Adam's apples and down necks, and the customers think he's just doing his job. Soon, when the beard's done, this one will ask for a friction too. He always does. Simon thinks it's more because he likes the feeling of having someone massage his scalp, rather than for the scent or the supposedly beneficial effects. His hair is thick and full, and he's arrogant enough to think it will stay that way forever. Maybe he thinks about his girlfriend while Simon is rubbing his scalp.

'I mean, would you phone somebody if you're about to crash to your death?'

'Ach,' says Simon. That's the third word he uses. *Ach.* They don't even notice because he just keeps working. He's using the old-fashioned straight razor, with the ball of his left thumb pressing against the young guy's jaw to keep his head up and slightly to one side. The thick carotid artery winds down below his hand.

'No way,' the young guy says. 'Really not. At a moment like that, everybody's just thinking about themselves, surely?'

He's probably right. Simon is thinking about something completely different too. Crashing to your death. Knowing there's nothing you can do about it. Although in his father's case that moment must have been very brief, seeing as the plane he was on was just taking off and only reached an altitude of about twenty metres. Maybe thirty. He's always kept it at arm's length, the whole story about his father — it was his mother's story, hers and hers alone. It was her disaster, her grief. They were her memories. He runs his hand over the young guy's throat. He calls him a young guy, but he's not much older himself. About ten years. Maybe fifteen. He traces the course of the carotid with his index finger, the thin skin, the weak and inaccessible throbbing of the blood. The barber who has no reason at all to touch a customer's throat like this. The customer who doesn't notice, or lets him do it anyway. Simon rubs an expensive cream into his throat.

'Can you quickly do my hair too,' he asks.

'Of course,' says Simon.

'Lovely,' he says. *Lovely.*

At night, in bed, he thinks about Aleksandr Popov. That belly with a knife in it, his index finger, which still seems to hold a memory of that weakly throbbing blood. The straight razor — that's another one of those things — they love it. They think being shaved with an old-fashioned cutthroat heightens the experience, making it more intense, more authentic. A shave's a shave. He's got an electric shaver himself. It doesn't make the slightest bit of difference.

6.

The next morning he makes some coffee. It's six o'clock, not much is happening yet outside. The radio's on. He doesn't eat. He'll do that later when he gets back, before the first customer. Today the first customer's not till half twelve. He drinks the coffee standing at the kitchen window. It's getting light. The collection of branches out the back is breaking free of the buildings on the far side of the gardens and becoming a tree. Not long now, and there'll be leaves on the branches. A few birds are singing. He's not thinking about anything. He slept well. No dreams, and if he did have any, he's forgotten them. There aren't any lights on in the windows in the buildings at the back. He rinses the coffee cup, puts it on the draining board, picks his bag up off the kitchen table, and goes downstairs.

'Morning,' says the lifeguard.

'Morning,' says Simon.

There are already a few people in the pool. Nobody looks up. He wets his goggles and puts them on. Lane 1 is his lane, he likes swimming on the side of the pool. There's nobody else in Lane 1. He swims. One hour. Back and forth. After ten or so laps he stops thinking about what he's doing. His arms and legs do what they have to do. The timing of his breathing gets better and better. He doesn't hear much, but notices that he's no longer alone in the lane. Nobody's bothering him, he keeps to the right, the others do too. This is the time of day when it's quiet. The swimming centre only gets noisy later.

In the showers, the man next to him goes a bit wild shaking his head, flicking shampoo into Simon's eyes and making him think of his mother's mentally handicapped non-swimmers.

'Hey,' Simon says, 'watch it.'

'Sorry.'

'Doesn't matter.'

The man smiles. Or rather, he raises one corner of his mouth. Simon can't remember having seen him before. He dries himself and gets dressed in the cubicle. Instead of going straight to the exit he walks down the corridor that leads to the second pool. The water is completely smooth. The rectangular pool is a good bit larger than he'd imagined and he's not sure he's ever seen it before, although he knew it was here, of course. They give aqua aerobics for the elderly here too, swimming lessons for kids, some hours are even reserved for rehab. It doesn't smell like the big pool, there's a sweet scent in the air. The atmosphere must change a lot here depending on the various activities. The elderly don't shout. People doing rehab groan softly or make determined little noises. It's probably only the mentally handicapped who make a racket. He shakes his head and turns away.

The man with the newly washed hair is standing near the exit, smoking.

'Hey,' he says.

'Hey,' says Simon.

It is now completely light. In the bed of dark soil in front of the swimming pool there are dozens of narcissus, some of them broken. The air is fresh and clear. Simon sees the spring flowers. They register, but spring doesn't get through to him. The man throws his cigarette between the narcissuses. Together they look down at the smouldering butt. 'Filthy, really,' the man says. Now Simon can say that he's right, that it is filthy, but he doesn't.

7.

Almost nobody else comes into his bedroom, but he's not embarrassed by the posters. He got them framed; they're not posters in a boy's bedroom anymore. They've become art, the frames much more expensive than the pictures. The curtains are drawn, and there's a reddish light in the room. The man has fallen asleep on his side. His skin was dry from the chlorinated water. No matter how long you shower, no matter how much shampoo or bath foam you use, chlorinated water sticks. His breath smells slightly of ammonia, because of the cigarette. 'Sexy,' the man said when he saw Popov on the wall. Simon's lying on his back with no intention of falling asleep. The first customer will arrive soon. He doesn't know what time it is. Simon will have to wake the man up and send him on his way. First, lie still for a while, on his back.

Cut and shave, eat and drink, swim. Dead, unknown father, slightly hysterical mother. Never had a steady boyfriend. It was too easy, maybe, having an occupation thrown in his lap. He'd gone to hairdressing school, of course, but that didn't mean it was something he wanted to do.

He turns his head to the side and inspects the back of the man's defenceless neck. He's got red hair, straight. Redheads often have a lot of hair on the nape of their necks. It seems to grow faster than the hair on their heads, and the hair on their necks is the first to turn grey. I could offer to shave his neck for him, thinks Simon. 'Hairdresser!' the man shouted after following him into the shop. He sat down in a chair and looked at Simon in the mirror. 'Barber,' Simon said. He doesn't have a clue what the man does, why he can fall asleep here on a weekday. Simon thinks, At least I'm enough of a barber to always see hair the way a painter sees peeling window frames or a gardener sees overgrown shrubs. I've adjusted to it. What he's never adjusted to is another man asleep in his bed.

8.

'It's worse than I thought! Now she's not coming back at all. At least, that's what she says. Ko's taken on a job. A big job, a house for some Brit. The place is crawling with Brits. They all go there for those cheap and nasty holidays. The kind that drown here in the canals by the dozen when they're off their heads on booze or drugs. "It's still so divine here," she writes, "it's like I'm blossoming," and under that she's put another photo of Ko in his trunks, with his flat stomach and a gold chain. And he's not thirty, right? He's about sixty or so. How'd she manage that? She's gone mad! Henny in her floral swimming costume. They went on an excursion to the top of a volcano. "It stank to high heaven," she writes. What are you groaning for? What are you doing?'

(The man is getting out of bed. Which means climbing over Simon. It reminds him of a dream where Ian Thorpe kept having to climb over him to answer the doorbell. Thorpe was heavy, and Simon was like a ladder in a swimming pool — something to climb up and down. The swimmer kept coming back, no matter who was at the door. The complete certainty of that returning. It was a magnificent dream that smouldered within him for quite a while. For days Simon had a vague suspicion that the Australian swimmer really was his boyfriend and that he, in turn, was now wandering around thinking of Simon. While his mother rattles away without expecting a reply or a reaction, the man dresses silently. Strange — that body Simon was granted such natural access to a little earlier has already become a kind of forbidden territory. By pulling on jeans and a T-shirt he's turned them back into two different, distinct men. The man zips up his jacket, holds his thumb to his ear and his little finger to his mouth, turns, and leaves the bedroom. He can make a telephone of his hand as much as he likes, Simon doesn't have a number, and neither does he. No number and no name. Simon leaves his mother to it for a moment and checks the screen for the time. Quarter to twelve.)

'… never seen a volcano before and then she's stuck with this Ko …'

'I've got a customer soon,' Simon says.

'A customer? Well, they can put that in the paper. As long as you don't have a customer this Saturday because then you have to come help me. And don't think it's only going to be the once. Unless Henny's making it all up, we're not going to see her around here anymore. I've already told them to start looking for a replacement for Henny because you're not actually allowed to help at all because you're not qualified, but they can't do something like that from one day to the next, and they realise I can't do it by myself, so they're over the moon you're coming to assist, even though I told them it's stretching or even breaking the rules, but then I said, "That boy swims three times a week. That swimming pool's in his blood. It's second nature to him, and he definitely won't let anyone drown," and I told them that you're very good with that age category because you're still a kid yourself, a big kid with a barber's shop. No, I didn't say that, of course not, but I did think it. My God, Henny and Ko. Do you think I'm jealous? Am I jealous? I do wonder how a woman like Henny can end up with a slim builder on a tropical island. Is it tropical there? Or subtropical? What has she got that I haven't? Are you still in bed? Do I hear that right? Why don't you just say yes if I'm asking you to help me? Do I have to beg? Do you want me to beg? If you don't help me, I'll have to call the swimming off. I really can't do it by myself.'

'Fine,' Simon says. 'I'll come. I'll help you.'

'Was that so difficult? You won't get anything for it, by the way. I can't do anything about that. They can't just transfer Henny's pay to you. I don't need to explain that to you. But you're not short of money anyway, are you?'

'No, Mum, I'm not short of money.'

'Good. Lovely. It starts at eleven, make sure you're there at half ten. Don't expect them to be like us, though I know you wouldn't. Some of them hold on to you the whole time. Those people have a very different kind of, yeah, how can I put it? A very different way of dealing with physical things. Doing things like wanting to kiss you the whole time. They don't give it a second thought. They like it, the way it feels. It doesn't occur to them that people like us don't just do things like that. That it's inappropriate or unde—'

'Fine. I'll bring a stick to beat them off with.'

9.

The customer is the young guy with the beard's girlfriend. One of his few female customers. They came into the shop together one day, and right away the woman took a deep breath. 'It smells really good in here,' she said. It was the first and last time they came together. It's a good thing Simon generally limits himself to interjections, otherwise he could tell her that when it came down to it, her boyfriend would have better things to think about. Maybe their intention is to use him, Simon, as a go-between. You never know what people really want, what they really mean. In any case they both love talking. Especially about themselves. While trimming her split ends, Simon runs through their earlier conversations. Has either of them ever asked him a question?

'Jason's beard looked sharp again,' she says.

'Hm,' Simon says. The woman, who's called Martine, has fabulous, thick dark-blonde hair, which somehow always falls well of its own accord. It's not too thick, in other words, because then it would be unmanageable. Simon has never had hairdressers' eczema. The friction lotion he uses is all natural ingredients — that alone makes it quite pricey — and if he can avoid it, he doesn't use any shampoo when washing. He's wet her hair, and when he's done he'll blow-dry it. She doesn't want a scalp massage. She thinks they're something for men who love having another man rub their skull.

'We're going on holiday next week,' Martine says. 'That's why I'm here now. Old-fashioned, huh? Going on holiday, off to the hairdresser. Birthday? To the hairdresser.'

'Where are you going?' Simon asks. He looks at her in the mirror for a moment, almost as if to see if she's as surprised by the unexpected question as he is.

'The Maldives. Gorgeous place. Three weeks. With any luck, spring will have set in for real by the time we get back.'

'Hm,' Simon says. And just hope they don't crash. Or wait, they'll be on the plane together. Jason won't have to call her to tell her he loves her. He can tell her on the spot. Or not.

Simon has flown once in his life, but he doesn't remember it at all. He was three or four. A flight to Reina Sofia. They'd already stopped using Los Rodeos for international flights. Too misty. Too emotionally charged. The wrong side of the island. He flew back the next day after he and his mother had taken a bus along the motorway to the other side of the island, looked around, and taken the bus back. He knows he did it, he's been told, but no matter how much he digs, he's never unearthed a single memory. False memories at most, on the very rare occasions he looks at the photos his mother took on the day. Shots of empty runways and the square control tower, hazy mountains, clouds over those mountains. Maybe he would have remembered something, if only a smell, if there hadn't been any photos.

Blow-drying Martine's hair, he thinks for the first time since the telephone conversation with his mother about the man with red hair who crawled over him to get out of bed. Martine interrupts him.

'We've been together five years,' she says. 'That's why.'

'Hm,' says Simon.

'Why we've booked this holiday. Nice, huh?'

Only now does it sink in that his mother said that Henny and her builder are on a Canary Island. Is that why she's so wound up about it? Are they on Tenerife? Not necessarily, of course. There are plenty of other islands in the Canaries. Gran Canaria. Lanzarote and ... he doesn't know any others. Don't forget to ask Saturday. He turns off the drier and walks over to the counter, where there's a thick appointment book. In the corner of his eye he sees Martine running her fingers through her hair. That annoys him. Don't people realise how rude it is? Then he looks out through the window with CHEZ JEAN on it. It's started raining. The Saturday is free, completely free, just as he expected.

'Done?' Martine asks.

'Done,' says Simon. And with feigned jollity he calls out 'Have a good holiday!' as she walks through the door.

He sits down in the chair in front of the window. The only barber's chair in the shop he never uses for its purpose. There's never anyone in it because it doesn't get crowded enough; he cuts and shaves almost exclusively by appointment. The idea of having someone or even more than one person sitting behind him waiting for him to finish doing somebody else's hair doesn't bear thinking about. The OUVERT and FERMÉ sign is almost always turned so that FERMÉ is facing out to the street. His regulars know that, and aren't deterred. The only two who comment on it are his mother and his grandfather. 'It frightens people off,' says the latter. Simon answers that maybe that's the idea. 'Weirdo,' his grandfather says, but he must be able to tell from his grandson's voice that it's not a joke, and he doesn't press it.

In his Chez Jean days it was always packed in here. And not just with people waiting to get their hair cut. There was a coffee maker, a Wigomat, and everyone in the neighbourhood knew how to use it. Instead of a hairdressing salon, it was more like a community centre for their part of the Jordaan, and that was exactly how his grandparents liked it. Simon's father — who was called Cornelis — hated it. Apparently there was quite a lot of disagreement, with Simon's father in particular complaining about the place being full of 'spongers', as he called the local women and older men. For Simon, these were stories. All second-hand. People much preferred his grandfather to his father. But can he believe an almost ninety-year-old who brags about how many women chase after him in the old folks' home?

Not many people pass through the narrow street. It's not a shopping street. A little further along there's a bicycle repairman, and past that a picture-framer slash art-supplies shop. Two therapists, but neither has a shop window or an open door. There can't be many left of the locals who used the hairdressing salon as a community centre thirty or forty years ago. Unless they're in assisted living in Almere. I should go to Westgaarde with Grandpa, thinks Simon while staring unseeingly at the wet buildings across the street. It's mid-March. With Grandpa or by myself. He gets up and grabs the soft broom. Carefully he sweeps Martine's hair into a pile before clearing it away with a brush and pan.

Then the red-headed man is standing in front of the window, pointing at the sign on the door with his shoulders raised. His hair is damp. Simon shakes his head and gestures for him to come in. The man steps over to the door and tentatively pushes it open. Pretending to be shy. 'Would you …' he says.

'Sit down,' Simon says.

He takes off his coat and sits down without another word.

Simon doesn't put a hairdressing cape on him. That's to let him know this isn't a normal visit to a barber's shop. He takes a neck razor from the cart next to the chair and starts to carefully scrape away the messy grey hairs. I still don't know his name, he thinks. Was he outside in the rain, up the street a little, waiting for Martine to leave? The man evades Simon's gaze in the mirror. All very unclear. Is this the end or a beginning? He puts the razor down and uses a soft brush to clear away the hairs. Then he rests his hands on the man's shoulders. 'Done.'

'Thanks,' says the man. He runs a hand over the back of his neck and stands up. 'I'll see you,' he says and walks to the door. He hasn't even made a show of wanting to pay. He turns the sign around so that passers-by — if they notice it — can read OUVERT instead of FERMÉ. 'Bye, Jean,' he says. The bell echoes through the shop after he's left.

Simon goes upstairs to the kitchen and makes himself an espresso with an expensive Siemens espresso machine. The days of the coffee-maker are over, long gone. *Wigomat*, he thinks, what's that name doing in my head? I'm still fairly young, but kind of old too. He doesn't feel rejected. He doesn't feel relieved. He doesn't think 'prick'. Someone called him 'Jean', and that's not his name. He doesn't actually feel anything at all. Even the fact that downstairs the shop is inexplicably open rather than closed doesn't make him nervous.

10.

'I'm working on a new novel,' says the writer who used to have straw-coloured hair.

'Ach,' says Simon.

'With a hairdresser as the most important character.'

'Hm.'

'So now the question is, would you mind me sitting here for a few days?'

'Here?' Simon asks.

'Not in this chair, of course. There, maybe,' he nods at the chair in front of the window, 'or against the wall.'

'And then?' Simon asks. Against the wall is impossible, the very place Simon doesn't want anyone, where they could watch him from behind.

The writer whose hair is now grey has been coming here for years. A couple of small rings in his left ear, hands clasped together under the hairdressing cape, shoes planted firmly on the footrest against the skirting board. He almost always says what's brought him here. A literary festival in London. A book launch at the Dutch embassy in Berlin. An award ceremony in

Spain. He's like Jason and Martine. Old-fashioned, somehow. There's something on, something involving other people, a party, a holiday, a meeting — so you get your hair cut. But he's not completely like Jason and Martine, because the writer is terrified of flying. He goes everywhere by train. Simon wants to take the request seriously: this isn't just anyone, he's not the kind of person who only writes for himself. He's a translated author who's won prizes abroad, someone who lives from his work. Simon is, in his own estimation, an average reader. He has every book this writer's written, for the simple reason that he's given them to him. Simon has read the novels, and every time the writer sits down in his chair, he worries about being asked what he thinks of them, though he knows the writer would never do that because somehow it doesn't seem to interest him. There is one book, *The Only Child*, about a daughter who puts her mother in the cellar because she can't bear her anymore — he liked that one a lot.

'You can just ignore me,' the writer says.

'Yeah …' says Simon.

'What I'd like is to see what you do, and hear the words you use, words related to cutting and shaving, words I don't know.'

'But I hardly ever say anything.'

'You don't?'

No, Simon thinks, not usually. But with this man he does. Because this man asks him questions. He's not your average customer.

'Be a bit careful, by the way,' the writer says. 'There, on the back of my head, above my right ear, there's another one of those lumps. Fifty, and I still get bloody pimples. And I'll take notes, of course, the kind of things that get said.'

Carefully, Simon steers the clippers around the lump. 'Most people just start talking,' he says. 'About all kinds of things, it doesn't matter what. They don't need me to set them off.'

'And I won't come right away tomorrow. I'll come when I need you.'

'As long as you let me know. Some days I only have one customer.'

'Fine.'

Simon reaches for a guard. A half on the back and sides, number two on top. The writer has a nice brush cut. He sees the old, weathered face of a dead writer before him. A writer with just one name, which escapes him for the moment. It's a pseudonym.

'I have to go to Aachen tomorrow.'

'What's in Aachen?'

'Oh, a reading. Nothing special. Or, actually, it is special. It's with Daniel Kehlmann, who wrote a fantastic book a while ago about Till Eulenspiegel.'

'Never heard of him,' Simon says.

'No reason you should have,' the writer says. 'I always assume nobody knows me. That way I'm never disappointed.'

Yes, thinks Simon.

'I'm a bit in awe of this Kehlmann guy. He's quite a writer. I actually look up to almost all other writers. I feel like they're real writers and that I've ended up in their company more or less by accident, like a walrus in a colony of seals.'

'A walrus?'

'Yes, or a cormorant in a flock of seagulls. I don't know. Either way, a different species, one that looks around with a daft expression on its face and wonders how it got there.' The writer disentangles his fingers and pulls one hand out from under the hairdressing cape. He rubs his nose. Then whispers, 'All bullshit.'

'What?'

'Bullshit,' the writer says, a little louder now. He straightens the cape and wraps his hands neatly together again. He doesn't need a shave because he's hardly got a beard. In general, people with red or blond hair don't have much beard growth. They have some, but sparse. Usually not enough for a beautiful, full beard. Simon knows the writer is single, like him. There was a time three or four years ago when he, without any immediate attraction, wondered if this was someone he could live together with. The writer comes often, that's inherent to the use of clippers, and the writer seemed interested. 'Hey, barber,' he says when he comes in. Other people say, 'Good morning,' or 'Hello.' There's even one who says, 'Here I am,' as if Simon's been anxiously awaiting his arrival for hours. Sometimes just hearing the name of your profession spoken out loud is enough. They call each other by their professions the way others use surnames. Sometimes interest is enough. It didn't last long, that wondering, because you needed something to set things in motion, something like Jason's carotid — a sudden discovery or awareness of the other's body. The writer's head remained the writer's head — nothing more, nothing less.

'Walruses, with those bizarre tusks of theirs, they can look really daft,' the writer says.

'What?'

'Plans for the weekend?'

'No. Or yes, tomorrow I'm going swimming with the mentally handicapped.'

'The mentally handicapped? Swimming?'

'More splashing around, I think. Making sure they don't drown.'

'That's noble work. You don't get paid for it, I suppose.'

'No. My mother's regular colleague, Henny she's called, has suddenly left for the Canaries. I'm standing in.' He draws the finest comb through the writer's eyebrows, and carefully runs the small trimmer along them.

'And that book, if it ever comes, won't be about you, of course.'

'Ach,' says Simon.

Friday. After he's had something to eat, Simon googles Daniel Kehlmann. Already written quite a lot of books. Born in 1975, older than Simon, and younger than the writer. A run-of-the-mill face, somewhat dopey hair. One-and-a-half million copies of *Measuring the World.* Filthy rich, in other words. The writer once told him that an author gets 10 per cent. Two euros a book, three million euros. 'No dearth of humour and therefore accessible to a broad readership,' he reads on Wikipedia. Then he watches TV and drinks an espresso. Coffee before going to bed doesn't bother him. He always sleeps well.

In bed he reads the editorial of the latest issue of *The Hairdresser.* 'Entrepreneurs can get a head start by anticipating the trends of tomorrow.' Sure, he thinks, and lays the magazine aside. Just before he falls asleep the word 'noble' pops into his mind. Noble work. The writer in Aachen with Daniel Kehlmann, him in a paddling pool with a gang of mentally handicapped kids. And his mother, of course. He turns over to one side, sees Aleksandr Popov before he turns off the bedside lamp, and realises for the first time that he lies here in the dark every night while that same Popov — with Biondi and Spitz — watches him from the wall. No, in that moment each of them is doing or not doing things in their own place in the world. Concurrent existence. It's a thought he quickly shucks off. Some things are too big. He turns onto his other side, sniffs the man with red hair's residual scent for a moment, imagines the shallow pool by daylight, realises that he didn't ask the writer what his new book *was* about, and falls asleep.

11.

Simon wasn't prepared for his mother's garish orange swimming costume. It was Henny who had a floral one. And of course he knows who Henny is. Not from here in the swimming pool, but from birthdays and other special occasions, even Christmas sometimes. His mother and Henny have known each other for three-quarters of a lifetime. He loves Henny for the way she gently navigates his mother's birthdays, glancing at him now and then when his mother succumbs for a moment. *Succumbing* is what Henny calls it when his mother breaks down. Which is something you can expect on festive occasions. His mother winds herself up — almost literally, as if she's one of those tin toys and turning her own key — until a release becomes inevitable. He's never seen Henny drunk. Strangely enough, he felt a tinge of jealousy when his mother told him about the wiry builder with the half tooth and a glass of rosé.

'Simon!' his mother calls, though he's only a metre away.

'Yes,' he says, 'here I am.'

'Are you eating properly?'

'Sure. I cook every day.'

The orange swimming costume is dripping, she's already been in the water. No sign yet of any people with mental handicaps. 'You have to go in for a moment too, then the temperature won't come as a shock.'

'Is it that bad?'

'Try it.'

'Your swimming costume hurts my eyes.'

'I am completely indifferent to your boring navy trunks.'

The pool is too shallow to jump in. He goes down six wide steps into the water. Almost immediately his forehead feels clammy. He dives under and swims from one end to the other. You can't swim properly here, and he's decided that after his forty-five minutes of noble work he'll do at least half an hour of laps in the fifty-metre pool. His mother has taken a seat on the top step. 'The minibus will arrive soon,' she says.

'Where from?'

'A few come from home, a few from *a home*. There aren't any parents with them. That's the whole idea of this hour, giving parents with children who live at home some time to themselves. After swimming, they go to a day centre. The driver has a coffee at the restaurant and looks in here towards the end. When she turns up, you'll know it's almost over. And if necessary, she helps the children get dressed.'

'How old are they?'

'Between thirteen and eighteen? Twelve and nineteen?'

'So they're not all children.'

'What do you call that age group?'

Simon has to think about it. 'Youth?' he says.

'Fine. Youth. Youths, whatever. You'll get to know them. I'm not going through their names now.'

'How many are there? It's not a very big pool.'

'Eight, nine maybe? There's always at least one of them sick. If you ask me, these children get sick a lot more than normal kids. Youth, I mean. Sorry, youths.'

Simon wipes water and sweat off his brow. The water comes up to just above his navel. The sun is shining, the low spring light glaring into the hall at a sharp angle. He can count the hairs on his mother's shins. When he looks at her face, he doesn't see anything of himself in it at all. Apparently he looks like his father. Another one of Henny's sayings, whispered on maternal birthdays with the succumbing imminent or having just occurred: 'Thank goodness you take after your father.' His mother is wearing a bathing cap. It's not orange, but red. She couldn't care less. The hair on her shins, the clashing colours. As if she can tell what he's thinking, she says: 'They're like puppies, or other pets. They love you, they grab hold of you, they slobber all over you. Whether you're as handsome as you or as ugly as me. But pet dogs can give a nasty bite too. For no reason. They're unpredictable.'

'Why is it so boiling here?' Simon asks. His mother's not ugly at all. He doesn't understand why she's never been able to find another partner.

'I think it's mainly for people doing rehab. They have to keep the water temperature constant. It'd be way too expensive to adjust it all the time. And the warmer the water, the calmer our clients.'

'Hm,' Simon says. 'If I need to ask something or call you, I'll say Anja, not Mum.'

'Fine,' says his mother.

'Thanks.'

Simon is nervous. His mother is relaxed, and splashes her feet in the water. She's been doing this for years. He goes up the steps out of the pool, and when he's at the same level as his mother, she quickly squeezes his calf muscle. He shakes his leg, then goes

over to stand in front of the enormous window with his hands
on his hips. This is idiotic. People in thick coats are sitting or
walking around in the park behind the swimming pool. It might
be spring and the sun might be shining, but it's not warm. And
him here in his boring navy trunks, dripping lukewarm water.
He waves, but not to anyone in particular. It's not his kind of
place. Simon is someone who needs a wall behind him, the kind
of person who feels most comfortable in a corner. A boy in a
sandpit sees him and waves back. His father looks in Simon's
direction and says something. Simon undoes the bow in the cord
of his swimming trunks, pulls it tighter, and re-ties it. He turns.
From the corridor comes the sound of a schoolyard.

His mother — Anja, from more or less this moment on — is off
helping the mentally handicapped youths where necessary into
their swimming trunks or costumes. 'You shouldn't do that just
yet,' she'd said. Maybe I should never do it, he'd thought. One after
the other they emerge from the changing rooms. He soon notices
that it's quite a mix. There are two Mongs and, yes, he knows he's
supposed to call them 'people with Down's syndrome' even in his
thoughts. 'Hello!' he calls from the pool, where all kinds of things
are floating in the water: balls, rings, rods, an inflatable raft. They
look at him as if he's been standing here waiting for them for
years, as if he's Henny, but stay on the steps, apparently having
learnt to wait until everyone has got that far. Simon counts them:
seven. One of them towers over the others — a well-built youth
with black hair. Simon can't see what's wrong with him, not
Down's anyway. He looks like Aleksandr Popov.

   'Go on, guys,' his mother says.

   A girl wearing goggles leaps over the steps and into the water.
She starts swimming with a kind of breaststroke. The others

walk down the steps, his mother bringing up the rear. The two with Down's immediately grab a couple of floating rods and start hitting each other. Is it because it's been three weeks since they were in the pool, or do they always do that?

'Do they always do that?' he asks his mother.

'Yes, Sam and Johan like to hit each other. Just ignore it. Those pool noodles hardly weigh anything. Soon they'll start hitting you too.'

'Who are you?' asks Sam or Johan.

'I'm Simon,' he says.

'Are you a good swimmer?'

'That's Sam,' his mother says.

'Yes, Sam,' Simon says, 'I'm a really good swimmer. I used to swim in races.'

'Did you win?'

'Sometimes. Not always.'

'Have you got a kid?'

'No, I don't have any kids.'

'A dog?' Johan asks.

'No dogs either. I'm all alone.'

Sam hits him right in the middle of his face with the foam rod.

'Have you got a dick in your trunks?' Johan asks.

'Of course,' Simon says.

'Me too,' says Johan. He throws his rod away, pulls the elastic of his trunks forward, and hauls his dick out with his other hand.

'Gosh,' Simon says.

Sam too reaches into his swimming trunks.

'Leave it, Sam,' Simon says. 'I believe you. I can see you're a boy.' To his surprise, Sam does as he's told, and Johan too puts his dick back in his trunks. Now that this has all been established, the two boys go back to hitting each other with the rods, which are apparently called pool noodles.

'Good start,' his mother says.

'Shouldn't you introduce me?' Simon asks.

'Not at all. That takes care of itself. Look, Jelka's trying to go underwater. We have to keep an extra-close eye on her for the moment.' Jelka is a small girl with blonde hair who's wearing a swimming costume with built-in floats that make it virtually impossible for her to disappear underwater. She keeps saying 'Tut'. It's the only word Simon hears her speak. He limits himself to the ones who are walking back and forth in the pool, and tells everyone he encounters that he's called Simon, though none of them seem to care. A girl with an enormous forehead calls him Henny. Is that possible? he wonders. Can your intellectual faculties be so limited that you really can't tell the difference between me and Henny? He saunters around, getting whacked on the head with a noodle by Sam or Johan now and then, and avoiding any physical contact, something that clearly doesn't bother his mother at all. He can tell she's been doing this for years, how familiar she is with people with mental handicaps, with Down's syndrome. She holds them tight, rocks them to and fro in the lukewarm water, tosses a ball to the big youth with black hair. She even squeezes snot out of noses after saying, 'Blow!' The light is bright on the bodies, facial expressions, garish flotation devices, the light-blue tiles, his mother's red bathing cap. Everything in the same merciless spring sun.

'Igor! How many times do I have to tell you! What is it about Melissa that you can't just let her swim?!'

Igor starts bellowing.

'No, don't shout, that won't get you anywhere! Come here, so I can rock you a little.' But instead of going over to Anja, he heads straight for Simon, pushing Jelka underwater on the way. She pops back up again immediately.

A cormorant in a flock of seagulls. Simon sees it before him as if the writer was trying to prepare him for this yesterday. The cormorant grabs hold of him — a seagull — while the rest of the flock cough up water, swim on imperturbably, bash each other on the head with noodles as hard as they can, figuratively fighting for a scrap of food. Igor has wrapped his arms tight around him, pressing his head against his midriff. Simon tries to free himself by accelerating backwards, but Igor doesn't give up, he even tries to hook his legs around Simon's too. Simon tugs on the boy's arms, and when that doesn't help, he tries to prise his fingers loose behind his back. Igor lets go of his torso, but keeps his legs around Simon's. The boy is now lying on his back in the water in front of him, and Simon can see all too well that he, like Sam and Johan, and like he himself, has a dick in his swimming trunks. A belly almost as flat as bloody Aleksandr Popov's, an Adam's apple, black hair floating in the chlorinated water. Simon takes another couple of steps back, but Igor keeps his legs hooked around his and undoubtedly thinks it's a game, like throwing the ball back and forth or taking Melissa's goggles. Simon feels the back of the boy's knees against the back of his own and a glow inside his trunks, the last thing you want when you're standing almost naked in a sun-drenched swimming pool in water up to your navel. He grabs Igor's legs and wrenches them loose. The boy's head goes under and comes back up spluttering. Simon is free. Melissa swims past, touching his arm with one hand and a foot a second later. Sam and Johan are yelling somewhere behind him. Jelka says, 'Tut. Tut. Tut.' Simon lets out a breath, but Igor grabs him again, his head even lower this time, his nose against Simon's belly, against Simon's navel, his mouth close to the top of his swimming trunks. Comparative thoughts regarding cormorants and seagulls are far away. 'Anja!' he calls.

His mother walks over calmly and starts stroking Igor's back. 'Let go now, Igor,' she says. 'Simon's not used to that. He doesn't like it.'

Igor seems to hesitate. Simon feels his grip relaxing. The boy is incredibly strong. Again he prises his fingers apart while his mother tries to talk him round. The boy lets go of him and grabs hold of his mother, but differently, now more as if he wants to be consoled. Gently.

'Yes,' his mother says, 'Igor does that. I think he has separation anxiety.'

Simon is standing under the cold shower. He's embarrassed, although his mother's assured him nobody will have noticed it because 'things like that aren't an issue with the mentally handicapped,' and 'if it is an issue, they don't know what to do with it.' After that she thought for a moment. 'At least that's my impression.' Luckily Sam and Johan didn't spot it. They would have been sure to provide detailed commentary. The others, including the driver, are getting ready to leave for the day centre. Simon is in a shower cubicle, a staff shower. He said goodbye to his mother right away while climbing out of the pool. What does she feel when that boy hugs her?

Five minutes later he's in Lane 1. The only lane reserved for laps at this hour, the rest of the pool is free recreation. The racket is enormous. The fifty-metre pool is so bright in the sunlight it too feels like it's outside. He swims and swims, he pants, gulps in air, turns. The half hour becomes an hour. Swimming, turning, gulping in air. Cormorant, he thinks, as he hangs off a ladder to catch his breath — what rubbish. The writer just put that into my head.

12.

Simon is on a 63 bus with his grandfather. They took a train from Amsterdam Central Station to Lelylaan and changed there. It's Sunday.

'What made you come up with this all of a sudden?' Jan asks.

'All of a sudden?' Simon says. 'I had a customer this week who started talking about plane crashes.'

'I've been there about five times. The first was on the seventh of April, and the second was when they placed the monument. I don't remember when that was.'

'I've never been there at all.'

'Doesn't matter.' As usual, Simon's grandfather is looking very dapper. If this was England, he'd be a gentleman. Straight-backed and not an ounce of fat. Well-dressed. Simon sometimes imagines him as a veteran, though his grandfather never fought in any wars. He looks around with interest as the bus drives through a neighbourhood Simon wouldn't be seen dead in. It's a grey day. 'The third time,' Jan says, 'was 1987, ten years after. Ten years, not nine, not eleven. Nonsense really. And twenty-five years after too, in 2002. They made a big fuss of it then, some people even came from America.'

'Baden Powellweg,' announces a female voice.

'Almost time to get off,' Simon says.

'And once just to visit, without any special reason,' Jan says. 'That was in autumn.'

The signposting is extremely vague; at one stage, Simon and his grandfather end up in the Chinese section. There's a gate there, 'the gateway to heaven', Jan says. Leaning against it is a blue container with a brown lid and a big white sticker on the side saying NON-RECYCLABLE. There are Chinese characters above it on the wooden upright. A couple of Chinese people are rummaging around a grave. They don't look up as Simon and Jan walk past.

'I have no idea,' says Jan. 'It's fifteen years since I was last here. The weather was completely different then too.'

Simon searches for a sign. After finding it, he walks slowly in the direction indicated, looking around carefully, but a few minutes later they're back among ordinary graves with no trace of a path or a monument. 'How's this even possible?' he asks. 'That sign said we had to come this way.'

'Yes.'

They walk back even more slowly. Then Simon sees an entrance, a gap in a yew hedge. Beyond the gate is an enormous stone table, round. TENERIFE, 27 MARCH 1977. They sit down on one of the red-painted benches. The burial site is an enclosed square, hedged on all four sides. They've let the hedge get too tall. If you didn't know it was a monument, you'd overlook it. The round stone table is stained a dirty green, and looks old and shabby. All from long ago, partly forgotten, the place unvisited. There are shrubs with stones placed here and there between them. 'Not really a pleasant cemetery,' Simon says.

'No,' Jan says. 'When they were buried here, Westgaarde had only been open six years. It was just a field, divided into burial plots.' He's sitting up straight and doesn't seem particularly moved, and for the first time Simon sees him as a father who has lost his son. There are three of them left, and besides a dead son, he's a dead husband and a dead father too, but the dead father is a complete unknown and could have been anyone as far as Simon is concerned. A strange image comes to mind: his mother showing him a photo of a different man, a different person, a stranger. He wouldn't have noticed.

Jan lights a cigarette. The smoke blows into Simon's face. He stands up and starts reading the names on the metal plates. Is that zinc? Bronze? He reads them all and has already shuffled around the corner before he realises he's reading from A to Z. A moment later he sees that another name has been added. At the end of the row of names, around another corner, a plate has been screwed onto the stone plinth: OF THE VICTIMS NOT BURIED HERE, THE FOLLOWING NAMES HAVE BEEN ADDED AT THE REQUEST OF THE NEXT OF KIN. Then he looks at his grandfather.

'He was never identified,' Jan says. 'Forty-four people weren't identified. I know that an entire family from Friesland is buried here and not in Friesland, not at home, because one of the children couldn't be identified and KLM wanted to keep them all together. It was either all here, or four in Friesland and one here, and that was unacceptable. You can see from that plaque with names how people feel about something like that. They wanted the name here with all the others. Altogether on a plane on the day, so here together in a single grave. Then and now. Or at least as many as possible.'

'So why isn't his name written here too?'

'Your mother didn't want it to be. If you think about it, it's incredible that they already held a funeral here on 7 April. What did they actually have? Jewellery, scraps of clothing, teeth, medical records. The way they do it nowadays with DNA and everything didn't exist back then. Just eleven days afterwards, but with forty-four unidentified bodies.'

'So everyone they couldn't identify is buried here?'

'Yes.'

'And Mum didn't want my father's name on that plinth?'

'That's right.'

'Why not?'

'Well, because he wasn't identified. She was in denial at first, I think. She couldn't believe he was on that plane. He'll turn up, she said. But the days went by, and Cornelis didn't come back.'

'And you? What did you want?'

'It was fine by me. I know he's buried here, one name more or less on the plinth doesn't matter.' Jan blows out a column of smoke, throws his butt on the ground, and squashes it flat with the toe of one shoe. 'Filthy,' he says.

Really, thinks Simon. He walks past the names again and sees an off-white stone between the shrubs with REST IN PEACE, DEAR COBBY written on it. 'I don't understand,' he says. He swallows. What a name. It's probably a boy's nickname, although there are sure to be fifty-three-year-old men called Cobby too. The names of the loved ones under the inscription move him more than the idea that his father is buried here. Partly because of the way it sounds. *Cobby*. 'So there's not, what was it, a hundred and twenty people buried here, but a hundred and sixty?'

'No,' Jan says. 'There are 125 people buried here, including more than forty who are fully named but whose bodies weren't identified.'

'And the others somewhere else?'

'Yes. There's nothing strange about that, of course. They had an ordinary funeral in the town or village they lived in. Look at the Vs again.'

Simon walks back. The first name to start with a V is J.L. Veldhuyzen van Zanten. Simon reads it out.

'The pilot,' Jan says.

'Among his passengers. Are there cabin crew here too?'

'No idea. And he's here because he wasn't identified. The crash was his fault. Do you really not know anything about it?'

'No.'

'You could have asked me.'

'His death was part of Mum's life.'

Jan looks at him. 'And mine.'

'Yes,' Simon says. 'Yours too, of course.'

As they're walking back to the entrance, a distant argument reaches them from behind a tall hedge. They can't see anything, but voices are raised against each other. Then a black man in a white robe and a brightly coloured bowler hat emerges through a gap in the hedge. He smiles. Simon sees an almost square beard, with edges that are a little too straight, a rectangle around his mouth. He'd do that very differently. The man is holding a jar with hyacinths. Not an argument at all, just a different way of interacting. Invisible voices, no longer as loud, talk on. The three men greet each other with a nod.

'Did my father have a nickname?' Simon asks.

'A nickname?'

'Yes, something for short, a pet name.'

'Your grandmother sometimes made the mistake of calling him Cor.'

In the bus back to Lelylaan, Jan is less attentive of the surroundings. His hair is too long at the back. Simon feels like his grandfather has put him in his place. He may be pursued by women at the rest home, he may look smart and healthy, he may have smoked his whole life without getting lung cancer — he's still eighty-eight years old, and he lost a son.

'You mustn't forget,' he says after a long silence, 'that same year a train was hijacked and a whole primary school was taken hostage. That was in May. May, June. People died. The interest, if there was any, in the air disaster faded away.'

'Yes, I've heard about that,' Simon says. Apparently his grandfather feels the same way he does. 'Were you ever actually approached for an interview?'

'An interview? No.'

'As someone who'd lost family,' Simon says.

'Come on, in those days they didn't do stuff like that.'

The bus turns onto Pieter Calandlaan.

'Are you coming this week?' Simon asks.

'Hm,' says Jan. Just before they get off the bus, he says, 'And to think that there's a much bigger grave somewhere in America.' And later, in the train to Central Station, 'Fancy a genever?'

'Of course,' says Simon.

13.

That same evening, Simon is on the computer. Next to the computer is a glass of whisky. Once he's had a drink — two glasses of Rutte Oude in his grandfather's flat — it's easy to keep drinking. 'Look on the internet,' Jan said, and now he's surprised by how much you can still find about it. He knew the plane his father was on wasn't supposed to be in Tenerife at all, but he didn't know why.

A bomb *and* a bomb scare at Las Palmas. The bomb exploded in a florist's. Shop assistant Marcelina Sánchez was badly hurt and ended up dying from her injuries sixteen years later. All flights were diverted to Los Rodeos. Both planes were headed for Las Palmas, both planes were full of people on their way to something fun: the Dutch had booked a holiday with Holland International; the Americans were going to board the cruise-ship the MS *Golden Odyssey* in the harbour of Las Palmas de Gran Canaria. A Holland International hostess got off at Los Rodeos — along with all the other passengers — but didn't get back on because she had no reason to go to Las Palmas. She was off work and had planned to travel from Las Palmas on to Tenerife, where she lived. For her, the diversion was a lucky break. She still remembers the exuberance of the flight out, 'like a school excursion'. Later she became known as the only Dutch survivor. There was talk of congestion, talk of sudden fog, talk of an impatient KLM pilot who had his plane refuelled so he could save time by flying from Las Palmas back to Amsterdam without any further delay. There was talk of 'miscommunication'. There are photos taken just after the crash that show the emergency services putting out fires among the debris. That must have been before the bodies of the victims had been recovered.

Simon realises that he's looking at the spot where his father was burnt, the spot where he must have still been lying there somewhere at that moment. There is footage of an incredible number of coffins in a hangar at Schiphol, footage of those same coffins, but now in a long row in, as Jan said, a virtually bare field that must be Westgaarde — lots of people looking on. He replays the clip a couple of times in search of his grandfather. There are photos of passengers standing on a runway and staring at the burning planes, with others on or in the grass between them, people who have come from the American aircraft, sixty-one of them, or no, on another website he reads that there were seventy, and nine people died later after all. An aerial photo shows that the planes ended up a good distance from each other, the Dutch Boeing some hundred metres further along. It flew another hundred metres — if you had to swim it, it would take you two or three minutes — so the chance that a Dutch body is buried in California is very small, and vice versa. He reads an interview with the father of one of the victims from Sneek, who says that not one but three members of the family were unidentifiable; an interview with a stewardess who shoved people out of the American plane; an interview with the son of the Dutch co-pilot, who became a pilot himself. In some interviews the relatives get annoyed when it comes to the question of blame. Simon even finds a list with the names of the victims. His father's name is there in black and white, age in brackets, place of residence. He takes a sip of whisky and sees that almost two hours have passed.

Died instantly, it says somewhere. The expression always makes Simon think of a blind fruit fly with a thumb descending on it like an elephant. It dies instantly, crushed without even a leg sticking out on one side. Those people must have felt an enormous smash, and they would have definitely had two or three seconds to realise what was happening. That's far from dying instantly. That's two or three, maybe even four seconds of terror, despite the complete unexpectedness of the event.

Father. He hardly knows what to imagine by the word. *Unidentified*, that's something he can imagine, and he feels now how open that really is. How unfinished. You'll never know for sure. What was his father doing on that plane? Surely he hadn't signed up for a package holiday with Holland International? By himself? It was a charter flight, but that wouldn't necessarily mean they would leave seats empty. It was a very different time, a time when there wasn't a mass interest in funerals and frivolous ways of burying people, a time of not talking about things, suffering in silence, a time of picking yourself up and carrying on, a time in which terms like 'victim support' and 'trauma counselling' were virtually unknown. He reads somewhere that the haphazardly chosen group of people who were flown out to identify the victims went on to form the basis of the Netherlands' Disaster Victims Identification team. Only in 2007 was a monument unveiled on a mountain near the old airport — a spiral staircase climbing to infinity. The mountain could be in one of the photos his mother took dozens of years ago.

Simon types in *Monument MH17* and goes straight to a beautifully designed official website, and sees that in Vijfhuizen, besides 298 trees — on the website you can click on them to see the victim's name and the species of tree — 170,714 bulbs have been planted, all 'glory of the snow'. An idiotic number until you realise you have to google with dots: it's a date. They thought about it. Everything there means something and has a symbolic value, and it was completed in three years. Not thirty, but three. The list of victims of 1977 includes misspelt names and missing ages, whereas Tree Number 166 in Vijfhuizen is a Fraxinus ornus 'Ebbens Column' (manna ash) (including picture), linked to the name Hadiono Budyanto Gunawan.

Simon pours himself another whisky. He gets up and goes over to the bookcase where his books are standing upright or lying stacked, and puts the writers' four books, which aren't arranged alphabetically, together, then stares at them for a while. *The Only Child*, *The Day Tour*, *April*, and *Almond Trees Blossom Red*. I'll have to ask him sometime how something like that emerges, he thinks. How you decide a title. In one of those books there's a man who's not all there. Sometime in the last few days, that came back to him. The book with the ditch on the cover. Then he draws the curtains, street side first, then at the back in the open kitchen. He takes a sip and pours the rest of the whisky down the drain. That's not unusual for him: pouring himself a glass, then realising after the second or third sip that he's had enough, that whisky is actually filthy, just like cigarettes. How can you die from the injuries sixteen years after you were hurt? he wonders. It's dissatisfying. He takes *April* off the shelf and goes to bed. Tomorrow's Monday.

14.

'Sometimes I'm so glad I'm a woman,' his mother says.

'What?' says Simon. Monday morning. He's had breakfast, and he's already had a second espresso. It's a free morning. He wants to do a load of washing and clear the stuff off his enormous kitchen table. He doesn't understand how exactly it happens, but within a week or two the table is always covered with junk again. Clearing it is something you can do on autopilot. You do it without thinking about it, and suddenly it's three hours later. His phone is on the table on speaker.

'Things like that don't show with us. We can get excited without anyone noticing.'

'I wasn't excited,' says Simon.

'Yes, that's another thing about men. Their body reacts totally independently. Apparently they even get an erection when they're raped or hung.'

'Mum!' Simon says.

'Sorry,' says his mother.

'I don't want to talk about it.'

'No? But on Saturday you have to come again.'

'I'm not so sure about that.'

'I'm counting on you.'

'Have you heard anything more from Henny?'

'No.'

'Which island is she on?'

'Tenerife.'

'Is that what's making you think about my father?'

It's quiet on the other end. A bird is singing in the garden. A blackbird, Simon thinks. It sounds like spring.

'Who says I'm thinking about your father?'

'It seemed like that to me.'

'*This* is something *I* don't want to talk about.'

'OK. I went to Westgaarde with Grandpa yesterday.'

'What did I just say?'

'Yeah. Afterwards, last night, I spent hours online. Did you know you can find all kinds of stuff about it? Not masses of information, but quite a bit.'

'Simon!'

'Yes. But you forget sometimes that he was my father.'

'Come on, father, *father*. He got me pregnant.'

'He's still my father.'

'No getting round that. You were great yesterday with Sam and Johan. Sam and Johan are my favourites.'

'What's actually wrong with this Igor guy? It doesn't show with him at all.'

'Hm. Does it show that you're gay?'

'That's completely different.'

'How? Why?'

'I'm not retarded.'

'Challenged. Intellectually challenged.'

'Sure. And Sam and Johan are challenged by Down's.'

'With those two you can at least see that something's

wrong with them.'

'Yes, that's why I asked you what Igor's got.'

'I don't know, Simon. Something probably went wrong when he was born. Not enough oxygen maybe. He's a strange boy. Did you notice he's got it in for Melissa? He always has to get Melissa. It's like he can't stand her being able to swim, really swim.'

'I'll look out for it Saturday.'

'And don't worry about a thing. I think you did very well. Henny and I once had a girl who wanted to work with the mentally handicapped, who was planning on doing a course, but that was a disaster. She — how can I put it? She tried too hard to do her best, and the kids felt that. We already had Sam and Johan back then, and Melissa, but not Jelka, and Igor came much later. Melissa grabbed her by the boobs, and Johan kept hitting her with his noodle for so long and so hard that she crept off in tears. We never saw her again. If you get another stiffy, just realise I'm the only one who'll see it and I'm your mother, so there's nothing to get upset about.'

'That's the worst thing about it,' Simon says.

'No, come on. I don't understand how you turned into such a prude.'

'I'm not prudish at all.'

'You are totally prudish.'

'The other day you didn't want to know what Henny and her builder got up to at night.'

'That's different.'

'Really?'

'Yes.'

'Is he Russian?'

'Who?'

'Igor!'

'Not as far as I know. I've never heard him say anything.'

'I'm going to do a load of washing now.'

'Yes, you can't put it off forever. Have you got customers today? Or are you going to take it nice and easy again?'

'Now you put it like that, I think I might take it nice and easy today. It is a Monday.' He taps the red button and slides the phone away.

Three hours later, Simon has not only done a load of washing and hung it out, cleared the table of junk and wiped it down, but also watered the plant, done the vacuuming, and cleaned the TV screen. What's got into me? he thinks, sitting at the spacious table with a third espresso. The blackbird in the garden is singing nonstop. Why am I cleaning and tidying like a man possessed? He stares at the plant, a thing with large, leathery leaves, and tries to feel something. Where he is, how to go on from here, his place in it all. He can't really picture that 'all', but he knows vaguely what it means. The world. Life. On the day his grandmother was buried, he did the dishes and scrubbed the kitchen right up to the moment he had to leave for the funeral. Apparently it's a repression mechanism.

Five hours later, he's back at the monument in Westgaarde, sitting on one of the red benches. As he's alone, he's come by bike. That was more or less as fast as public transport, although Sloterplas turned out to be an enormous obstacle. When he checked the route on his phone after arriving at the cemetery, it turned out he'd turned the wrong way when he reached the lake and done almost a complete circuit. Sitting at his tidied and spotless kitchen table, he had suddenly had no idea what to do with his Monday. Before he could fall prey to a kind of paralysis, he'd gone out onto the street and unlocked his bike.

Today the sun is shining, which makes everything inside the square hedge look a little less shabby. His grandfather and his mother might not mind, but he finds it very strange that his father's name is not included on the plinth. Does he have to simply believe that his father's remains are buried here? Simon tries to imagine what it would be like to run Chez Jean together with his father. Giving people shaves and haircuts together, sweeping up the hair, taking coffee breaks together, doing the bookkeeping. For some reason, he doesn't picture his mother with them. It's easy to imagine them being divorced. Maybe Chez Jean would be called Simon & Cornelis, Men's Hairdressers. Simon and Cornelis, because that sounds a lot better than Cornelis and Simon. Simon's father would be around retirement age by now. Which year did Jan change the name anyway? Was that before 1977? Did they argue about it perhaps, or was it afterwards, as a consequence?

He stands up and walks past the names again. Again, like yesterday, he feels that it is all forgotten, so long ago, so dusty, possibly supplanted by the train hijacking. Those people had the bad luck that it happened when even TV was only just out of its infancy. Not really bad luck, they don't know anything about it, of course, it's his own interpretation, and now, here, he realises that he's too late, that he's been treading water, that he's effaced himself in favour of his mother, going so far as to overlook his grandfather. Is losing a child worse than losing a husband? An idiotic question. Maybe it's even worse to lose your father before you were born. There's the stone with Cobby on it. Underneath those four names: Klaas, Ina, Rense, and Tilly.

He takes a direct route back to the buildings at the cemetery entrance. Somebody is cycling towards him, somebody who uses Westgaarde as a through-route. Apparently that's allowed. It's a young woman with spiky, dark-blonde hair. A good women's hairdresser would have a field day on hair like that. 'Hello,' she says cheerfully, clearly in high spirits. Otherwise the place is dead. No shouting behind tall hedges. But, he thinks, if my mother had remarried after a year or even two, I wouldn't have known any better. My father would have been someone from a story, and Jan would have been a strange kind of step-grandfather.

Before falling asleep that night, he reads a bit of *April*. He still hasn't found what he's looking for. Just keep reading, he's resolved, not especially gripped by the story. Keep reading until I've found it.

15.

Simon is honing his razors. He finds it a calming job. Hone, thumb test, a drop of oil. He also uses shavettes if he doesn't have a sharp razor at hand, but only the blades are disposable. His shavettes have olive-wood handles. Simon loves beautiful things, and he can afford them. He cleaned the two mirrors earlier to make sure the customers have a clear view of themselves. It's Wednesday. He swam for an hour; it was very quiet in the pool. So quiet he did a couple of laps of butterfly. He can still feel it in his shoulders. Is it the spring holiday already? Things like that escape him; he doesn't have children or an office job. He doesn't have anyone, well, a grandfather, and he's due soon. And the writer, who's texted him sooner than anticipated that he's ready to come and listen. It's very quiet in the barber's shop, as if the spring holiday has descended outside too — if it *has* started. It's bright in the street, the sky must be clear above the buildings opposite. A reflection in one of the chrome armrests of the chair in front of the window is shining straight in his eyes. He gets up out of the barber's chair, sees himself moving in the mirror, and takes the hone and the razor over to the straight chair behind the counter.

The job is actually finished, the razor sharp enough. An empty ashtray is waiting next to one of the chairs. His grandfather is the only one who's allowed to smoke here. How could Simon forbid it? The man spent dozens of years casually smoking in this shop.

'You know what's strange?' the writer asks before immediately providing the answer. 'Not a single Dutch writer has ever written a word about that disaster.'

'Oh,' Jan says.

'At least not as far as I know,' the writer adds. 'I haven't read everything, of course. You can't.'

Simon looks at him. He's sitting on the chair in front of the shop window and staring out at the street, as if that makes him less intrusive.

'I don't want to either, of course,' the writer says. 'Are you ever jealous of other barbers?'

'Other barbers?' Simon says. 'I don't know any.'

'No? Don't you have meetings? Or trade fairs?'

'Fairs galore,' says Jan. 'I used to like going to them, abroad sometimes too. But Simon here doesn't find that necessary. Oh, those fairs in France.'

'No,' Simon says. 'I do read the trade journal.'

'What's it called?'

'*The Hairdresser*.'

'Ah, of course.'

'I used to like training people too,' Jan says. 'We always had a trainee here.'

'Really?' Simon says.

'Sure. I thought it was fun. Your father hated it. Not your grandmother. She was just crazy about my trainees.'

Simon scrapes the hair off the back of his grandfather's neck.

'What do you call that thing?' the writer asks.

'A nape razor,' Jan says. 'Simon honed it this morning. Just for me.'

'Hm,' says Simon.

'Simon's sitting on a goldmine here,' Jan says. 'Nowadays young guys just love going to the barber's. A barbershop isn't just a place to get your hair cut. It's a lot more than that. Recently I read in *The Hairdresser* that it's a "total experience". You've already got barbers who serve drinks during a haircut. But recently you've also had a remarkably large number of barber shops being shot at. That's odd.'

'Do you still read that?'

'Sure,' Jan says. 'Once a hairdresser, always a hairdresser.'

'Could you cut your own hair?'

'No.'

Simon leaves them to it. Maybe it's advantageous for the writer that he's got Jan of all people here today. Bits and bobs from the old days. Two hairdressers for the price of one.

'So you're a writer?' Jan asks.

'Yes.'

'What kind of things do you write?'

'Books,' says the writer.

'What are they about?'

The writer sighs. Simon sees it, but Jan might not have heard him.

'Yeah,' he says. 'All kinds of things.'

'Thrillers?'

'No, literature. Novels.'

'Historical?'

'No. I can't stand research.'

'You're doing research now, aren't you?' Jan pronounces it 'reesursh'.

'You've got me there,' the writer says.

'And now the friction,' says Simon.

Later they're sitting in a circle — Jan with a scented and tingling scalp in the barber's chair, rotated away from the mirrors — the window chair turned back towards them, and Simon having slid the straight chair out from behind the counter. He went upstairs and made two espressos. Jan is drinking a Rutte Oude. They've been talking about muguet, what it means. Only Jan knew. It's French for lily-of-the-valley, and Jan admitted that it's quite a feminine smell, but that didn't matter, because he still had all of the women in the rest home chasing after him, maybe because of the smell.

'Simon takes after his father,' he tells the writer.

'Do I?' says Simon.

'Yes. You keep things to yourself, just like he did. And you act like you don't enjoy it — working here. Sometimes I worry that one day I'll come by and you'll have just disappeared too.'

'You're supposed to talk about the hairdressing business,' Simon says. 'That's why he's here.' He gestures at the writer. *He*, as if he doesn't have a name.

'Ach,' Jan says, 'we're sitting here now, aren't we? You two with your disgusting little coffees, me with my genever. It's Wednesday afternoon, what else are we going to do?'

'Just disappeared?' the writer says.

'He was suddenly gone, and a day later he was dead, or, well, they said he was dead, and I've never seen him since. Not that I noticed he was gone. It was a Sunday.'

'Didn't you know he was going to the Canaries?'

'Not at all.'

•

Simon looks at the writer. Is he committing all this to memory? Jan is starting to enjoy himself. Is it because he has a neutral listener? Someone other than his grandson, someone he can be frank with? He wonders if this is how a book arises. An idea, a hook in your thoughts, and the feeling that it could turn into something bigger, grow into a rounded whole? He thinks about Jason, and from Jason to his visit to Westgaarde, and from the visit to Westgaarde back to today. It's strange with Jason, how stealthily stroking his throat felt so much more emotional than the actual physicality with the man with red hair. Does that have something to do with writing too? That describing something is somehow more important than what really happens? That it's detached from reality? He immediately resolves to reread all of the writer's books.

'So you're going to write a book about a hairdresser?' Jan asks, smoke spiralling up around his head.

'Maybe,' the writer says.

'But not about me,' Simon says. He stands up and grabs the broom. You can say, 'Everybody out!' or you can keep your mouth shut and grab a broom.

'That's a shame,' Jan says. He knocks back the last drop of genever, stubs his cigarette out in the ashtray, and gets up. He takes his coat off the hook. 'I'm off,' he says.

'Don't you have to pay?' the writer asks.

'No,' Jan says. 'And I get a genever thrown in too.' Before leaving the shop, he turns the sign on the door. Seen from inside, OUVERT becomes FERMÉ.

The writer stays seated.

'I was planning on doing some shopping,' Simon says.

'Yes, I'm about to leave,' the writer says.

Simon starts sweeping.

'Your grandfather opened you.'

'He thinks I should have more customers.'

'Why don't you have more customers?'

'I've already got enough. Plenty. I have no desire to spend the whole day trimming one beard after the other.'

'Why not?'

That's something Simon has to think about. Why not, actually? Why doesn't he spend the whole day on his feet? 'I think I find it too stressful, one customer after the other. A customer is a person, and people suck energy.'

'They give you energy too,' says the writer.

'I don't feel that. My grandfather used to rabbit on about football the whole time. With everyone, even me, despite knowing full well that football leaves me cold. I preferred talking about swimming or swimmers, but that was lost on him. The things he said, the things he asked, it was all just routine. He never actually listened. It took no effort on his part at all. Maybe he was just as fresh at six as when he started at nine. I can't do that. For me, every customer's a new person.'

'And your father?'

That's something Simon doesn't need to think about. 'How would I know?'

'What are you going to do for the rest of the day?'

Simon looks at the clock. It's just gone half four. 'Rummage around a bit. Cook, eat.'

'Our professions aren't really that different,' the writer says. 'You cut and shave, not too much, and I write, also not too much, and I spend the rest of the day rummaging around, cooking, eating, watching a bit of TV, reading.'

'You have to go,' Simon says.

'Yep,' the writer says. He stands up. 'Thanks. Fine that it turned out to be your grandfather. Old school.'

'You're welcome,' Simon says. 'Was this enough?'

'If I could come again sometime, that would be great.'

'Of course.'

'"Rummaging around,"' the writer says. 'What a beautiful expression. A way of making it through the day more or less without noticing.' He puts on his coat, and turns the sign back. 'I like coming here anyway,' he says with his hand on the door handle. He's talking to the door, not Simon.

'Really?' Simon says.

'Really,' says the writer. He pulls open the door and steps out onto the pavement. In front of the window, he stops to pull a packet of cigarettes out of a coat pocket, lights one, inhales deeply, blows out an enormous cloud of smoke, waves his hand in a gesture that says goodbye while clearing the smoke away from his face at the same time, and walks off.

Simon stares at the sign for a moment, which is swinging slightly to and fro, then notices that he's still holding the broom, leaning on it, like a council worker standing by a big hole in the road.

16.

Standing in the Albert Heijn aisle, Simon is at a loss for a moment. Food. But what? Every day you have to eat, and every day you have to come up with something to eat. The music playing on concealed speakers is distracting him. When did that start? In the end he buys prawns and cherry tomatoes, rocket, and some garlic just in case — he might have run out. A bottle of white. Bread, spaghetti. Outside, a very well-behaved dog is waiting for its owner, glancing up every time someone leaves the shop. 'Hey,' Simon says gently holding a hand out to the dog without any real desire to pat it. The dog ignores the hand and tries to look through him. Yes, Simon thinks, I'm getting in the way. There's just a hint of light left in the sky, the streetlights are already on. Another month, he thinks, and it will already be light an hour longer, or an hour and a half. I should eat out more often. If I eat out, I don't need to think about what to cook. On the corner there's a small restaurant, The Grub Shed, the kind of place where it's no problem to eat by yourself with your back to a wall, small tables. He used to eat there sometimes, but for no obvious reason he got out of the habit. It's Wednesday; in three days it will be Saturday. It's only when he's walking past the framer's shop window, almost immediately followed by the sign for one of the therapists — *For Wynia please ring 3 x* — that he realises what he was thinking. That boy keeps looming a little too large in his imagination.

When he gets home he puts the wine in the fridge and the rest of the shopping on the worktop, goes over to the bookcase with his paltry collection of books, and grabs the other three novels by the writer whose hair has turned grey in the meantime. He stacks them up neatly on the coffee table next to the sofa. He didn't pull out a cigarette until he was on the pavement, he thinks, instead of asking if he could join Jan the moment he saw him lighting up inside.

'Yeah,' his grandfather says. 'Me again for a sec.'

'I hear it,' says Simon.

'About one of those trainees.'

'Yes?'

'They were actually always guys. I don't know why, your grandmother did the interviews. She arranged it all.'

'And?'

'One of them was on the plane too.'

Simon is sitting at the kitchen table with a game of FreeCell open on his iPad. Next to the iPad is a glass of white wine. It's a difficult game. He's already started over again four times because it seemed unsolvable. He stares at a queen of spades blocking a seven of hearts. 'Huh?' he says.

'One of the trainees was on that plane. A trainee who had a placement with us at the time.'

'What?'

'Am I talking Chinese?' his grandfather asks.

'No,' Simon says, a bit stupidly. 'Together with my father?'

'No idea. There's nobody left to ask.'

'No.'

'But of course it is — was — well, odd.'

'And my father and the trainee knew each other?'

'Yes, your father worked in the shop a lot, but like I said he wasn't keen on the trainees — it was like he was jealous of them — so I don't know how well they knew each other.'

'Why didn't you say anything about it this afternoon?'

'Well, with that bloke there, a writer, so, you know …'

'What do I know?'

'He'd milk it for all it's worth, of course!'

'Oh.' Simon is still staring at the queen of spades and the seven of hearts, trying to force a breakthrough in the game while listening to his grandfather at the same time. 'Does Anja know this too?' he asks.

'Absolutely. When the boy's mother phoned, your mother was at our place. That was on the Wednesday. To tell the truth, we'd forgotten he wasn't coming in. We were closed, of course.'

'Bizarre,' says Simon. He suddenly spots a red five and a black four and an open slot on the upper left. All at once, the queen of spades is out of the way and the seven of hearts too, and his glass of wine is empty. 'Did you stay in touch with the family afterwards?'

'No. That's the way of things like that. You plan to do something, but before you know it, weeks and then months have gone by. He'd booked a trip, you know, one of those package holidays. The parents are probably dead by now.'

'You're not dead yet.'

'True. Far from it.'

'Did my father have one of those packages too?'

'Not that we know. Your mother never found anything about it. Not a single letter or anything at all from Holland International.'

'But it can hardly be coincidental?' says Simon.

'I don't know, son. Nobody does anymore.'

'No,' says Simon. He stares at the new game that's already laid out in front of him because he unthinkingly tapped *New game*. He hears a sound, not where he is but at his grandfather's. A kind of foghorn.

'Hear that?' his grandfather says. 'Dinner!'

'Enjoy your meal,' says Simon.

17.

Jelka is sick. Not Sam and Johan, they're just extremely quiet today. They haven't hit each other or anyone else on the head with a noodle once yet. Sam's asked Simon if he's got a bum too and Johan's already shown him his. When Simon remarked that it was a pretty fat bum, Johan surprised him by cracking up laughing. It's like indignation is completely foreign to them. Today the sun's not shining, and everything in the swimming pool looks more pleasant. Softer, greyer, even the noise seems muffled. Melissa is swimming to and fro imperturbably, Simon's mother is standing at one end of the pool and keeping a vocal count of how many laps she's completed. The girl with the enormous forehead who called him Henny last time has shaken his hand. 'I'm Simon,' Simon said. The girl said her name too, but it came out so strangely that Simon now thinks she's called Buari. Igor is sitting on a raft with his arms behind him and his head down, as if he's just swum five kilometres and is now exhausted, upper body bowed. His eyes are fixed on Simon. For some reason, Sam and Johan don't like him sitting there like that, and tip the raft over. Igor disappears underwater, comes up spluttering, and grabs both boys, one under each arm. 'Calm down, Igor!' Anja calls. 'What are you doing with Johan and Sam? Twelve!' Igor's not listening to her, or at least not looking at her. Melissa starts her thirteenth lap.

Igor brings Sam and Johan over to Simon. Like two puppies, they let Igor move them through the water, kicking their feet to help him. Once they've made it over to Simon, Igor lets go of them. They line up in front of Simon and look at him.

'Thank you,' Simon says. 'Igor.'

'Reuaahhh,' says Igor.

'Is she your mother?' Johan asks.

'Yes, Johan, she's my mother.'

'Wow,' says Sam.

'Fifteen!' calls Anja.

'She's good at counting,' says Johan.

'She is.'

Sam bends forward, looks to one side, then says, 'Four.'

'You're good at counting too,' says Simon.

'Go away, you!' Sam shouts at Johan. Johan waddles off.

'Three,' says Sam.

Igor stands there and doesn't say anything.

Sam waddles off too. When he's halfway across the pool, he calls out, 'Two!'

Two. Igor and Simon. 'Hey, Igor,' Simon says. The boy doesn't say anything, but takes another step forwards. Simon looks at his mother. 'Sixteen!' she calls before glancing in their direction. Then Igor takes Simon by the shoulders and gently shakes him back and forth, as if testing the firmness of his footing. 'What are you doing?' Simon asks. He has to say something, he can't just stand there, even if he knows that posing questions is completely pointless. They are about the same size, Igor maybe a couple of centimetres taller. The boy lets go of Simon's shoulders, sticks his arms through under Simon's, and grabs Simon's shoulder blades with his big hands. He pulls Simon towards him and takes a last step forward himself. Now he can't get any closer. Two bodies pressed against each other in an overheated swimming pool. Simon can see minuscule droplets of water glistening on the boy's lips. *Cormorant*, he thinks. *Seagull.* Now that's in his head, it's hard not to think it. He suppresses a childish inclination to call his mother, and hears her voice telling him that 'Things like that aren't an issue with the mentally handicapped,' and also 'They don't know what to do with it', but now he's not so sure, and suddenly he wishes there was nobody else in the pool, nobody except him and Igor, nobody to see what's happening here, especially now that Igor's started licking his throat and pressing his lower body tight against his. And he's doing it to me, Simon thinks, not to Melissa or Sam and Johan or Anja, or that girl with the big forehead, what's she called, Buari or something like that. To me. He doesn't want to think any of this, he wants to be set free, he wants to get out of this tepid pool, he wants to be alone in his barber's shop, or with a customer if necessary, an easy customer. He doesn't want to be here, he curses his mother, it's all —

'Igor!' Anja bellows. 'Stop it!'

The boy lets go of Simon immediately, then looks him in the eye for a moment before turning away. He roars something and leaps, as far as that's possible, through the pool to the other side, where Sam and Johan are waiting for him with their noodles.

'Fucking hell,' says Simon under his breath.

'Seventeen!' calls Anja.

Melissa doesn't see or hear anything. Calm and collected, she starts her eighteenth lap.

'You OK?' his mother calls.

'Sure, no problem,' says Simon.

Simon almost always looks at people indirectly. Through their reflection. Even on the street or in shops, anywhere really. He habitually avoids looking people in the eye. Simply because he has no desire to make contact. Eyes that meet yours in a mirror are at a remove, askew, the way you can suddenly see in a mirror that somebody's face is skewed, noticing something you don't normally see, probably because you're used to it. That look Igor gave him in the brief moment between being shouted at and turning. Straight in the eye, no filter, no mirror, not askew. As if there was somebody else inside the boy's magnificent Popov body. It was almost a shrewd look. Shrewd, not skewed. Straight through him, as if the roles were briefly reversed: Simon the intellectually challenged man, and Igor the one who was trying to fathom him.

Simon has to wank himself off, of course. The moment lingered in his body as a languid horniness all through the rest of the Saturday — one customer, cooking dinner, watching TV. He can't banish the objections entirely, but the excitement wins out over his reservations, and after it has ebbed he's left with the way the boy looked at him, and it's Igor's eyes — greenish-grey — that he takes into the night with him. Cormorant, he thinks again, because it's easier to reduce the boy to a bird, an animal. Easier, and somehow not as bad. Seeing himself as a seagull as well makes it even less worrying.

18.

'It's going better and better.'

'Definitely,' Simon agrees.

'You'll know all there is to know about working with people with special needs before you know it.'

'Henny will come back at some stage, surely?'

'Ha! I don't think so. I haven't heard anything from her for a while now. I think she's getting established there.'

'With Ko.'

'Yes, with Ko.'

'Hm.'

'Offer me something.'

'Sorry. Coffee? Tea? Wine?'

'Wine. White.' His mother looks around the room as if she's here for the first time. She always does that, a little surprised, as if she's wondering how it's possible that her son can have a whole house to himself, a three-storey house with a beautiful, streamlined open kitchen, a large plant, a washing machine, an iPad on the coffee table in the living room — things other people have too. Things that are completely normal, but not when her son has them.

Simon gets up and walks to the kitchen, where he pours two glasses of white and empties a bag of crisps into a bowl. He wasn't expecting his mother and had been sitting on the sofa with a book, reading a book like a real grown-up, and that had felt good. The TV hadn't been on, no distractions, no naked men on his iPad.

'Are you putting crisps out for me?'

'Yes.'

'I haven't eaten crisps for years.'

'Then don't.' He takes a big handful for himself and starts crunching away. Just to fill his mouth.

'What a pig,' his mother says.

Simon swallows. 'Would you like something else? Cheese?'

'No, wine will do me.'

'Should I cut your hair?'

'No, why, for Pete's sake? Do I look like I need a haircut?'

'No,' Simon mumbles.

'And what's more, you don't even do women. You don't enjoy it.'

'But I can. Don't you remember I used to dye your hair?'

'Yes, I remember.'

'I cut Grandpa's hair just last week.'

'Oh. What did he say?'

'*What did he say?* What do you mean?'

'What did you talk about?'

'Nothing. Nothing special, this and that, things in general, my father. There was someone else too, a writer who comes here often. He wanted to see what happens in a barber's shop.'

'A writer?'

'Yes.' Simon points at the book on the coffee table, *April*.

His mother gives it an uninterested glance and makes no effort to pick it up. 'Never heard of it,' she says, and sips her wine.

'Grandpa loved the attention. He leant right back. You know what he's like. Glass of genever. Cigarette.'

'You shouldn't let him smoke in your shop. But why were you talking about your father?'

'Oh, it just came up. The way things do. We'd been to Westgaarde, of course.'

'Yes, you told me,' his mother says. She drains her glass and holds it up to send him back to the fridge for the bottle. He fills her glass and tops his own up, to be polite.

'Two glasses,' his mother says. 'Always two glasses.' She leans back, rests a hand on one knee and balances the glass on her other, fingers loosely touching the base. Like a man. 'I don't think I really meant that much to your father.'

'What?'

'I don't *know*, but that's what I think. It was like his thoughts were always somewhere else.'

'How do you mean?'

'Oh …' She stares at the glass on her knee. A scooter goes through the street, a sound that's much louder at night than it is in the daytime. The rows of buildings box it in, and in the dark, without any background noise, it sounds much fuller. *Your father.* That's how she always describes him, as if he was only there for him. Never his name, never Cornelis, never 'my husband', although that last one would sound somehow ridiculous. 'He was always so dutiful. In everything.'

'And?'

'Yes, nothing really. No idea. But still.' She thinks for a moment and comes up with a better description. 'He took me for granted.'

Simon is about to ask a question he's never put to her before, because he'd never stopped to think about it before, until recently at Westgaarde. 'Did he know you were pregnant?'

She hesitates, sips her wine, then puts down the glass, not on her knee this time but on the table. 'Yes.'

'Is that why he left?'

'Could be.' She bends forward and pulls the bowl of crisps over. She puts a couple in her mouth. 'What flavour's this?'

'Salt and vinegar.'

'Nice. English.' She washes the crisps down with some wine, and holds up her glass again.

'Three glasses?' Simon says.

'Sure, let my hair down for once.'

Simon hopes his mother doesn't succumb. It's not often she visits him. She's the kind of mother who assumes that children visit their parents. What's more, she's busy. Choir, cooking lessons, all kinds of voluntary work, lots of friends, bridge club, book club. Now he stops to think about it, he wonders whether in all those clubs and associations she couldn't have found someone to help her out at the swimming pool. There's no point asking. He knows her, he knows he shouldn't press her. What she's just said took two glasses of wine, almost three. The new information from his grandfather is something he should hold back for now. As far as he's concerned, she doesn't need to stay much longer. He's the kind of person who needs to work through things on his own.

She looks straight at him. 'How on earth,' she says, 'did you come to be so indolent?'

'Indolent? What kind of word is that?'

'It popped into my head. Hard to motivate too. I had to nag so much, almost beg, before you promised to help me.'

'Yeah.' He thinks for a moment, but of course an answer doesn't occur immediately. 'Was I like this before as well?'

That's something she, in turn, has to think about. 'You were quiet. Calm.'

'I think I just let things come to me.'

'Yes, you are a bit of a follower.'

'Now, now.'

'It's not so bad.' She takes a sip of wine. 'What do you make of Igor?'

'What I make of Igor?'

'Yes.'

'Nothing. What you'd expect.'

'You don't think he's special?'

'Ach. I think Sam and Johan are pretty special.'

'They've all got something, each in their own way. But not Igor. And you can't tell anything by looking at him. I always expect him to start talking to me. As if one day the sounds he blurts out will turn into words and sentences.'

'No, I don't have that. He talks with his body.'

'Yes, he does. But he could do with a haircut too. It's as if they don't notice things like that in those homes.' She screws up her face. 'Not a good idea, this third glass.' She stands up, goes over to the kitchen, pours the wine down the sink, rinses the glass, and fills it with water. Which she drinks. 'So,' she says. 'I'm off.'

'OK,' Simon says. 'See you Saturday.'

'Yep.'

After she's gone, Simon doesn't return to the book. He sits down at the computer and types in the word *indolent*. Apathetic. Dull. Idle. Inactive. Inert. Lackadaisical. Languid. Lax. Lazy. Lifeless. Lumpish. Otiose. Plodding. Shiftless. Slack. Slothful. Slow. Sluggish. Torpid. Work-shy. Twenty descriptions. I'm not lumpish anyway, he thinks. Then he looks at everything he can find about the plane disaster, clicking link after link, trying to find new pictures. More. He wants to know and see more. He pours himself a third glass too. He watches a *Reporter* from 1987

all the way through. Putting up with Fons de Poel's annoyingly
nasal voice. Where before Simon paid attention to other things,
mainly searching for pictures and eye-witness accounts, he
now sinks his teeth into why the planes crashed. An American
from the National Transportation Safety Board relates that the
collaboration between the Americans, the Spanish, and the
Dutch National Aviation Authority went smoothly at first.
Until the moment when it began to emerge that the Dutch
pilot of the *Rhine*, Veldhuyzen van Zanten, was largely to blame
for the accident. 'Lack of cooperation from the Dutch became
apparent at that time,' says the American, Dreifus by name. Only
the Dutch Aviation Authority published a report concluding
that the crash was caused by a series of events and that 'human
factors' played no role, while the other reports, both Spanish and
American, took those same 'human factors' as a given. Simon
finds the Dutch expert from the Aviation Authority annoying.
He has a smirk on his face through the whole show. He realises
it's because this guy's father didn't die in Tenerife. He's there to
represent the technical side of things, and has to do his utmost
to remain plausible. He'll have known that the journalists have
already talked to or will talk to the Americans and Spaniards too.
He's not one of the next of kin.

I'm a next of kin, he thinks. For the first time in his life. Again he
feels how the disaster was hidden away in a corner, the dustiness
of it, the sense of it-happened-and-now-we-have-to-get-on-
with-our-lives. The enormous difference between 1977 and 2014.
It's weird, but he feels jealous, though he realises that in 1977
there were probably only two TV channels. The impact was much
less, people couldn't express themselves as directly as they can
now. Now they stand rows deep on the side of the motorway

when victims have been transported back to the Netherlands after a disaster in a foreign country. They even applaud.

The only survivor — if you can call her that — the hostess from Holland International, said in a 2017 interview with the *Reformatorisch Dagblad* that there really wasn't such a thing as support for victims. Don't talk about it, and just carry on. She told the KLM desk she was going home, she lived on Tenerife. Officially, it wasn't allowed because her name was on the passenger list and her suitcase was still on board. She asked her colleagues to take care of it and just went home. Clearly, in those days, or because of the circumstances, a suitcase in the hold without an owner wasn't an insurmountable problem.

Then he finds an interview he missed last time, with Veldhuyzen van Zanten's daughter in the *Trouw* of 27 March 2007. She saw the hand of God in the events: 'He [God] was there, even if it went completely wrong. That doesn't reduce the sorrow, but I do see God through my tears. I always prayed for my father when he was going to fly. I only realised later that I didn't pray that Sunday morning. It was as if God said, "Don't pray because I can't answer your prayer." And if I had prayed I might have rebelled.'

The disbelief about the death of her father was heightened by the fact that his body was no longer able to be identified. The crash was followed by a fierce kerosene-fuelled blaze. The family dentist provided a description of his teeth, the family were shown photographs of recovered items of clothing, but it didn't help. 'For a really extremely long time I had a vague idea that my father was still alive. Perhaps — I thought — he'd suffered an enormous blow, been hurled out of the plane and lost his memory. Soon my mother will call me and say, "Papa is back, what do you think of that? Come quick to Sassenheim." You cling to that minimal chance, hoping even when you know there's no hope. That makes it harder to process. But the longer ago it is, the more rational you become and you know — he didn't survive it. There's nothing left of you after such an enormous conflagration ... In all these years we've been to Westgaarde maybe six times. I have no memories of my father, I don't even know if he's buried there. He could also be buried in America or nowhere, in a manner of speaking.'

In a manner of speaking, thinks Simon. He drinks his fourth glass of wine, and turns off the computer.

If, he thinks, later in bed, a suitcase without an owner can and may be left in the hold, you could also have a false name on a passenger list. The situation was confused. He can't put it out of his head. Something sour repeats on him — that's what you get for drinking four glasses of white. He tosses and turns, then gets out of bed. Downstairs he turns on the computer. He searches for the interview with the hostess. And it really does say so: 'Several days later the Royal Marechaussee came to her door. Two gendarmes had to officially ascertain that she has survived the disaster. Her name was on the passenger list. She herself was the living proof she had survived.' Then he goes in search of the passenger list, remembering having searched for it before and seeing one that looked like a photocopy of an original document. Now he can only find a corrected list on www.project-tenerife.com that doesn't include the hostess's name, but does say that it might contain errors because of the coexistence of various 'definitive' lists.' Somewhere else he reads that the initial assumption was that there were 225 passengers, but the figure was later adjusted to 235, 'as there were several babies on board who were not included on the passenger list'. He counts the one- and two-year-olds, and comes to eight. But can you still call a two-year-old child a baby?

19.

'Half one,' the writer says.

'As usual,' says Simon.

'Is that easy or boring?'

'It doesn't bother me,' Simon says. 'In a while I've got one of those young guys coming for his beard.' He puts a number two on the clippers. If he felt like it, he could be done in ten minutes, but generally he works slowly and meticulously, if only to give the writer the idea that something's happening for his twenty euros. Number two on top, a half on the back and sides. Not that much comes off. After all, it's not that long since the writer was here. To tell the truth, Simon really doesn't understand why he's back again so soon. 'Do you have to go somewhere?' he asks.

'Marseille,' says the writer. 'In three days. A literary festival.'

'By plane?'

'You crazy? On the train. These days it only takes eight hours. You go to Paris first, and change there.'

'Yeah?'

'Yep.'

'Is something like that fun?'

'Ah, fun. I mostly look forward to it, but once I'm there, I feel lost. What am I supposed to do in Marseille?'

'Do you give readings?'

'Yeah, I don't mind that. I don't speak a word of French, but that's their problem. I keep making the same mistake. I always add a day or two extra because it takes so long to get there, but I forget that the other writers will all have left and I'll end up having breakfast by myself in some hotel restaurant with no idea what to do next.'

'Hm,' says Simon.

'You can say that again. One day I'll give up on it.'

There's an unusually large number of cars driving past. There must be roadworks somewhere. They're going very slowly, giving the drivers plenty of time to peer in through the big window.

'What am I wearing now?' the writer asks.

'What?' Simon says.

The writer moves his arms under the hairdressing cape. 'This thing. What do you call it?'

'A cape,' Simon says. 'Or a gown.'

'See. Now I'm getting somewhere.'

'Have you already started?'

'Yep.'

'And?'

'What do you mean, *and*?'

'Are you making progress? Is this helping? What's it about?'

The writer looks at Simon in the mirror.

'Sorry.'

'Doesn't matter. But I don't know either. No idea where it's going.'

'Rather you than me.'

'Ah, it's not really that hard.' He looks at Simon again. Skewed. 'You know what's really terrible?'

'No …'

'Me thinking after my last visit, why don't I have a father like that? Why don't I have a story like that of my own?'

'You can make it up.'

'Yeah, sure. Other writers are always better off. They've got something. An alcoholic father, Iran as country of origin, a brother who killed himself, a grandfather in the resistance, a mother with a pigsty full of rescue pigs, a grandmother who knew Queen Juliana, Asperger's. Haven't you ever felt an urge to delve into that plane crash a little more?'

'Yes.'

'Last time, I got the impression you weren't involved with it at all.'

'Oh.'

'And how's it actually going with that swimming you're doing? Is that OK?'

'It's nice, yeah.'

'Nice? Apparently you're not allowed to say that anymore.'

'Why not?'

'Because it's meaningless.'

'I don't know how else to put it. And I wouldn't really call it swimming. There's only one of them who can more or less swim, Melissa. The rest just splash around. It's about making sure they don't drown.' Simon has no desire to say anything about Igor. Or, rather, he's on his guard about mentioning him.

'Would you like to go swimming with me some time?'

'Huh?'

'Or catch a movie. Go out for a meal. Somewhere other than here. Neutral territory. We've known each other for years.'

'OK.'

'You are single, aren't you?'

'Yes.'

'I'm single too.'

'As if it's that simple …' To finish off, Simon uses the small trimmer to remove the hair in the writer's ears. Before he realises what he's doing, he's blown the little hairs out of one ear. 'Sorry,' he says. 'I was distracted for a moment.'

'No problem,' the writer says. 'It's been a long time since anyone blew in my ear.'

Simon removes the cape with a tug. 'Done,' he says.

The writer runs a hand over his head. 'Excellent, again. Worthy of Marseille.'

'My pleasure,' says Simon.

'And now I want a friction.'

'Really?'

'Yes. I have to try that sometime.'

'Then you have to choose a scent.'

'You do it. I wouldn't have a clue.'

Simon goes over to the cabinet with the lotions, chooses a bottle, and comes back to the chair.

'What have you got?' the writer asks.

'Eau de Portugal.'

'Sounds good.'

Simon cups his hand, tips a big splash of lotion onto it, and starts massaging it in.

'Lemon!'

'Amongst other things.'

The writer has closed his eyes. He moves his feet up and down, looking very content. 'Yes,' he says quietly. 'A father and a plane crash.'

'Shall we arrange a day now?'

Simon looks at him from behind the counter. 'Go to France

first. We'll arrange something when you're back. OK?'

'Fine.' He waits a moment, then pulls a wallet out of his back pocket. He takes out three ten-euro notes. 'Thanks,' he says.

'My pleasure,' Simon says again. 'Have fun in Marseille.' He stuffs the money he would normally place neatly in the till in his trouser pocket. After their conversation, this money feels different. He tries to calculate how much he's received as a tip from the writer over the years. If he only uses the clippers, he charges fifteen euros.

Again the writer lights a cigarette the moment he's stepped out of the door. This time he doesn't wave to Simon. It takes a couple of seconds for the bell to stop tinkling. Simon glances at the clock. Almost an hour before the guy with the beard is due. He sweeps the hair together while one car after the other drives past. They all see a barber sweeping up somebody else's mess, he thinks. Then he goes upstairs to make an espresso.

20.

Another sunny day. This spring has been tremendously sunny. Bright light shining in through the big windows. Sam and Johan have abandoned the noodles and are getting a swimming lesson from Melissa, who has given up her usual imperturbability to teach them.

'I didn't know Melissa was such a good communicator,' Simon says.

'Ha. She once literally told me that she didn't understand why they always put her with all these retards,' his mother says. 'She did have to repeat it three times before I understood, but still.'

She's holding both boys by one foot. They're lying — more or less — on rectangular floats, and thrashing their arms to move forward. Melissa decides whether or not to let them, pulling them back if she feels like they're not following instructions well enough. Jelka and the girl Buari are floating in a corner of the pool. It's like Jelka's telling whole stories, her 'tat, tat, tat,' intoned as if every 'tat' means something else. The stories aren't making much of an impression on Buari, who's picking her nose.

'Where's Igor?' Simon asks.

'He's coming.'

'Separate from the others?'

'He wasn't ready when the minibus arrived. Someone from the home's bringing him.'

'Not ready?' Simon says.

'No,' his mother says. 'Maybe he couldn't find his trunks.'

They're sitting on the steps and staring at the bare crowns of the trees in the park. Anja is up to her breasts in the water, Simon with just his lower legs.

'Strange,' his mother says. 'Sometimes you can forget yourself and think it's summer, but then it's really weird to see the trees without any leaves on them.'

'Summer's still a long way off.'

'Yes.'

'Tell me …'

'Uh-oh.'

'What?'

'I feel something coming.'

'That morning, that Sunday morning. How did he leave?'

His mother sighs. She pushes herself up for a moment with her arms, as if to find a more comfortable position on the hard-tiled step. 'I didn't notice.'

'How so?'

'I was off doing a training circuit with a couple of friends. You know how popular it was back then, jogging around one of those circuits with all that fitness equipment. Oh no, of course you don't. Anyway, half of Amsterdam was doing chin ups, jumping from concrete block to concrete block, zigzagging between dead tree trunks, and running from exercise station to exercise station. That was what I was doing. Early Sunday morning.'

'And when you got home, he was gone.'

'Yes, I didn't even realise at first. We didn't always tell each other where we were, but when I went to have a shower, I noticed things were missing from the shelf in front of the mirror.' She thinks for a moment. 'You don't see them anymore, those training circuits. I wonder what happened to them all. Do you think the council cleared them away?'

Simon ignores that. 'And when you heard about the accident, you didn't think anything of it?'

'No. Why would I? But by then I'd spent a whole Sunday home alone. That was unusual.'

'When did you first hear something?'

'Late that night, I think. No idea how they found me.'

'Wasn't there anything on TV?'

'Probably. But not much. I remember watching the next day. They had pictures by then, and Harmen Siezen had travelled to Tenerife. He was there in a little studio with an enormous photo of a mountain behind him. Or maybe it was a window, and the mountain was real.'

'Harmen Siezen? Was he already doing the news back then?'

'Must have been. Melissa! Let them swim! Don't keep pulling on their legs. You don't like it when Igor does that to you either!' She stands up and walks down the steps.

'Did you believe it?'

'Of course not. What would he be doing on that plane? That's enough now.'

What's enough — Melissa's antics, or his, Simon's, questions? 'How old is Harmen Siezen actually?' he calls after his mother, who has now reached Jelka and Buari.

'How would I know? Ninety?'

'You do realise!' Simon calls over Melissa, Sam, and Johan's heads.

Sam looks up in fright. 'What's wrong?' he asks. 'Aren't we doing it right?'

'You do realise this involves me too? My father was gone before I had a chance to get to know him?'

'Hey! Quiet!' shouts Johan.

'Be glad! Calm down a little. Your father might just as well have been someone else.'

Simon can hardly believe it. What is wrong with this woman? He's suddenly enormously wound up about it. The way she's always shrugging off everything, or walking away. Swimming off.

'Go and help Igor in the changing cubicle instead. Look, here he is.'

Simon turns. Igor and a woman have come into the hall. The woman gestures that her task is over, and disappears.

'No,' he says.

'No? What do you mean, no?'

'Do it yourself. I'll keep an eye on them here.'

'Come on!'

'I'm sick of Igor using me as a scratching post.'

'What are you saying now? A scratching post?'

'Yes, he's the cat and I'm the scratching post. You've noticed the last couple of times. Does he ever grab anyone but me? You? Melissa? No, Simon's the one to rub up against.'

'Come on!' his mother says again. 'You're only a few steps away.'

Igor has now been standing rather vacantly at the side of the pool for a while, near the changing rooms, a backpack hung off one shoulder. 'Beuh,' he says.

'Insubordination,' says Simon's mother as she passes him on her way out of the pool.

'"You shouldn't do that just yet." That's what you said not so long ago.'

'Yes, OK, fine.'

'And I'm thinking of stopping.'

'Put that right out of your head.' Anja disappears into the changing room with Igor.

'You've got loads of acquaintances, haven't you?' he calls after her. 'All those people in your clubs.'

'Acquaintances, yes. Ha! I can just see Linda from the book club splashing around in this pool. Or Harold from choir.'

Simon looks out through the windows at the bare trees. In the park there are people jogging, others are walking their dogs, young mothers are pushing strollers, a police car is driving extremely slowly along one of the paths. He knows that it's cold out, but, despite the bare branches and the low sun, all the people in the park look like it's summer, simply because the sun is shining and it's at least thirty degrees here inside.

That night he finally discovers how the writer described it. On page 185: 'What's the point of that? Klaas wonders. Johan's hair is thick, long, and gleaming. His body is broad and muscular. His teeth are white, and his lips are full. Who decided that someone like him should be so good-looking?'

It's much shorter than he remembered it. Shorter and different. Stranger too. Who could possibly decide something like that? God or what? Things like that happen. Things like that are completely normal. But it is true. Igor is incredibly good-looking, and that's of no benefit to anyone. He closes the book and puts it aside. Reading lamp off. Just start by getting up again tomorrow morning, he thinks, turning onto his side and pulling up his legs.

PART II

21.

'What are you doing?' She's lying with her back to him.

'I'm getting up. I feel a bit off.'

'Why don't you just stay in bed then?'

'No, I have to get up. I'm going downstairs.'

'I'll be up soon too.'

'You're going to do the circuit, aren't you, with Liesbeth?'

'Yes. Irene too. I don't want to think about it just yet.'

'I'll see you downstairs.'

She mumbles something he doesn't catch and stays where she is. He gets out of bed. There's hardly any light coming through the curtains. He doesn't get dressed, but goes downstairs in his underpants. He has clothes laid out there and a small suitcase in the cupboard under the stairs. He doesn't make tea or coffee, doesn't eat. I'm sneaking off, he thinks as he closes the door quietly behind him. Doing a flit. Maybe running away. It's cold and dank, and every now and then he shelters in a doorway or under a tree, but as the trees are bare, there's not much point to that. It's annoying, this rainy weather. He doesn't want to arrive at Schiphol like a drowned rat. The streets are quiet — early Sunday morning. In the small suitcase he has a spare pair of slacks, some underpants, two shirts, three pairs of socks, a toilet bag. He walks to the Overtoom, where he catches a 15 bus. There are almost no other passengers. He looks out of the window. Amsterdam is wet and grey. He's tense, he's never flown before. There's hardly anybody at any of the stops. The bus stays quiet. The city gives way to a messy landscape. Fields, industrial buildings, a solitary hotel. Approaching Schiphol, he sees they're building something new there. It's just before seven, still grey and wet. He can tell from the bare trees that it's not very windy.

The trainee is at the entrance. His jacket is too thin. He's dressed for a sunnier clime, but that will take a while yet. He knows that the hairdresser's son is married, but as far as he's concerned they'll act like this is a holiday where they happened to bump into each other. He, the trainee, as a member of a group that has booked a holiday with Holland International; the hairdresser's son as an individual traveller who managed to get a seat on the charter flight fairly easily because it was far from full. The trainee has let them know he won't be coming in tomorrow and why, but he has no idea if Cornelis has said anything to anyone. He suspects not.

Initially not much happened; Cornelis seemed to ignore him. The trainee felt like he was getting the cold shoulder, as if he were an intruder, even though the old hairdresser, Jan — who Cornelis rather sarcastically addressed as Jean — and his wife in particular had been so enthusiastic about bringing him on board. He didn't understand why Cornelis was being so hostile. But then a moment came when they were alone with just the two of them at the end of the day, a busy day, a typical day with more visitors than customers, the neighbourhood women animated, the men drinking coffee, calmly and proudly discussing their new Simca or their job, and at one stage one of the men fetched a cream cake from the baker round the corner, and Cornelis got angry because the man whose hair he was cutting was given a piece on a saucer too, and then ate it, hindering his work, but still, the trainee could tell he didn't really mind the commotion, and afterwards, it had already gone six, came that moment with the two of them, which started with accidentally looking at each other in one of the mirrors while sweeping up the day's hair, which turned them into two different people, no longer the hairdresser's son and the trainee, just two young guys. At least that's how he, the trainee, sees it. Since then they've met up a couple of times outside of the salon: Cornelis, invariably wary and noncommittal; the trainee, bold and assertive because he knows what he wants. He wants this good-looking guy who keeps him at arm's length and acts so gruff. Not happy, not relaxed. Once, just once — after seeing *Logan's Run* at Tuschinski, they were in the narrow alley that leads to the Amstel — did the trainee get the feeling that they were about to kiss. Cornelis agreed when he suggested going away with him. The two of them. Just leaving — they'd see where it led to. And here he is getting out of a bus, his head bowed to avoid the rain on his face. He's really come. The trainee looks at his watch. It's a little past seven. Time to check in.

A radio's playing in one of the shops. *All through my wild days, my mad existence, I kept my promise.* The trainee is walking ahead of him. *Don't keep your distance.* Cornelis tries to keep his mind blank. Don't stop to think. He's no longer as tense, but still has a jittery feeling in his stomach. He's tempted to do an about-face, but realises that's no longer possible. They've already gone too deep into the building, and the trainee has already checked in his large suitcase. They're actually already on their way. The trainee turns and smiles at him.

'Good morning!' chimes the stewardess. She's wearing a cobalt-blue suit with a colourful scarf.

'Yes, good morning,' he says. Through a chink in the movable gangway he's seen that the plane is called the *Rhine*, and finds that strange. Why name a plane after a river? Why not something like a bird? Sparrowhawk. Osprey. Cormorant, for all he cares. Stork.

'A jumbo jet!' the trainee told him. 'I've never been on one of them before.'

They walk onto the plane. It's enormous. And noisy — there seem to be quite of lot of kids on board. He searches for his seat, 28H aisle.

'I'm a lot further along,' the trainee says. 'But if you ask me, it's nowhere near full. I'll arrange something once we're in the air.' He takes Cornelis's suitcase and pushes it into a space above the seats. 'See you in a bit.'

'OK,' he says. He sits down and buckles up immediately. There's a couple sitting next to him, the man in the window seat. 'Hi,' he says to the woman, who is leafing through what looks like a KLM magazine.

'Good morning,' the woman says.

So they say, he thinks. He closes his eyes. He swallows. He wants to get off. It's a few minutes to nine. Jet engines roar. He opens his eyes again and looks back. In that same instant, the trainee bends out into the aisle as well and raises a hand. Really far away. What an enormous thing, Cornelis thinks. How's it even supposed to get off the ground? He waves back, sits up straight, and turns his head to look out of the window. The trainee is no help to him now. He hardly knows the guy. There's nothing reassuring about him at all. He can't see out of the window because the male half of the couple has his head in front of it. The woman rustles the KLM magazine. Children are yelling, adults are laughing too loudly, a baby is crying. Stewardesses walk past and close the overhead lockers. Jet engines roar even louder. Swift, he thinks. Heron. Bittern. The plane starts driving. It's called taxiing, he knows that. He closes his eyes again. From memory he counts the seats in one row. Ten. Then he tries to count the rows. Hundreds of people can fit on this plane. And did he just see stairs? Stairs on a plane? He rubs his breastbone. A little later his body is pressed back against the seat. It feels like the floor of the plane is sinking beneath him. Breathe, he thinks. Breathe calmly. 'Whoo!' shouts a child. Then the plane starts to curve away, and Cornelis inadvertently moves his body in the other direction. As if he and he alone is trying to get the aircraft under control, and he succeeds, because shortly afterwards it seems to be flying straight again. He realises he still has his eyes closed, opens them, and looks to the side. The woman is still peacefully reading the magazine, the man has moved his head back from the window. Cornelis can mainly see grimy clouds, but look, there: green meadows, little cars, another wisp of cloud, and is that the North Sea?

When the light for the seatbelts goes off and the light with the cigarette goes on, the trainee gets up and starts walking forward. From the smell of things, people in the back have already started smoking. The plane is hardly even half full. He can't work out why an airline would then cram the passengers all in together. Or has Holland International arranged it like that? Does it have something to do with weight distribution? They've emerged from the rainy grey skies. Outside the sun is shining brightly, with an immense field of clouds passing under the plane like snow-capped mountains. On reaching Row 28 he lays a hand on Cornelis's shoulder. He feels the hairdresser's son tense up. 'It's me,' he says. 'Shall we ask a stewardess if we can sit together somewhere?'

'Are you travelling alone?' the stewardess asks quietly.

'Yes,' Cornelis says. 'Or at least *I* am. He's with the group.'

'Yes, but you're together too.'

'Definitely,' says the trainee.

Cornelis feels uncomfortable. And he's scared. Really scared, and the general commotion is only making it worse.

'It's a bit noisy here, isn't it?'

'Rather,' says the trainee.

'Come with me,' says the stewardess.

Cornelis gets up. Standing up and walking around on a plane — incomprehensible. But it's just like standing on the ground.

'Do you have any hand luggage?' the stewardess asks.

'No,' the trainee says. 'But this gentleman does.' He gets Cornelis's suitcase out of the locker.

The stewardess leads the way to the front of the plane. They pass a small kitchen, and then the stewardess climbs the stairs. Upstairs is deserted. The seats are wider than downstairs, more spread out too. 'Business class,' the stewardess says. She gestures at the nose of the plane. 'That's the cockpit.'

Cornelis feels calmer immediately. As if the absence of other people gives him breathing space; he can be scared here without anyone noticing. 'Is this allowed?' he asks.

'Of course,' the stewardess says. 'There's nobody else up here.'

'You take the window seat,' says the trainee.

'Is this your first flight?' the stewardess asks.

'Yes,' says Cornelis.

'May I offer you a glass of champagne shortly?'

'Certainly,' says the trainee.

'And you have a toilet each, just over there.'

Cornelis sits down and puts his case on the floor in front of him. He can do that here. Champagne, and it's not even ten o'clock yet.

'We've struck gold here,' the trainee says, stretching and slumping on his seat. 'Business class.'

Lucky me, thinks Cornelis. He wants to go with the flow somehow, but he's not managing. Not yet, perhaps. Put this nightmare behind him first.

'Check it out,' the trainee says. 'That soft white blanket. It's really calming. There's nothing up here. You don't have to do anything. Just drink a glass of champagne.'

Very cautiously Cornelis looks out of the window. It really does look soft. It looks as if the plane, if it unexpectedly dropped, would just start gliding on its belly. But still the depths below him feel fathomless, with nothing but air between him and the ground — or is it the sea? It's quiet here. The sun is shining in from the left. Behind the door in the front are men who know what they're doing. Maybe they're drinking coffee, joking, talking about nothing in particular — the work they do so familiar that they hardly need to pay attention. The plane is probably on autopilot. The trainee leafs through the KLM magazine he's pulled out of a pocket in the back of the seat in front of him. 'Hey,' he says.

'What?' Cornelis asks.

The trainee lays the magazine on his lap. 'That's our pilot.'

'How do you know that?' Cornelis asks.

'He introduced himself, remember? He just told us what time

we're going to land and what the weather's like on Gran Canaria.'

Cornelis looks and reads. The man has a broad smile and grey hair. He tells the readers that KLM is punctual and reliable. There are all kinds of photos randomly positioned on the page, including one of clogs. 'Clogs again,' he says. 'Can't they come up with something else for once?'

'Ha,' the trainee says. 'Apparently not. Clogs, tulips, and windmills. That's us. But it doesn't make us predictable.' He points at the article. 'It says so right here.'

The reliable airline of those surprising Dutch. Cornelis closes the magazine and puts it away. He looks out the window again. The layer of cloud seems to end up ahead.

'Look at me for once,' the trainee says.

Cornelis looks at him.

Then the stewardess arrives with the champagne. 'Gentlemen, enjoy,' she says.

'Ladies and gentlemen, due to unforeseen circumstances at the airport of Las Palmas de Gran Canaria, we are being diverted to Tenerife. As a result, our flight will take a little longer than anticipated. We will provide further information regarding the continuation of our trip as we receive it.'

'Oh, flip,' says the trainee.

After two glasses of champagne Cornelis has become almost overconfident about looking around. He's even been to the toilet. A cubicle just behind the cockpit. After flushing he stayed there for a moment in the hope of hearing something. He couldn't hear anything.

'Landing,' Cornelis says. 'That's what I feel like.'

'No doubt,' the trainee says. 'But after that we'll have to take off again.'

22.

Half an hour later, it's almost one thirty, PH-BUF *Rhine* lands
at Los Rodeos. Around two, the also-diverted *Clipper Victor*
lands. It's already had two intermediate landings, in Chicago
and New York, since taking off from Los Angeles International
Airport hours earlier. They're not the only planes on the tarmac
that shouldn't be there. It's busy. And everyone is waiting for the
all-clear at the airport on Gran Canaria. At first, that waiting
takes place on the plane itself, but once it starts to seem like it
could be quite a while, so the Dutch passengers are allowed to
get off and wait inside the terminal. Around three o'clock, the
airport of Las Palmas is given the all-clear; after the telephone
call threatening a second explosion, no bombs were found.
Now air-traffic control can start to deal with the planes on the
taxiway. Fernando Azcunaga, one of the controllers, is facing a
complicated situation: because of the congestion, a number of
planes are unable to taxi on the taxiway; the runway will need to
be used for both taxiing and taking off.

•

Cornelis didn't enjoy the landing — he'd been looking forward to the plane getting closer to the ground at last, rather than being ten kilometres up in the air, but it didn't go as smoothly as he'd hoped. And waiting in the crowded terminal, the glow from the two glasses of champagne has faded. He's standing near a KLM desk, where a woman in an orange Holland International uniform is — if he's understood it correctly — checking herself out. He tries to follow her with his eyes as she walks away, and thinks he sees her leaving not only the desk but also the terminal. Can you just do that? he wonders. I didn't check out at home either, he thinks, and remembers something he'd completely forgotten until this moment: the extremely keen sense of relief he felt as a kid when the dental practice called his mother to inform her that the dentist was off sick.

'Why have you got your suitcase with you?' the trainee asks.

Cornelis looks down at his case. 'It was between my feet. I just picked it up. It seemed strange to leave it there.'

The trainee is getting agitated. Before, he'd said that it should be easy enough to find some way for Cornelis to join the Holland International group; maybe he could even let him sleep in his room at the hotel. They'd work it out once they arrived. If necessary, Cornelis could arrange a hotel of his own. But now this has come up, and it's getting later and later.

Cornelis looks at him, and it's like he's looking a complete stranger in the eyes. Who is this guy? Yes, he knows who he is, he knows that he's called Jacob, and yes, he's got a placement in his father's salon, but how did he suddenly end up here? What was that just now in the plane when Jacob said, 'Look at me for once'? Why?

He realises, almost in a panic, that he doesn't understand what he's doing here — Sunday, mid-afternoon, on a Canary Island. Only a few hours ago he'd lied to Anja, he'd left her because she'd told him something that was way too big for him to deal with. He'd walked through a cheerless Amsterdam and got on a Number 15 bus, and since then he'd let himself be carried along on this trip as if he didn't have a will of his own. He'd got onto a plane feeling more than nervous, and now, through the terminal's enormous windows, he can see planes parked everywhere that all have to take off again. He has a sinking feeling in his stomach, the ground under his feet feels unsteady. I'm not doing it, he thinks, I can't. And here too, just like at Schiphol, he hears — when they're walking around the terminal for something to do — Julie Covington singing over concealed speakers or from a shop with a radio. *Though it seemed to the world they were all I desired, they are illusions, they're not the solutions they promised to be.*

'What a crap song that is,' the trainee says. 'I'm sick to death of it.'

There is next to no information about the time of departure, no information at all, really.

'Do you think there's a toyshop here?' the trainee asks.

'A toyshop? What do you want a toyshop for?'

'Well, no reason.'

Cornelis swallows. 'Jacob,' he says.

'Yes?' says the trainee.

'Jacob, listen.'

The two planes are in each other's way. The crew of the *Clipper Victor* — Captain Grubbs, First Officer Bragg, and Flight Engineer Warns — are not amused when Captain Veldhuyzen van Zanten decides to refuel before flying on to Gran Canaria. That way he'll save time on the other island and be able to fly back to Schiphol with a plane full of holidaymakers sooner. The decision is partly motivated by an approaching cut-off point: the crew's maximum working hours cannot be exceeded, and if they are unable to leave Gran Canaria on time, they will have to spend the night there. The passengers have now been back on the plane for more than an hour. The holidaymakers on Gran Canaria have already been waiting six hours for their delayed flight. The Pan Am aircraft is ready and could have left earlier, but has not quite been able to get past the KLM plane. The American passengers didn't get off at Los Rodeos.

As the planes taxi onto the runway, the weather changes. A bank of fog slides down the hills and settles over the airport. That's not uncommon here. Sometimes the fog stays put; sometimes it clears again ten minutes later. Just before five, the *Rhine* receives instructions to backtrack the entire length of the runway and make a 180-degree turn at the start. On the way, First Officer Meurs asks if they're meant to turn at Exit C1 ('Charlie One'). Air-traffic control repeats that they have to backtrack the entire length of the runway. By this time, the *Clipper Victor* has also started taxiing and has been instructed to leave the runway at Exit C3 and continue to the start of the runway on the taxiway, which is clear from that point. Once the American plane has left the runway, the Dutch plane will be able to take off. Exit C3 will require the crew to make a 140-degree turn, and then — as the plane would then be facing in the wrong direction — make another sharp turn to the right. In a 747 this is a virtually impossible task. Taxiing in the fog with only a simple map of the runway, they miss Exit C3 and continue on to Exit C4, an easy turn that will let them join the taxiway without having to turn sharply there either.

·

After the backtrack, co-pilot Meurs reads the checklist. 'Body gear disarmed. Landing lights on. Checklist completed.'

Veldhuyzen van Zanten advances the throttles. Meurs is startled and says, 'Wait a sec, we don't have ATC clearance.'

'No, I know that. Go ahead, ask.'

'KLM 4805 is now ready for take-off and we're waiting for our ATC clearance.'

'KLM 4805, you are cleared to the Papa Beacon. Climb to and maintain flight level 90, right turn after take-off, proceed with heading 040 until intercepting the 325 radial from Las Palmas VOR.'

Veldhuyzen van Zanten advances the throttles again.

Meurs reads the route back to the tower, but meanwhile Veldhuyzen van Zanten has commenced take-off, forcing Meurs to rush through his reading of the route.

During this reading, Veldhuyzen van Zanten says, 'Let's go,' in Dutch. 'Check the thrust.'

Fernando Azcunaga says, 'OK, stand-by for take-off. I will call you.'

In the cockpit of the *Rhine* the crew only hears 'OK,' the rest partly lost because of a squealing noise.

But the plane is already six seconds into take-off.

The squeal is caused by simultaneous radio contact between the *Clipper Victor* and the control tower. 'We are still taxiing down the runway, the *Clipper* 1736.'

'Roger Papa Alpha 1736, report runway clear.'

'OK, we will report when we're clear.'

'Thank you.'

Because of the cockpit arrangement, Flight Engineer Schreuder is sitting a little behind the others. Normally he sees very little through the small windows, but now he can't see anything at all. It's grey outside. He does partly hear the exchange between the *Clipper Victor* and the control tower. 'Is it not off yet, then?' he asks.

'What are you saying?' asks Veldhuyzen van Zanten.

'Is it not off yet, that Pan American?'

'Yes, it is,' Veldhuyzen van Zanten and Meurs say simultaneously.

The trainee is Jacob Willems, twenty-one years old. Son of Klaas Willems (51 years old) and Ina Willems-Klein (47), road-mender and housewife respectively. He still lives at home in East Amsterdam. Brother of Rense (23) and Tilly Willems (26). As the youngest he is sometimes called 'Cobby' by his brother and sister. He's almost finished hairdressing school. Since the age of six he has collected Dinky Toys, and although he considers the hobby childish, he can't resist buying a missing model now and then. He likes going to movies. He's just come out of a relationship with an instructor. The instructor, who is twenty-one years older and has seen plenty of future hairdressers pass by, arranged things to make sure nobody noticed. Grown devious over the years. Jacob saw through his ploys from the start and thinks he's learnt something from them. He thinks he knows how to manipulate Cornelis. Or rather, he *thought* he knew how.

Jacob hasn't gone back upstairs. He's gone to the seat on his boarding pass. Nobody pays him any attention; even the stewardess who took them up to business class walks past him.

As he's alone in a row of three, he's slid over to the window seat. It's like a school excursion where the children have been allowed to leave the coach for a moment and been told things like 'Listen carefully' and 'Don't go too far', but when they get back on the coach nobody pays any attention. Everyone gets on, and off they drive. The kid that's been left behind is only noticed kilometres later. He's thinking of a coach trip because the passengers are even more rambunctious than earlier, as if waiting on Spanish soil has stoked their enthusiasm for the coming holiday. The atmosphere is almost boisterous.

Fuck, thinks the trainee. Suddenly he's alone again. Suddenly it's the way it was meant to be. 'Come,' he'd tried when everyone was asked to reboard the plane. Maybe he'd said it a little too forcefully, maybe he should have tried to coax him with, 'Come on.' It had all been fairly chaotic. A couple with children next to him had just walked through without showing their boarding cards. 'No,' Cornelis had said. He'd stood there like a horse that won't drink. Did I see it all wrong? he thinks. Was I wasting my time on Cornelis? Jacob decides that he won't go back to Chez Jean. I'll find another placement, he thinks. No shortage of hairdressing salons. He looks out. Even the weather's joined in. It was lovely and sunny, and he could already see himself in a swimming pool with Cornelis, in a bed too, wherever it happened to be, in his hotel or a hotel Cornelis had found, but now it's suddenly foggy. He can't see a thing, just the tarmac. Yes, he thinks, it's gone back to how it was planned. That's how I have to see it. Forget the rest. Go on holiday. Who knows who or what will cross his path on that other island? I have to forget Cornelis. They can all get stuffed in that bar in the Jordaan that pretends to be a hairdresser's. The pilot advances the throttles. The plane starts to pick up speed, the tarmac below the window is passing faster and faster.

•

'Let's get out of here, get the hell out of here.'

'Yeah, he's anxious, isn't he?'

'Yeah, after he held us up for an hour and a half, that son of a bitch.'

'Yeah, that …'

'Now he is in a rush.'

'There he is. Look at him, he's coming.'

'Get off. Get off, get off!'

The Dutch plane takes off so steeply that the tail scrapes the tarmac for a distance of twenty metres. The landing gear hits the Pan Am plane's right wing and body, and Engines 2, 3, and 4 slam through its upper deck. It's only the speed it's built up that makes the *Rhine* hang in the air for a moment before it crashes down onto the runway, where it immediately catches fire and explodes. Captain Grubbs would later declare that he didn't realise at first how great the impact of the collision had been. 'He hit us, but I didn't even think he had done us any damage. Because the airplane shook very quickly, not very much noise.' Then he saw that there was nothing above him — where twenty-eight first-class passengers had been sitting. The right wing was on fire. Crew members and a number of passengers managed to get out of the *Clipper Victor* through a hole in the left side of the front part of the plane, some with the help of a stewardess who simply shoved out the people who were too scared to jump, but shortly afterwards one of the engines on the left wing exploded. There were no eyewitnesses because of the fog. The Airline Accident Report of the American Air Line Pilots Association stated that four passengers from the Pan Am plane were found by Dutch investigators among the remains of Dutch passengers — and identified. For months afterwards, holidaymakers landing at Los Rodeos could see pieces of wreckage on the side of the runway.

Purser Dorothy Kelly's survival was entirely due to the sensitivity of her colleague Francoise Colbert de Beaulieu. Stories like hers are standard fare with plane crashes, and in the case of Dorothy Kelly it got even crazier in December 1988 when a colleague asked her if she would like to swap shifts. Dorothy wanted to accommodate her, but declined as she preferred to spend Christmas with family in New York, and a flight on 21 December was too inconvenient. The flight she turned down was Pan Am Flight 103 from Frankfurt to Detroit via London and New York, which ended in Scotland in the small town of Lockerbie. But that was later, much later. On the *Clipper Victor*, Francoise was so painfully aware of her French accent that she had asked her fellow purser to take over first class and the intercom announcements. Dorothy was more than happy to accept a temporary promotion from junior to senior purser.

The *Clipper Victor* was taxiing. Dorothy was standing near Door R1, holding a coffee and talking to a colleague. That coffee had been brought to her by Miguel Ángel Torrech, who then climbed the stairs back to the upper deck without a second thought. In 1977 cabin crew didn't sit with seat belts on during taxiing. The floor disappeared from under her feet, and she ended up in the hold below the upper deck. She lost consciousness for a moment, and when she came to she thought: bomb. Somewhere above her she saw a strip of light. She climbed up and emerged on the top deck, where — as she said later — the KLM plane had torn the top off the Pan Am plane 'just like peeling off the top of a sardine can'. There were two people there. 'How did you get here?' she asked. They didn't know. She saw that an engine was still running, she saw flames, she heard explosions. 'Jump,' she said. They didn't, so she pushed them and jumped herself. The landing was fairly soft — the earth had been ploughed up by the nose landing gear. She saw more people coming out of a hole above the left wing, got back on her feet, and started leading people — mostly quite a bit older, some badly injured from the jump — away from the plane. The engine was still roaring. She saw a white figure standing under the nose in a daze. It was Captain Grubbs. She grabbed him by the arms and dragged him, shuffling backwards, away from the plane. In that instant, the engine that was still running exploded. The aircraft's gigantic nose groaned and moaned and sank agonizingly slowly onto its side 'just like a great beached whale that had given up the will to live because it couldn't get back in the water and had put its head over and died'.

Co-pilot Robert Bragg was suddenly beside her, and together they got the last people away from the plane. She didn't want to see it, but she saw it anyway: passengers pounding on windows, mouths wide open, screaming silently, but there was nobody to rescue them, nowhere a door that could open. She heard later from a colleague who survived that people didn't even unbuckle their seatbelts, simply remaining seated to hear what was expected of them. Not even knowing that there was a completely destroyed, burnt-out Dutch 747 a little further along.

They took her to the hospital, where she, as she spoke Spanish and had some medical knowledge, helped peel clothing off burnt people. It was only when she noticed that she couldn't cut properly with the scissors that she found out she had broken her arm. She stayed in a hotel for a few days, did her best to avoid the international press, and flew back to the US. She took six months off on medical advice, but then resumed flying, a little more alert to unusual noises, a little less calm during turbulence, but with the knowledge that flying is the safest means of transport. And anyway, what's the chance of experiencing two plane crashes in one lifetime? She was spared Lockerbie. Francoise Colbert de Beaulieu and Miguel Ángel Torrech died.

In the airport terminal a twenty-eight-year-old Belgian tour guide from Airtour Belgium saw a red glow in the fog over the runway. She had just checked in approximately three hundred passengers and was waiting for a new group to arrive on a Sabena flight. She hadn't heard a thing. She thought later — to be precise, twenty-five years later, in an interview with the *Reformatorisch Dagblad* — that it must have been because of the fog. But that can't be right. It's only because you see almost nothing in fog that you think the air is 'thick' and that sound doesn't carry as far. A commotion arose in the terminal. Spaniards started yelling because they thought a Spanish plane had crashed. 'Inside we didn't hear any explosions or anything like that, but that red column in the distance was very ominous.' The terminal was full of people who only really knew that 'something had happened'. There was something in the air, that was all, and after a while three badly burnt people were brought in who turned out to be Americans. 'They were in shock, didn't know their own names, looking around with empty, bulging eyes,' she remembered twenty-five years later.

Her husband was home watching a football match. Spain–Hungary, a world cup qualifier. 'The transmission was suddenly interrupted by an appeal for all medical personnel present on the island — doctors, nurses, paramedics — to go to Los Rodeos as fast as they possibly could.' He jumped in the car and drove at top speed to the airport. The Guardia Civil stopped him, and he had no choice but to drive back home, some eighty kilometres south. There, he waited for a call from his wife. It was a long time coming because there were only three public telephones in the whole airport. He also said, 'After Catholicism, the second religion in Spain is football. It's no surprise then that, despite the ban on listening to the radio in the control tower, the air-traffic controllers had tuned in to such an important qualification match anyway. With all the consequences that had for their ability to concentrate on air traffic, which was already so chaotic that day.'

He said this to back up something his wife had told the journalists. She had bumped into a friend and colleague who had a relationship with the airport manager. While they were discussing the chaos in the terminal, the airport manager joined them. 'Those bastards in the tower were listening to the football match! How is it possible?! The imbeciles, they know it's irresponsible and prohibited! Don't say a word about this, or I'll kill you. Keep quiet about it, please, girls! Not a word!' The women (the expression 'girls' really was the manager's) had to keep it to themselves, and that was what the Airtour travel guides did. According to her husband, it was to avoid a conflict with the Spanish authorities that might have led to their work permits being revoked. Her husband brought up something else as well. He said that 'he could still clearly picture' yet another of his wife's colleagues and an 'older lady with grey hair and gold-rimmed glasses', whose name escaped him, having seen a so-called ghetto blaster being dropped or thrown from the control tower shortly after the disaster. According to him, it was an open secret in Tenerife that in the control tower they were not only listening to the football match, but also watching it on a small black-and-white TV. 'The sound was turned off because the radio commentary was more enthusiastic.'

A preliminary investigator from the Dutch Aviation Authority was '100 per cent' certain that he could hear 'football noises' on the tapes from the control tower and the two planes. He went in search of people who could confirm it, 'but when you need them they either can't be found or are unwilling to make a statement'. He remarked that only the American crew became alarmed, while the Spanish air-traffic control remained noticeably calm, 'almost inattentive', which surprised him given that they had two jumbo jets taxiing 'one after the other along the runway'. Neither the Spanish nor the American report includes any reference to the football match at all. 'Placing the blame entirely on the KLM crew was very much to the benefit of the Spaniards, and we couldn't get the Americans onside either. The Spanish conclusion suited them too.'

In fact, this football story is not relevant at all. Contact between Spanish air-traffic control, the *Rhine*, and the *Clipper Victor* was maintained throughout. There wasn't a single moment when the air-traffic controller seemed distracted. And for that matter, years later the 'preliminary investigator' quoted in the article seemed a little less fastidious about the truth. In 1999, twenty-two years after Tenerife and three years before the interview in the *Reformatorisch Dagblad*, he was head of the National Aviation Authority's Flight Operations Department *and* a Martinair pilot. In that year a letter he had written was included in a compilation of abuses and failings that the next of kin from the Faro air disaster sent to the parliamentary committee of enquiry into the Bijlmer Disaster. The next of kin believed that transparency was badly needed: all investigations leading up to a final report by the National Aviation Authority and the Aviation Safety Board are confidential. Only the final report is public, but even then the aviation authority can decide to hold back certain findings. The next of kin pleaded for a parliamentary inquiry into all plane crashes. The letter by the preliminary investigator/pilot/ head of Flight Operations stated, among other things: 'Martinair is considered a sufficiently safe company. There is no (official) reporting requirement for non-functional systems on Dutch aircraft. An airline company has its own responsibility in this area.' And why did the journalists refer to him as a 'preliminary investigator'? A recovery team from the Netherlands was present the next morning. There was hardly anything to preliminarily investigate. Was that how he had described himself?

On Tuesday 5 April 1977, at 11.00 a.m., a memorial service was held at St. Agnes Church on 43rd Street in New York, led by R. Rosenberg, C. Johnson, and J. Brew, rabbi, minister, and priest respectively. The service was organised by the Pan Am Employee Awareness Committee. The most important memorial of the disaster in the United States is in Orange County, California, in the Westminster Memorial Park and Mortuary — an inconspicuous monument made up of four horizontal bronze plates with around one hundred and twenty names, set in a bed of cut stone. Above the plates, also horizontal, is a plaque saying: IN LOVING MEMORY OF THE VICTIMS OF THE AIR TRAGEDY OF MARCH 27, 1977 AT TENERIFE, CANARY ISLANDS. This is where all of the unidentified bodies on the Pan Am flight are buried. Westminster can actually be considered an outer suburb of Los Angeles, the city where the *Clipper Victor* took off. Many of the passengers came from Orange County.

•

Missing from the bronze tablets is the name Eve Meyer, who was born Evelyn Eugene Turner in Griffin, Georgia, on 13 December 1928. She was probably the most famous person on board, even if her fellow passengers didn't recognise her. During secretarial training she had started earning some extra money as a model. A sideline that led in June 1955 to every pin-up's dream: Playmate of the Month in *Playboy*. From 1952 to 1969 she was married to Russ Meyer, writer and director of sexploitation movies. He summed it up later with the words: 'I knew I'd marry her the minute we met, and she was the greatest love of my life. We broke up because I'm a no-good son of a bitch.' She acted in a number of his movies, including *Eve and the Handyman* (1961), an attempt to blend humour and eroticism — not much plot, and lots of large breasts. Eve Meyer played all of the female roles. Pictures of her will have hung in garages and workshops. Mechanics and burger flippers will have dreamed of her. There were indications that she suffered from depression after an operation on her 'lower body'. She was compared to Marilyn Monroe and Jane Russell. She produced a lot of movies with her husband, even after their divorce, the last one being *Black Snake* (1973), where Russ Meyer took the leap from sexploitation to blaxploitation. It was an enormous flop. Eve Meyer didn't have any children. On 27 March 1977 she was forty-eight years old. A cabin had been reserved for her on the MS *Golden Odyssey*, a cruise ship that was due to sail the next day. She would see Morocco — Morocco! — and later Venice, a city from the movies, an almost mythical place. Maybe she would meet someone, an Italian with good manners, brown eyes, and long black lashes. She is buried at the Sunny Side First Baptist Church Cemetery, in Sunny Side, Georgia. 2,210 miles from Westminster. Written on her grave: 'THREE TIMES A LADY'.

Cornelis had no difficulty leaving the terminal. The trainee walked off, and he turned away. After showing his passport to a Spaniard in a booth, he was outside. Not for a second did he consider checking out at the KLM desk. He started walking, because he didn't know what else to do. Making a decision was one thing, but that decision had consequences, and he had no idea what those consequences might be. So walk. This is an airport; there must be a city or a town nearby. There were a few stray buildings right outside the terminal, and he soon reached a more built-up area. San Cristóbal de La Laguna, he saw on a sign. It wasn't far. He walked into town. A hotel, where can I find a hotel? And then, how will I ever get away from here again? Do boats sail from here too? Can I leave on a boat? And where will it take me? Morocco? Somewhere in the back of his mind he knew that this was the idea, that it had always been the idea. Go on holiday, and don't come back. The town turned out to be a city. He went into the first hotel he saw and asked in English for a room. They had one — no problem. Holiday? Yes, holiday. Ah, then make sure to see the Iglesia de la Concepción. Beautiful, on the square, you can drink beer or coffee there too. It is in any case a magnificent old city. Just give me the key, thinks Cornelis, who's having great difficulty understanding the man at the desk.

23.

It was only on 28 March that he found out what had happened and realised what had caused all the commotion late yesterday. Ambulances, fire brigade, police — everything in the distance, and he hadn't known what was what. Dutch sirens sounded different. He had to ask people what it was all about, after making it clear to them that he didn't speak or understand Spanish. At an outdoor café on a square with a rather unusual church tower, an American tourist told him that two planes had crashed into each other on the ground. One Pan AM and one KLM. Almost everyone killed. Fire. An explosion. 'Terrible, terrible,' the American said. So many of his countrymen. Is this the Iglesia de la Concepción? thought Cornelis. 'Almost everyone killed?' he said. 'Yes.' A little later again, on that same square — it was now dinnertime, and Cornelis had chosen something at random from the Spanish menu — he heard from two Swedish tourists that the only survivors had been on the American plane. They showed him a local newspaper, a special edition. Bold headlines, photos. He'd ordered another glass of wine. He knew by then that he had to ask for *vino blanco*. The meal he had ordered turned out to be squid.

•

After dinner he lay down in his hotel room. It was very quiet. His room was on a kind of courtyard with trees and bushes. There had been birds singing in it earlier, but they had now fallen silent. He looked at his case, which was sitting on a small table. Above the table there was a mirror on the wall. In that mirror, which was tilted slightly forward, he could see himself and the other side of the case. Does this mean I'm dead? he wondered.

PART III

24.

Simon is lying in bed. It's morning. He looks at the posters of Biondi, Popov, and Spitz. They have to go, he thinks. A grown man with posters of swimmers in his bedroom. I'm not even a swimmer anymore, he thinks. I'm a barber with a barber's shop and responsibilities, and like thousands of other people all over the Netherlands I swim laps. Nothing more, nothing less. And it's not art at all, of course, despite the expensive frames. They're posters for a boy's bedroom.

Just as he promised himself last night, he starts by getting up. He lifts the three frames off the wall. After he's taken the posters out of them, he wavers for a moment. Then he rolls them up one after the other. Ripping them would be a bit too drastic. He puts the frames in the cupboard where he also keeps the vacuum cleaner; the rolled-up posters go on the top shelf. So, he thinks, a clean sheet. Then he sees the white rectangles on the wall. He tries to work out how long it's been since he did up his bedroom. A long time.

•

While he's drinking an espresso at the kitchen table and staring at the mess that has grown back again unnoticed, his phone rings. *Writer,* he reads on the screen. Before starting the conversation, he realises that there must be a lot of telephones on which he's called 'Barber', not Simon. 'Hey,' he says. 'You're back from Bordeaux.'

'Marseille, barber,' says the writer.

'Oh yeah, Marseille. How was it?'

'Ah. Eleven people showed up. That's what I travelled more than a thousand kilometres for.'

'But you still got to go to Marseille.'

'True. They can't take that away from me, as my mother would say.'

'Is she still alive?'

'Absolutely. Film? Tonight?'

'Sounds good. Do you want to choose something? I don't keep up with it.'

'Will do. I'll message you.'

'OK,' Simon says, and swipes the writer away. I am my work, he thinks. Maybe there are customers who, like the red-headed guy, think I'm called Jean. He stands up and makes another espresso. He hasn't got dressed yet, nobody's coming today. It is Sunday, after all. He could buy a tin of wall paint and repaint his bedroom. First he opens his laptop. He's already gone so deeply into the material that a report from the Air Line Pilots Association is on his reading list. Unfortunately it's mainly about the American plane. There are quite a few pictures: schematic representations with seats in black and white; causes of death, by fire or suffocation, by trauma. He reads the report — which isn't dated — all the way through. His English is fairly good and he takes it slowly, but there are still a couple of sentences that require quite a lot of thought. 'Five bodies were subsequently identified as belonging to persons manifested as assigned to the KLM aircraft. Four passengers manifested on board the Pan American airplane were subsequently identified among the remains of those persons thought to be travelling on the KLM airplane.' Does it really say that the bodies of five Dutch passengers were found at the site of the American plane? And four Americans at the site of the Dutch plane, quite a bit further along? How was that even possible? That would have to mean that the KLM plane was already more or less destroyed and didn't just smash to pieces further down the runway. And are there then Dutch people buried in America, and Americans in the Netherlands? What a mess. What a lack of resolution. And so many questions. If you delve deeper into something, shouldn't you find answers? He closes the laptop.

In the shower a bit later, he thinks about the writer. And the guy with red hair. And Igor, of course. And then about his father, in a confusing way. He doesn't know him and only has a couple of photos. A good-looking young guy. A good-looking young guy he wouldn't have minded getting to know a little better. In a particular way.

They go to see *1917*. In an arthouse. It's not an especially recent film, but the writer wanted to see it because he'd missed it the first time round, so for two hours they run, walk, climb, creep, leap, and shoot along with a British soldier who has to deliver a message to some general or other (Benedict Cumberbatch). First there are two soldiers, but more or less halfway through, the other one gets murdered by a German pilot they've dragged out of a burning plane. That was a nasty moment in the film, with the fanatical German stabbing the British soldier who'd saved his life. Simon thinks it's a beautiful film; the writer is less enthused. Afterwards they go at the writer's insistence to a gay bar on Zeedijk. Simon never goes to gay bars, he doesn't see the point. It's quiet, they're not even playing any music. They sit at the back, next to a window that looks out over the smooth water of Oudezijds Voorburgwal. They drink beer. The barman greets the writer as if he knows him well. Simon has the idea he got some drinking in before the film too. Maybe even here.

'It did have beautiful music,' the writer says.

'Definitely,' says Simon. 'I should go to the cinema more often. It's really not the same on TV.'

'Often I only take a film like this half in, especially if I'm writing. Then I see something, and my thoughts drift off to what I'm working on myself. I suspect that elements from quite a lot of films have made it into my books without my being aware of it.'

'That doesn't bother me. I just sit down and watch.'

'Cheers!' says the writer, clinking his half-empty glass against Simon's. 'We're on a date!'

'Never thought I'd live to see the day!' the barman calls from behind the bar. That's how quiet it is.

'Mind your own business,' the writer shouts back.

'It is my business. We're in the business of bringing people together.'

'Or do they come together?'

'Same difference. Two more?'

'Sure,' says the writer.

Last one, thinks Simon. Then I'll have had enough of this place. He drains his glass and thanks the barman, who's brought their beers over to the table. They clink again.

'Who's your friend?' the barman asks the writer.

'This is my barber.'

'Oh, that's convenient.'

'Are you done now?'

'Yes, I'm done now.' He walks back to the bar, where he looks around for a moment. Then he puts on some music and immediately turns down the volume.

'I'm not sure what to say,' the writer says. 'In the barber's shop it always comes automatically.'

'Are you a regular here?'

'Yeah, I come here quite often. It's not as overwrought as other places.'

'That better?' the barman calls.

'Yep,' says the writer.

'Not too loud, so you can talk. About important things.'

'Unbelievable,' says the writer.

'Come on, I'm helping you to get going. That friend of yours looks a little timid. Does he know who you are?'

'What do you mean?' the writer asks.

'How famous you are?'

'What's that matter? Anyway, it's not even true.'

'Well …'

'I can just leave,' Simon says.

'No, don't be crazy. Oscar, shut up.'

'Now, now,' says the barman.

'Bring us some of those munchies instead.'

'I don't have them today. Cheese? Sausage?'

'A plate of cheese and *ossenworst*.'

Simon looks out. The water in the canal is so smooth there are two rows of buildings, until a small boat emerges from under a bridge and wipes away the reflection. It makes him think of a friend's place near here, on Lange Niezel, one bridge further along. He's thought of it because he's suddenly realised where he is. When he rang the bell and was waiting for the door to open, he always had to stand in front of the window of the sex shop on the ground floor. It was uncomfortable. It wasn't that he was embarrassed — his friend happened to live above that sex shop, he had no choice — but maybe the barman is right and he is a bit timid. It was always so busy there too, all those foreigners, lots of Brits on their way to the red-light district. Eventually the friend moved to France and then he had no more reason to go to Lange Niezel. *Ossenworst*, it's been a very long time since he ate that. He doesn't drink beer very often either.

'What's on your mind?' the writer asks.

'Dildos and sex magazines,' Simon says. 'And now I stop to think of it, all kinds of other, what do you call them, attributes too. Things I wouldn't have a clue what to do with.'

'Gosh,' says the writer.

Simon finishes his beer. 'I wouldn't mind another one,' he says.

'Oscar!' the writer shouts.

'How did it actually go with that German writer?' Simon asks.

'Kehlmann? A disappointment, of course. Inflated expectations.'

An hour later, Simon is fairly drunk. They've long finished the slices of *ossenworst* and the cubes of cheese. It's still very quiet. 'Why is this place so deserted?' he asks.

'Oscar!' the writer calls. 'Why is it so deserted in here?'

'It's Wednesday,' the barman says.

'It's Wednesday,' the writer says.

Thanks to the beer, Simon feels so detached from everything that he orders another two glasses.

'See?' the barman says. 'He's getting into it!'

'How's your book going?'

'Do we have to?' the writer asks.

'Apparently,' says Simon.

'I feel like you've put me on track of something.'

'Yes, with those hairdressing things.'

'No, with your father.'

'Are you going to write about my father?'

'Not really *your* father … A father.'

The barman puts the beers on the table, then takes a moment to look out at the canal. 'What a fabulous city we live in,' he says.

Simon and the writer look up at him. 'Sorry,' says the barman. 'I'm going.'

'So it's about me after all?'

'You shouldn't take it all so literally,' the writer says. 'That's not how writing works.'

'Are you going to let me read it when it's finished?'

The writer looks at him and thinks about it. 'I don't know,' he says after a while. 'Shall we fuck?'

'Bingo!' shouts the barman.

Around four o'clock, when Simon gets home, he has to vomit. They'd gone on to drink a couple of old-style genevers at the writer's. 'Then you won't have such a bad headache in the morning,' the writer had said. 'You can take that from me.' As he leans over the toilet bowl, things he has absolutely no desire to think about pass through his mind. The writer's flat, the writer's body, the writer's fingers pinching his nipples really hard while he sits on him, or wait, no, it was the other way round: the writer was sitting on him, but it was Simon who was pinching the writer's nipples, following instructions. The writer seemed to find it incredibly exciting. As he remembers it, it wasn't the idea that he should do anything else or that there might be room at some stage for him to concentrate on his own body. The writer described, he executed. Or was that just an idea he'd got into his head? He can't even remember if he came or not. It hadn't been unpleasurable, but when you're sick as a dog you don't want to think of anything, you just want it to stop. He lets go of the toilet bowl and sits down on his arse for a moment with his back against the wall. He imagines the shop on a nice day with the door open. It has to be fresh and pristine, in the morning, before the first customer has arrived. The smell of hair lotion and sunlight on the wooden window seat, a woman riding past and cheerfully ringing her bicycle bell, cheerful and not angry at the car blocking the street. But then it surges up again. Vomiting is such a strange activity, the whole-body compulsion, the writhing, the peristaltic push to purge it all. The body wresting control from the mind. He washes out his mouth, cautiously drinks some water, then gives his teeth a thorough brush. He crawls into bed and hears, just before he falls asleep, the barman shouting 'Bingo!' again.

25.

Simon has an early customer before going to the swimming pool. The man is not talkative, and his hair is almost as black as Igor's. That's a good combination. They can both let their thoughts wander. The man — he's called Frank — regularly closes his eyes for long periods as if to better feel what Simon is doing. Feel, not see. The silence is only interrupted by Simon's 'Is this short enough?' and Frank's 'No scalp massage today, thanks.' Apparently he has less time today than usual. His hair curls, and curly hair is more of a challenge than straight hair. They don't know anything about each other. They're barber and customer. After he's paid and left with a 'See you next time,' Simon shakes out the hairdressing cape and calmly tidies up.

There's a new one. Frits, his mother tells him. 'I don't know what's wrong with him, but I've never heard him say a word.' Frits is a ginger, about fifteen. Freckles, pale skin, watery eyes. He seems to know Melissa well. The moment they hit the water, they both start swimming laps. 'He can swim,' his mother observes, 'but I already knew that, of course.' Jelka, Sam and Johan, Buari, Igor, the new boy, Melissa. He's starting to get used to it.

'Hey, Simon!' Sam shouts.

'Hey, Sam!' Simon shouts.

'Shall we hit you?' Johan asks.

'Yes,' says Simon. 'Feel free.'

As he hasn't said 'No', their noodles float in the air for a moment. Then, because he's confused them, they start hitting Jelka.

'No!' Anja cries. 'Stop it. Always hitting little girls, shame on you, hit each other if you're so keen on it.'

'Tat!' says Jelka.

'Yes, you tell them,' Anja says. Igor has sat down on the steps.

'Igor,' Anja says. 'Don't you want to swim today?'

'Beuahh,' says Igor.

'Are you not feeling very well?'

The boy doesn't answer. He looks out through the enormous window. It's overcast, the trees in the park are drab and motionless. A woman is walking a dog, a group of people pass on Segways. That agitates the dog, which jumps in the air and tugs on its leash. Igor makes a noise that sounds like laughter. It does look ridiculous, Simon thinks. A line of helmeted people riding those pedantic vehicles. No wonder the dog wants to bite the one at the back in the calf of his leg. It's as if Igor understands perfectly what's going on, as if he realises that the dog is seeing something inexplicable and maybe threatening, and reacting to it. Perhaps the boy also thinks those people are showing off, and knows that they could just as easily walk or ride bikes. But it's also possible that he'd like to be zooming along on one of those things himself, or walking a dog in the park, or just be somewhere else rather than here in this small, muggy swimming pool. He could just have stomach-ache too, or not understand anything of what he can see through the window. Fortunately there's Sam and Johan still, who suddenly seem to have figured out who they are allowed to hit with their noodles, but why they're shouting 'Bare bum, bare bum, bare bum!' while they're at it eludes Simon until they toss their noodles aside and try to pull down Igor's light-blue trunks. He stays calm and kicks out at the other two boys.

'Ow!' Johan cries.

'Bully!' shouts Sam.

'Ghhhh,' says Igor.

It's somehow quiet this morning. As if everyone has just woken up. Jelka and Buari are standing in a corner not doing anything, but not bored either. Frits and Melissa swim on in silence. Sam and Johan have stopped bothering Igor in the meantime and, although they're having an intense discussion, they're doing it quietly with just the two of them, not saying anything that's meant for other people's ears.

'How's it going?' his mother asks.

'Good,' says Simon. 'How are you?'

'Fine too. Did you come in the car?'

'Yep.'

'Why?'

'No reason. I can't just leave the thing parked in one spot for months on end.'

'True.'

Even this conversation isn't going anywhere and may already be over. Igor has moved down a step, the water now up to his navel. His hair is still dry. Simon can barely look at him.

'Heard any more from Henny?' he asks.

'No.'

'So no idea when my subbing duties will be over?'

'No. Not any time soon, I think. Yeah, Henny. Maybe she'll never come back.' She looks out through the window. The park is now completely deserted. 'With her ridiculous floral swimsuit.'

'Look at yourself.'

She does. Then shrugs. Even his mother is calm. Drained is maybe a better word for the atmosphere in the swimming pool. 'Have you ever had that, when you've done something or bought something, and never stopped to think about it afterwards? And other people have to point out you're not thirty anymore?'

Simon thinks about it. He sees himself taking down the posters of Spitz, Biondi, and Popov.

'That it's time to change? To swap orange for navy?'

'Yes,' Simon says, 'you can't keep everything the same forever.'

'Do you think it's going to rain?'

'It could do.'

'She may have a ridiculous floral swimming costume, but she's got this Ko guy too.'

'And you don't have anyone.'

'No. You neither, by the way.'

'True.'

'Frits! Melissa! Finished!'

The water in the fifty-metre pool feels cold by comparison. Simon swims for half an hour, thinking about what he's doing. Not very fast, but concentrating on his technique. As he's drying himself off, he realises again that it's something he dislikes. Drying himself off. Being wet feels good, swimming feels good, showering feels good, but there's always a moment when you have to dry yourself off. It takes a long time too, and more often than not your clothes feel hard and unpleasant afterwards.

Before leaving the swimming centre he goes back to the small pool for a moment. The water is smooth and still, all the toys have been packed away. It's as if nothing at all has happened here and nothing is going to happen later today. Outside the park still looks grey. It's still deserted. There are not many things as melancholy as a quiet, empty swimming pool, he thinks.

He drives from the swimming centre to the paint shop on Elandsgracht, where he buys ten litres of emulsion, a roller, a tray, and a brush. Just before leaving the shop, he thinks of something else, even though he's double parked with warning lights flashing. 'Do you have that thin plastic too?' he asks the shop assistant.

Of course they do. 'Ten metres by ten metres, is that big enough?'

'Don't you have it smaller?' he asks.

'Better too big than too small, surely?' the assistant counters.

26.

Instead of Igor in his bed, he now has a bed that's covered with thin plastic. While rolling the ceiling — if you paint the room white again after so many years, you have to do everything — he thinks about it. He hadn't driven to the swimming pool for 'no reason', of course, even if it only occurred to him when he saw Igor sitting on the steps and looking so lost, staring at what was happening in the park, almost longingly, as if he would love to be out there free and alone, maybe even riding a Segway. At that moment he realised what the car was for: it would be easier to get the boy in a car than onto the back of his bike. And if Sam and Johan could pull down his swimming trunks, then surely he could too. Do you, as a 'supervisor', need to remain above it all? Can't you just join in for once? Some paint splashes into his right eye. He doesn't rub it, but blinks a couple of times. He gets down off the low kitchen steps and rolls more paint onto the roller. His shoulder's already started to ache.

•

Igor in bed. Or on the sofa. On the floor, downstairs. In a barber's chair, in the swimming pool changing rooms. In his thoughts he can block out everyone else. In reality he can't, that's why he refused to help the boy into his trunks. Making that decision felt quite mature, but the truth was that he couldn't answer for the consequences. And who decided that someone like him should be so good-looking? That was why he announced he was stopping. A boy like a puppy. A puppy that wants all kinds of things too, shamelessly licking his groin, hind legs spread wide. Simon knows it, that total surrender, your mind completely blank, shamelessly spreading your legs, back arched, like a dog again, one that's taking a shit. Not like with the writer, that was awkward, something that was bound to happen sooner or later, or recently with the guy with red hair, who lay in bed here rather conceitedly, maybe already thinking about trumpeting his conquest around. Nice, if you're still allowed to put it that way, but nothing more than that. Igor unquestioningly and innocently naked, and him the one who's unable to say much more than 'Grrr' or 'Beuahh' or 'Oof'. How many times he's imagined himself flat on his stomach, arms spread, forehead on a pillow or on the floor, Igor on top of him, in him. He pushes the roller back and forth, jumps down, tugs the stepladder sideways, climbs back onto it, and rolls some more. This morning the car was parked directly in front of the swimming centre. It was chaos in the changing room. Jelka was bawling her heart out, the new boy, Frits, had water in his ears, and the rostered driver hadn't arrived yet. He could have almost taken Igor with him. There were moments when he could have done it without being noticed. The boy was sitting quietly on a bench, calmly waiting his turn, looking around almost benevolently, watching a red-faced Jelka and Frits, who said something for the first time, kicking up an enormous fuss because he thought the water had leaked into his head through his ears. 'Come on,' Simon had told him. And then he'd peeled down his trunks, dried him, and dressed him. 'Ghhhum,' went Igor, close to his ear. It was a satisfied sound. After that he and his mother took care of Jelka, and then the driver arrived, and with the driver's arrival, his plans, conscious or not, were thwarted. He rolls out the last paint-soaked roller and finishes the ceiling. He'd been dreading the ceiling most because of having to work over his head. Only now does it occur to him to open the window. The emulsion he's using is water-based, but it can't be healthy.

That night he reconstructs as far as possible the life of a pin-up who was on the American plane. He doesn't find it easy. She was quite famous, once, but not much sticks even with famous people. *Three times a lady* is written on her gravestone. Isn't that a Lionel Richie song? But that number can't be that old? He looks it up. August 1978. Not Lionel Richie solo, but The Commodores. Written after Richie's father called his wife 'a great lady, a great mother, and a great friend' during a birthday speech. How is that possible? Simon sighs, but he's not going to rack his brains about it. You'd almost bloody think Lionel Richie went for a walk in that cemetery in, where was it again, Sunnyside, Georgia. Is he from Georgia? No, he was born in Alabama. A neighbouring state. From Tuskegee to Sunny Side is just 119 miles. It's possible.

As he suddenly, very briefly, has no idea how he got from Tenerife to Lionel Richie, he closes Google Maps and opens boyfreepics.com. Half an hour later he's in bed. In his fresh white bedroom without any rectangles on the wall. He wanks, but doesn't call to mind a single boyfreepic while he's at it. He's dressing Igor in a changing room where nobody else is present. This time his forehead's not resting on a pillow, carpet, or a lower arm, but on hard white tiles. In his thoughts it's very easy to get the boy to take him.

27.

'Weiman.' She always answers with her surname with the stress on the first syllable. WEIman. It sounds inviting.

'Yes, Weiman here too.' He says WeiMAN. That sounds defensive. But he hardly ever says it, he answers with his first name. He actually only ever gives his surname when it's his mother, and then only because of how she answers. Plus, it's not even her real surname. It's his father's. Her own name is Wiegers. Maybe now he's not twenty-three or thirty-eight anymore he should start answering with his surname too.

'Oh, it's you.'

'Yes, it's me. Is that a disappointment? Were you expecting someone else?'

'Not at all. What's up?'

'Did you receive an invitation in 2007 for a commemorative ceremony on Tenerife?'

'What?'

'When they unveiled the monument.'

'Hang on, give me a second to adjust. I only just got up.'

'In 2007 they unveiled a staircase on top of the mountain.

There were next of kin there. Were you invited?'

'Yes, obviously.'

'Well, it's not obvious to me. How did they get your address, for instance?'

'Oh, yeah. That can't have been easy.'

'But you got the invitation?'

'Definitely.'

'And why didn't you go?'

'Pfff. What's there for me?'

'People who've gone through the same thing?'

'Hahaha.'

'Why laugh at that?'

'People who've gone through the same thing? Sure! Dig it up again after thirty years? Listen to me for once. He disappeared on a Sunday and never came back. I never saw him again. He is — so they say, but people can say anything — buried at that hideous cemetery. I don't even know how. I don't even know if all those people are really buried there under that ugly millstone. I don't know a thing! And I'd actually like to keep it that way.'

'But didn't you have any inclination to go?'

'Nope. And anyway, I'd already been there once. With you, I might add, but you were still little, so you probably don't know anything about it anymore.'

'Of course I know about it. I've seen the photos, haven't I?'

'Oh, yeah. That's true.'

'But why did you go there alone then? A couple of years after the crash?'

'I don't remember. It was at least partly to go on a plane for once. I really had to steel myself for that.'

'That doesn't sound like much of a reason.'

'Simon! I don't remember. Maybe I wanted to draw a line under it or something.'

'Did you never stop to think that I might have wanted to go to that commemoration?'

That's thrown her off her stride. He can hear her breathing. 'No, I'm sorry. That never even occurred to me.'

'Thanks.'

'Hey, enough of that! I'm not going to let you talk me into feeling guilty. And what would have been there for you?'

'Can't you get it into your head that that man was my father?'

'That man, as you call him, was my husband!'

'Oh, now I'm not allowed to have feelings about it? Now he's your husband? What about Grandpa and Grandma's son? Now you're acting like the queen being all friendly to a commoner until they say something disagreeable and then she says, "Do you realise who you're talking to!?"'

'What? Why are you talking about the queen all of a sudden? And can't you get it into your head that I don't want to talk about it? Has it never occurred to you how terribly painful all this is for me?'

Now it's his turn to think for a moment. And be quiet. But he perseveres. 'How did you feel about Grandpa's trainee being on that plane?'

Again he hears her breathing, and a motorbike going past. 'A trainee?'

'Yes. You know about that, right?'

'Do I?'

'Grandpa told me. A while ago now.'

'I don't know anything about it.'

'Yes, you do, you do know.'

'I mean I don't know what was going on. You'd assume they were going on holiday together, but I don't *know* that. That guy went away too, and never came back either. How am I supposed to know anything?'

'That's true too. I found it, yeah, how did I actually find it? Peculiar. You'd almost think they had something going on together.'

'Hahaha.' It's not really laughing, she blurts the word 'Ha' a few times in quick succession.

'Do you have to laugh again?'

'Yes. You probably like that idea. Exciting.'

'No. What was his name? Do you remember?'

'God almighty.' She sighs. Very deeply. 'Listen, I was pregnant with you. Six months later, you were born.'

'And?'

'What you mean, *and?*'

'Forget it. It's all so strange.'

'Your grandfather's pulling your chain.'

'No, Grandpa's just suddenly started talking about it, after all this time. Why didn't he do that before? Why haven't you ever talked about it?'

'How old are you anyway? You're like a teenager! A disgruntled teenager. Have *you* ever asked about it?'

She has a point there.

'You've really sunk your teeth into it, haven't you?'

Another point. 'Have you asked around in your clubs yet?'

'No, of course not. They're all people I do other things with. You're doing the swimming with me. Until Henny comes back.'

'But she's not coming back.'

'You never know. Yesterday I got a couple of photos of the house they're in at the moment. Temporarily. Ko's being passed around there among all those Brits. He shouldn't let it go to his head. He's not fifty anymore. It was twenty-three degrees, she wrote. And sunny.'

'I think I'll go and check it out there myself.'

'Yes, go and have a nice holiday. You've earned it.'

'I think I'm going to hang up. Bye, Mum.'

'Bye, Simon. See you Saturday.'

'No, wait! You just said something about a millstone. So you have been to Westgaarde.'

She hesitates. 'Yes.'

'And didn't you think it was a shame or weird that his name wasn't there with all those other names?'

She starts sniffling. It comes so unexpectedly, all he can do is listen. She's succumbing, he hears Henny say.

'Mum?' he says.

'I'm here,' she snivels.

'Are you crying?'

'Yes, I'm crying. Your fault.'

'That wasn't the intention.'

'I know that.' She sniffs loudly. 'You keep pushing.'

'Yes. I can't help it.'

'It's OK. I kind of understand it.' She sniffs again. 'Do you know what's just come back to me? When it all happened I hardly cried. I must have suppressed it. I wasn't in the mood for it, as idiotic as that sounds. And then, a year later, but this is something you don't know anything about, there was an enormous accident in Spain, in Spain again, a tanker that exploded near a campsite. In the summer. More than two hundred dead. And then I broke down. When I saw the pictures, or things on TV, well … Los Alfakese or something like that.'

'Strange.'

'It was like seeing how distraught all those other people were made me feel how distraught I was.' She's still sniffling a little. 'My God, people even died a hundred metres away floating on an airbed in the sea. Idiotic, isn't it? Remembering that?'

'Psychologists probably have a word for it,' says Simon.

'No doubt. Now I'm really hanging up.'

'You OK?'

'Of course. It did me good, having a little cry. When was the last time you cried?'

'I don't remember.'

'You're not entirely normal either.'

'You can cry on the inside too, you know. Maybe I do that.'

'Bye!'

Simon makes an espresso and drinks it standing at the rear window. The bushes in the gardens are already green. It's like everything close to the ground buds sooner than the trees. It's drizzling. In a kitchen in the row of houses at the back someone is doing something on a worktop; a bit further along, someone opens their bedroom curtains. I treat Anja like an equal, he thinks, and in the eyes of others we probably interact strangely with each other, but she's still my mother. I forget that sometimes. He checks the time. He has to go downstairs soon — Jason is in his appointment book. Apparently they're back from the Maldives. Without crashing. Strangely enough, Martine hasn't made an appointment. They mostly come a day after each other, or at least in the same week. And then he thinks, I can always cut Igor's hair of course. My mother suggested it herself. There's nothing suspicious about it.

Jason doesn't just want his beard trimmed, he wants a haircut too. Simon's done the cut and is now working on his beard with scissors and a fine comb. He could do it just as well with clippers, but that's not what customers want. They want to feel like they're at the barber's. The clippers or beard trimmer are for at home. Now and then Simon lets the comb float in the air for a moment to tighten the skin a little with his thumb. He can't help it, he has to feel the pulse in this throat. Jason didn't say a word during the haircut. Now and then he let out a deep sigh. Now he says, 'I suppose Martine hasn't made an appointment?'

'No,' says Simon.

'I'm not surprised.'

'Hm.'

'We broke up.'

'Gosh.'

'During the holiday. On the beach, of all places. With three days left to go and a long flight home ahead of us. Who does something like that?'

'Hm.' Jason's getting a bit agitated. Simon can see his carotid throbbing.

'It wasn't very pleasant after that. She said she'd wanted to do it there on purpose instead of at home. She wanted to give it a beautiful conclusion. A weird country, by the way, the Maldives. Not much country there, that's for sure. It's mainly sea. And that airport's spectacular. There's just an airport, that's all. A runway in the middle of the Indian Ocean. And then you have to go the rest of the way on a seaplane.'

'Hm.'

'I went on a binge. There's nothing else to do there. There don't even have any animals! There's sea and beach and booze. The last night we did have extremely good sex. Break-up sex. If only all sex was like break-up sex.'

'And the flight back?' Simon has to say something, he can't just hum in response to a story like this. What's more, he's imagining what that would be like, break-up sex with Jason. Maybe his cock has beautiful blood vessels on it too. He walks around his customer and then walks back again and ends up standing behind him. That's best at a moment like this.

'Oh, fine. I'd got used to it by then. I was actually looking forward to getting back home. Checking out the field. We didn't live together, you know. Technically not much has changed. Have you got a girlfriend yourself?'

'Nah,' says Simon.

'Nice and peaceful.'

'Yes, nice and peaceful.' He looks at Jason in the mirror.

'Satisfied?'

'Great,' says Jason. 'Another good job. I can start chasing the ladies again now.'

'Ha,' says Simon.

28.

It wasn't until the day after he realised he was dead that Cornelis thought briefly of the couple next to him on the plane. The man who blocked his view, the woman flicking through the KLM magazine. Of the pilot, whose photo was in the magazine. Of the stewardess who turned them into business-class passengers. Of Jacob, who had boarded without him. He was sitting at a small table having his breakfast. Apart from him there was a couple, two tables along. The hotel wasn't busy, even though it was the holidays. Or rather, it was holidays in the Netherlands, here probably not. He was doing his best to work out where the couple came from. They sounded Scandinavian. He'd slept well. The girl who served the guests had said something to him in Spanish. He didn't understand and said 'coffee', and he was given coffee. Apparently those words were similar. There were photos on the walls of the breakfast room. Photos of the city itself, by the looks of it, because he recognised the odd-looking church tower he'd seen the day before. Strange, he thought. We're here, aren't we? Why would you hang up photos of where you are? He pulled his wallet out of his back pocket and counted the pesetas.

It was an incredible amount, but converted back to guilders, not that much. He drank his coffee, gulped down a glass of freshly squeezed orange juice, and left the breakfast room.

Two hours later he had an idea of the city. He'd spent those two hours walking down one street and up another, finding alleyways that joined them, seeing fountains and churches, outdoor cafés, bakers, butchers, beautiful unfamiliar trees. Much later he realised that at the same time, terrible things were happening just a few kilometres away. That they were searching for bodies, that bodies were being identified, or not, that chaos and uncertainty reigned. But in the city itself life simply carried on, people bought bread and meat and sat down at outdoor cafés. A group of old men were playing a game with balls. He had thought about the people on the plane, fleetingly, the way you might think for no particular reason of an encounter you had yesterday. Just people, just a chance meeting, pleasant enough, but two days later gone from your memory forever. He too sat down at an outdoor café after finding a small Spanish-Dutch dictionary in a kind of tourist information office: *Wat & Hoe Taalgids Spaans*. He studied the book before ordering a coffee and a glass of water. A little later the smiling waiter put a coffee and a glass of water on the table in front of him. Cornelis found a bizarre sentence in the book: 'Is a Rutger Hauer movie showing here too?' It smelt different here than it did at home. There were quite a few tourists walking along the wide street. In the window of a house looking out over it, a young woman was watering her pot plants. She looked at him unsuspectingly. Yes, it really did smell very different here. Fresher. More spacious.

In the days that followed, the word 'home' didn't enter his thoughts. He was using his brains to store Spanish words and fragmentary sentences. He was soon able to ask for an egg at breakfast. The word for red wine didn't stick, that was undrinkable here. The white wine tasted good, and he became a white-wine drinker. After some time he'd figured out that there were eighteen barber shops or hairdressing salons in San Cristóbal de La Laguna. And that nobody called the city by its full name. It was simply La Laguna. He was pretty sure that *laguna* was a lagoon and meant a kind of lake, but there were no signs of a lake anywhere. He walked past all eighteen establishments several times, looking in as inconspicuously as he could. Where was it busy? How many people did they have working there — surprisingly he saw very few women cutting hair, even in the salons it was almost all men. He also looked at the upstairs. Was someone living there? He spoke little, but that wasn't unusual for Cornelis. In the Netherlands he often didn't feel like it; here he was simply unable to hold a conversation. Eventually he started paying attention to the clientele too. Was a *peluquería* exclusively for Lagunans, or did it also cater to tourists or other foreigners? *Peluquería* was one of the first words he learnt, of course, along with *barbería*. He walked past Barbería Juan Flórez more and more often. He'd seen northern types sitting there and heard scraps of English through the open door. Now and then he saw shoulders shrugging or hands going up in the air. It seemed to be a barber's shop that appealed to British expats, and when he realised that Juan was the Spanish Jean and Jan, he stepped inside.

He started the next day. The boss — who was called Manuel González, not Juan Flórez — had let him do a test cut. Anyone could say they had a hairdressing diploma. He seemed pleased

with what Cornelis showed him, and to top it all a Brit came in
and gave him a chance to show how good his English was. The
Brit wanted his beard trimmed. Without stopping to think or
asking any questions, Cornelis sat him down in a chair. Fifteen
minutes later the Brit was satisfied, and Manuel too. He could
live in the flat above the shop, which had recently been vacated as
the elderly tenant had moved into a nursing home. Cornelis had
an idea Juan was saying that his wages would be a good bit lower
as a result, but he could have misunderstood that. The flat was
sparsely furnished. There was a small TV. A bed. In the kitchen
he found pots and pans, plates, glasses, and cutlery. In a wardrobe
in the bedroom he found clean-looking sheets and pillowcases.
The previous occupant hadn't neglected the place. There were
even plants on the window ledge, about half of which were still
alive.

Manuel asked him to choose another name as he couldn't
wrap his tongue around Cornelis, no matter how hard he tried.
With the help of the *Wat & Hoe*, he came up with, 'Mi nombre
es Carlos,' although he wanted to say 'Just call me Carlos', which
he couldn't find readily. Carlos sounded extremely Spanish, the
second name of the new king. Carlos Weiman. But nobody
would ask about the surname, surely? He did some shopping. The
first night in his new flat he ate potatoes with a tin of something
poured on top of them, something with tomatoes. He drank
white wine — that was dirt cheap here. He read the dictionary,
and wrote some of the words down to better remember them. He
was so preoccupied with this new situation that the word 'home'
still didn't occur to him. He didn't think about his father and
mother in Chez Jean, he didn't even think about his pregnant
wife. He didn't think about a plane at all. He'd flown away and
landed here. That was it. Nothing else to it for now. He went in
search of a laundry. He asked Manuel González for an advance

(*adelanto*) because he'd spent almost all of his pesetas on the hotel. He got it. Manuel seemed to like the idea of having a young, blond Dutchman in his shop. Manuel himself was older, around fifty, and the other barbers — there were three more, working irregular shifts — were older too. They all looked similar, black hair and a black sheen on their cheeks, and it took Carlos a couple of weeks to stop mixing them up. Manuel, Santiago, Martín, and Felipe.

A month later they were friends. They were also the only people he knew. After closing time they often drank a few glasses of red wine, mostly in front of the shop, with the men constantly greeting everyone who walked past. Carlos didn't want to start off on the wrong foot by telling them he didn't want to drink their rotgut, and he had a vague idea that white was more for women. Besides, the third glass usually tasted a lot better than the first one. Vino tinto. He became an any-wine drinker. After three glasses they tried to call him Cornelis, and because they still couldn't, they had a fourth glass. All four of them smoked, even while cutting hair or shaving customers. They were disparaging about their wives. He asked them who Juan Flórez was. They didn't know. So where did the barber's shop get its name? They didn't know that either. Most of the customers smoked too, except the children. Men and children. It was rare for a woman to come into the shop, and if one did, it was the wife of Manuel, Martín, Santiago, or Felipe, who was then a lot more interested in blond, blue-eyed Carlos than in her own husband. More and more Brits came, and all the Brits were passed on to Carlos. Santiago, Martín, Manuel, and Felipe thought Brits were no fun — you couldn't talk to them. And most of them didn't even smoke. After a while, Manuel put a sign in the window that said not just WE SPEAK ENGLISH, but also HIER SPREEKT MEN NEDERLANDS. You never knew — a Dutch tourist could happen by. Santiago and Felipe arranged a couch for him and, after a while, a better TV. And didn't he need a double bed? They gave him big winks, and Felipe slapped him on the shoulder. *'Todavía no,'* he said. Carlos watched TV to improve his Spanish. The shows he saw didn't interest him in the least, they were all kind of shouty. Meanwhile at Los Rodeos, planes were landing and taking off in large numbers again.

Of course he sometimes lay awake. Of course he then tried to get a clear view of the situation he found himself in. It was beyond him. Things started getting mixed up. Manuel slipped between his father and a customer, his mother suddenly started talking Spanish to one of the Jordaanese women, who was filling the new Wigomat coffee maker. He was dead and then he wasn't. He counted the months since March. In August he dreamed of a birth, Juan and Jean swapped places, sometimes it took an effort for him to remember that his wife was called Anja, at others she was a loud, insistent presence, but this all happened in bed, in the time between waking and sleeping, when he couldn't remember whether or not he'd dreamed. On very rare occasions it was a nightmare, and he was a charred body that couldn't be identified because he had such good teeth he could hardly remember the last time he'd been to a dentist — then he'd wake up sick to his stomach. But a little later, in the bright sunlight, almost always at a pleasant temperature, he turned back into Carlos, the new barber at Juan Flórez, who attracted customers because he was so exotic and more and more often noticed a girl lingering in front of the shop. A young woman who seemed to think it was a shame that Juan Flórez wasn't a *peluquería*.

It wasn't until November that the first of his countrymen came into the barber's shop. After looking around, he gave Carlos a fright by saying in Dutch, 'You're the one I'm looking for!'

'Why's that?' Carlos asked cautiously. It was the first time he'd spoken his native tongue in months.

'It doesn't take a professor to see that you're the one who speaks Dutch here.'

'Oh, right,' said Carlos

'¡Bienvenidos!' called Felipe.

'Yes,' the Hollander said. 'Good morning to you too. Where do you want me?'

Carlos pointed out a chair. 'What were you thinking of?' he asked.

'Short, please. It's been a long time.'

'I can see that,' said Carlos. He worked in silence for a while. The man studied himself in the mirror with interest, turning his head slightly now and then. Felipe, the only other barber at that moment, was having a lively discussion with his customer, both puffing away.

'Filthy,' said the Hollander.

'Ach,' said Carlos. 'You get used to anything.'

'How did you end up here?'

'Ach, I wanted something different.'

'Different from?'

'Amsterdam.'

'Oh. I'm from Bodegraven.'

'Hm,' said Carlos.

'What's your name?'

'Carlos,' said Carlos, without a moment's hesitation.

'Yes, and my mother's Juanita.'

'Really?'

'No, of course not. She's called Rita.'

'Yes, that's possible too, of course.'

It was a strange conversation. Carlos hadn't stopped to think that putting up the sign he'd written himself would oblige him to talk to Dutch customers. Although the brusque Dutch way in which the man had said he was looking for him had turned out to only be about his job and had nothing to do with him personally, he was still keyed up from the fright it had given him. And suddenly, apropos of nothing, he realised he wanted a dog.

'I'm supervising a dredging operation,' the man said. 'These lazy islanders don't know the first thing about it. I work for Boskalis. I travel the whole world.'

'Is there much to dredge here?' Carlos asked, for something to say.

'You kidding me?' The man stared at him in the mirror.

'No. Why?'

'Just wondering. Can you make it a bit shorter around the ears?'

'Sure. However you like.' The man was full of himself, full of his important work all over the world. Carlos was just an obscure barber in La Laguna. That was the end of the conversation. Carlos thought about a dog. Felipe finished his customer at more or less the same time. Nobody had come into the shop in the meantime. A quiet morning. Unusual. Felipe was glad to have had the Dutchman. 'Even more customers,' he said.

'I'm just as happy without,' Carlos admitted. Then he started talking about a *perro*. If Felipe could arrange one for him.

'What kind of dog?'

'Not too big and not too small,' said Carlos.

'¿De raza pura?'

'No,' Carlos said. 'I want a mongrel.' He used the word *híbrido*.

'No problem,' Felipe said, then asked, 'How's it going with the paella?'

'Better, much better.' Carlos rarely ate potatoes anymore, and when he ate them it was in a tortilla de patatas. He liked making paella. It took a while, but that was the whole idea. The young woman strolled past. She looked in shyly, then quickened her pace when she saw there were no customers. Carlos opened the door. 'Entra,' he called after her. 'Unlike him' — gesturing at Felipe — 'I'm also very good at cutting women's hair.' At least that's what he thought he said.

'Now, now,' said Felipe.

'Am I wrong?'

'I don't know,' said Felipe. 'I've never seen it.' The young woman came in hesitantly. '¡Una cálida bienvenida!' he told her.

Two weeks later Carlos had a dog. A white dog with brown patches, including one around the left eye, which made him look very cute. Still young — Felipe couldn't say how old exactly. 'A few months,' he said. 'Maybe a year.' Where had he got it? 'Does it matter?' Felipe asked. The dog was free, it was a stray. Carlos bought an enormous cushion and food and water bowls. A lead, a collar. Whenever he could, he went upstairs. He walked the dog morning and night, and sometimes around midday too. It wasn't long before the dog was lying in the barber's shop doorway. 'I don't mind,' Manuel said, 'but if I notice it scaring off customers, it's gone.' Carlos found him a typical southern European dog: stretched out listlessly in the heat, wagging his tail, and displaying submissiveness at every interaction. He didn't scare off any customers, he was a gentle creature. Carlos called him Lobo. Thanks to Lobo he started straying further afield, taking the bus to Santa Cruz now and then to walk the dog on the beach. He'd been in Tenerife for quite a few months and only now saw the sea. Lobo stayed close and didn't really need a lead. Sometimes he would disappear for fifteen minutes, but he always came back. Carlos took the bus because it didn't occur to him to buy a car. Until Santiago asked if he had a driving licence.

'Of course,' Carlos said.

A couple of days later he had a car, a small one, but his for a ridiculously low price.

'How come it's so cheap?' he asked.

'Just pay and don't ask any questions,' said Santiago.

From then on he began heading out more often, not only down to the sea but also up into the mountains. Standing just below the peak of El Teide and looking round, he realised that he had spent almost an entire year in a very small circle. Lobo was running around and kicking up dust, Carlos took a deep breath. He wanted to go up higher, but was stopped by a man in a green coat. He wasn't allowed to go up there, he needed permission for the top. A pass, a permit. Carlos felt like running around in circles with Lobo. It was the most beautiful landscape he'd ever seen. Bare, dry, rugged, sharp. The moon on earth, if you blocked out the *teleférico*. A volcano. He was standing on top of a volcano!

A couple of weeks later, Lobo was joined in the car by Alanza. Not to the sea and not to the mountains, but a circuit, which came down to sea *and* mountains. The whole island was sea and mountains. His Spanish had got so good that he was able to have conversations with Alanza, and if he got stuck, he said, '¿Cómo se dice?' and they figured it out together. Alanza had become a regular, the only woman who dared venture among the men. Sometimes the others watched in silence while Carlos cut her hair, almost in reverence, even forgetting to smoke. When she was gone their silences were different. Meaningful. The usual winks now and then. Once Manuel said, '*That* is hairdressing,' as if realising on reflection what a terrible waste all these years of only cutting the hair of men and children had been, as if wishing Juan Flórez was a peluquería.

As Alanza smoked, Carlos smoked too. He found it no problem at all. They'd got out of the car near Punta del Hidalgo. Someone had painted an enormous mural of a stamp with the space dog Laika on a wall. 'Look!' Carlos told Lobo. Lobo looked at him expectantly, but didn't understand the pointing arm. Carlos found his dog incredibly stupid and extremely smart by turns.

'A dog doesn't see something like that,' said Alanza.

'No?'

'And if it did, it wouldn't be even the slightest bit interested.'

The dog ran towards the ocean across a pebble beach. Carlos and Alanza followed slowly behind. In the distance an enormous pyramid-shaped rock jutted up. Bare, sharp. Almost everything on the island was sharp and jagged. Wild.

'Is that the Punta del Hidalgo?' Carlos asked.

'No, this whole bulge — *protuberancia* — is the Punta.' Carlos committed the word to memory and looked around. It was March. The wind was strong. Enormously powerful waves were breaking on the rocks. The sky was blue, without a single cloud. Lobo barked.

'I think you're a handsome man,' said Alanza.

Carlos looked at her. What she'd said was so at odds with the way she'd first entered the barber's shop that he didn't know how to react. 'Gracias,' he said after a while. Fortunately Lobo crashed awkwardly into her legs at the same time. 'Ice-cream?' he asked.

'Stupid Lobo!' she said and then, 'Fine.'

The village was small, but every Tenerife village has an ice-cream salon. They sat down to eat their ice-creams at the outside tables, out of the wind. Lobo lay down on Alanza's feet with a sigh, as if sensing that he had something to make up for. Carlos too felt that he needed to redeem himself, but he couldn't bring himself to do it. Alanza was quiet. She licked her ice-cream and looked at the street. When the ice-cream was finished, she lit a cigarette and gave Carlos one too. Lobo looked up. They smoked.

In 1989 Carlos had been on the island twelve years. Lobo had grown old. Carlos had a subscription to *El Día*. He played cards once a week with Santiago's and Felipe's sons, and he went to their football matches, although he wasn't particularly keen on football. He took Gustava, Martín's mentally handicapped daughter, on regular excursions in his new second-hand car, which had been organised by Santiago, of course. Gustava was an adult woman who scarcely communicated with language. She could say, 'Aaiiii.' It was only to Lobo that she sometimes said something else, but if Carlos had tried to express that in writing, he wouldn't have succeeded. She seemed to enjoy their outings, especially when surrounded by parrots in Loro Parque. She loved ice-cream. Carlos had to tell from her facial expression how she felt, whether she wanted to go back home or stay longer, if she wanted Lobo close or a little further away. When he dropped her off, Martín and his wife nodded. Martín was in any case the quietest of the four barbers. Maybe that had something to do with the daughter.

He still lived above the barbería, although quite a few improvements had been made to the flat in the course of time. It was fairly small, but he was single, and the windows were open most of the year. He was thirty-six, and the longer he stayed dead, the more Spanish he became. Less and less a Dutchman who had left all kinds of things behind. Now and then he'd go to a disco with the barbers' sons: the barbers' sons to drink — they were almost all married, Carlos to pick someone up. After he'd been to bed with a woman, he could stick it out again for a while. He could live off the memory for a long time, and when he saw Lobo, he thought to himself, I've got Lobo. I've got somewhere to live, enough to eat. I can wash my clothes in the brand-new washing machine in the bathroom. *El Día* was a rather nationalistic newspaper and didn't make him much wiser about the rest of the world. More than that, it was as if beyond Spain, America, and the island itself, no world existed. He'd bought a video recorder and picked up or two or three new movies every week at the local *video club*. The weirdest event that year was a gathering of forty thousand people in the Parque Nacional El Teide because of a radio broadcast in which they tried to contact aliens. The islanders saw quite a few UFOs. Tenerife was a UFO hotspot. Carlos left them to it.

After him nobody else had been hired at the barber's shop. Santiago and Felipe in particular came when they felt like it. He himself was there every day. Imperceptibly he had become the head barber. He answered the phone, made appointments, allocated customers and shifts. 'We're turning into old men,' Manuel said to him one day. It was raining, but Lobo was lying on the doorstep all the same. It was one of those moments when he thought his dog was pretty stupid. It was as if getting up to lie down a little further along was too much bother just to avoid getting wet. I should get another one too, he thought. Then they'll have some time together. 'We're turning into old men!' Manuel said again, a little more emphatically.

Carlos turned his gaze from the dog to Manuel. 'Lobo's getting old too,' he said.

'Lobo's not a barber,' said Manuel.

Carlos felt where this was going.

'My sons aren't barbers either,' said Manuel.

'Yes, I'd like to,' said Carlos, to cut a long conversation short. 'If we can come to a good arrangement.'

In 1999 only Santiago was still working at Peluquería Carlos W. Manuel had turned into an old man sooner than he probably anticipated and had died of pancreatic cancer. His funeral was the first that Carlos attended on the island. For the first time he participated in a wake, immediately on the night of the death — a packed house full of singing, laughing, and drinking people. For the first time he saw a coffin being raised by a forklift. Manuel was interred four levels up.

Felipe and Martín came by at least once a week. When it was unexpectedly busy, when men had turned up without appointments, they'd lend a hand. They were adamant that they didn't want to be paid for it, they were doing it *por los viejos tiempos.* Conchita and Nilda didn't mind at all. They put in curlers, dyed grey roots black, and brought the women under the driers cups of coffee or glasses of water. The shop had been done up and looked like a hairdressing salon that could step straight into the twenty-first century. Five chairs, and four of those were almost always occupied. For that reason alone, Santiago couldn't retire yet. He was seventy-two, but still had no difficulty squatting to hug Oro. Oro wasn't white like Lobo, but an even sandy brown with a thick white stripe on his head. Otherwise his build was suspiciously similar to the old dog's. Carlos suspected that Felipe had got him from the same place. Lobo had lived another eighteen months, and when he died Oro changed from a high-spirited adolescent puppy to an introverted dog. Slightly fearful too. But he wouldn't hurt a fly, the customers just stepped over him, with the dog generally not even opening his eyes. In the evenings Oro liked to lie next to him on the couch — something Lobo had never done — and he reacted to certain sounds in the movies that Carlos watched on his new DVD player. The pounding of hooves was his favourite, and Carlos could say 'It's a movie!' as loud or as often as he liked. It didn't make Oro calm down any faster. He too became an old dog.

When Alanza came to get her hair done, Conchita and Nilda knew their place. Alanza was the boss's. They only saw each other in the salon. In the course of time, Carlos had learned that the men of the island didn't take kindly to their wives associating with an unmarried foreigner. They discussed everyday things. The children, bits of news, deaths. Nilda plied Alanza with cups of coffee. With Alanza he was always more aware of the touching that was part of the profession, more than with other, random women. After forty or fifty minutes she left again, smartly coiffured.

Carlos had become a man with a dog. Nobody knew he'd walked away from a plane. Nobody knew he was dead. He'd almost forgotten himself. He'd become a rambler too. Because of the dog, whichever dog. There were few places on the island he hadn't been. He could walk for hours, almost without thinking. Walking on the moon. Walking on the flanks of a volcano. Walking by the ocean. Sometimes he found La Laguna too big and too busy.

On New Year's Eve hundreds of people gathered on Plaza del Adelantado. Carlos was there too, with the sons of Martín, Felipe, Santiago, and Manuel and their wives. The children and Oro had been left at home. This was the Gathering Against the End of the World. As people on the island believed in UFOs, it was only natural for them to believe in the millennium bug too. They counted down. Quite a few people had drunk far too much in an attempt to calm their secret fear. But the world didn't end, the lights didn't turn off, the church bells rang everywhere, no planes or satellites fell out of the sky, and two days later all the computers turned on as usual.

In the spring of 2007 an article in *El* Día caught Carlos's attention. Lying at his feet was Pablo. A black dog with white front paws. Lobo and Oro had become framed photos on a sideboard, that was how much of a southerner and — with it — sentimental he had become. There was going to be a memorial service in the Auditorio de Tenerife. It was thirty years ago, and only now were they holding the first international commemoration. Along with the unveiling of a monument, but the artist wouldn't see it because he had died of a cardiac arrest at the age of sixty-three the previous year in Den Helder. *Desafortunadamente*, according to the newspaper. The artist's name meant nothing to Carlos, of course, but Den Helder all the more. It wouldn't evoke anything to the readers of *El Día*, but suddenly he was back on the boat to Texel, an eternity ago. Drizzle, wind making the boat sway, brazen seagulls, the smell of chip fat, salty air. He had to shake off the feeling, that's how strong it was. The Netherlands. The past. Despite shaking it off, he could still see himself coming home with wet hair. The street looked strange, like always after a trip, as if the bike shop had suddenly changed owners. Through the empty, silent hairdressing salon, up the stairs, his mother with her big leather shoulder bag. His mother! While giving his head another shake, he unwittingly started counting. She was getting close to eighty.

Pablo looked up with a start — his owner had made a sound he'd never heard before. For a moment he didn't know what was expected of him.

Carlos had already seen the work of art; he went that way regularly with Pablo. A spiral staircase. A beautiful thing, tall, made of rusty metal. The service was to be held on 27 March at 10.30 am. It didn't say anywhere that it was private or by invitation only. He heard the door opening downstairs, noisier than usual. Not Nilda, not Conchita. He held his breath for a moment. '¡Café!' Exactly. Santiago. Too lazy to make his own coffee, but also needing company when he's here. Of the four men in his life, he liked Santiago the most. A gentle man, less rigid than most of the islanders. Helpful without making him feel guilty. That was a skill. Santiago and his wife were the only ones who occasionally came to eat at his place, but each time it was a slight disappointment, simply because his wife was there. Not that she was annoying, far from it, but simply because Carlos got on best with Santiago alone. He stood up. 'To work!' he said to Pablo. *¡A trabajar!*

'But what do you want to go there for?' asked Santiago, after Carlos had told him why he wouldn't be working Tuesday.

'Ach,' said Carlos.

'I know what that word means by now,' said Santiago. 'Just tell me.'

'You remember that I'm called Cornelis?'

'Yes, now you mention it.' Once again he tried two or three times to pronounce the name.

Carlos waited calmly until he was finished, then said, 'I was on that plane.'

Santiago has to think about it for a moment. 'That's impossible,' he said at last. 'Then you'd be dead.'

'I am,' said Carlos. 'Somewhere.'

Santiago was seventy-nine, but with Nilda and Conchita there, he could still manage a day in the salon.

Carlos had one suit. For funerals or other special occasions. He left La Laguna around nine, and parked his car near the botanical gardens in Santa Cruz. At the kiosk he bought a pack of cigarettes and a lighter. The sun was shining, and there was a fairly strong breeze off the ocean. It was nice weather. They were digging up part of the gardens. Bulldozers were moving earth back and forth, and big pipes were waiting to be laid. Carlos sat down on a bench to watch. He lit a cigarette. He had to think of Alanza. And Lobo and Oro. Pablo would be lying in the doorway now, and Conchita, Nilda, and Santiago would be busy with customers. He was a bit nervous. He didn't know if he'd be allowed in, but the real nerves went deeper, of course, and that was why he was doing his best to think about the hairdressing salon and his dogs.

He lit another cigarette and walked along the coast towards the Auditorio. It didn't look crowded, at least. That calmed him a little.

After going in without any problems, he chose a seat at the back. The auditorium hardly filled up at all. Normally they staged operas here. He'd never been before; there were no opera-lovers among his friends and acquaintances. When it started, the place was only half full. That surprised him. He was slumped down on his seat as if afraid that someone might see him. As if someone would stand up, point at him, and shout, 'What are you doing here?' Why were there so few people? If there were two relatives for each of the victims that would be 1,166 precisely. Even then the auditorium wouldn't be full, but this was a very meagre turnout. On the stage were five flags and a few arty objects. They looked like willow branches with eggs dangling off them, which was possible, seeing as the next weekend would be Easter.

A woman on the stage started by telling them the pro-gramme. He had to get used to the Dutch, which she spoke with a vaguely Spanish accent. There was an invitation-only lunch. At three o'clock there would be buses available to take anyone who wanted to go to Mesa Mota. Carlos looked at the crowns of the heads in front of him. The woman informed them that the two musicians who were going to play were unable to attend due to health reasons. That too. A dead artist, a half-empty auditorium, musicians who couldn't make it. The president of Tenerife spoke. Carlos looked at the crowns of the heads in front of him. The chief of the public health service at the time of the accident spoke — very briefly. Then there was music after all: a woman played something on the piano, a soprano sang. One song and then another. Carlos hadn't recognised a single crown, and won-dered if he would recognise hers after thirty years. He wasn't just looking for the crown of an older head, he was also trying to see who might be sitting next to her. A young man.

The people applauded — the music was over. A small American woman came up onto the stage with measured, hasty steps. She mistakenly referred to 'two fully loaded 747s'. Her mother, a well-known and very successful real estate agent, had died. She'd won a trip to Hawaii for being one of her compa-ny's top sales representatives for eight years running. But since she'd already been to Hawaii, she had swapped that trip for a Mediterranean cruise. This was the remark that caught Carlos's attention. Several weeks after the memorial service that was held for her mother in Las Vegas on March 31st, she received a

letter from some army base or other. The envelope contained her
mother's pinkie ring. 'I shall cherish it forever,' she said. She was
fighting back tears, which made almost every sentence end with a
question mark. To conclude, she wanted to read something from
her scrapbook. A story about God creating mothers and being
interrupted by an angel while He was at it. She gestured occasionally while speaking, as if she'd rehearsed the story at home
in front of the mirror. 'Gracias, dank u wel, thank you,' she said
before leaving the stage with the same hasty little steps.

During the speech by a Dutch relative that followed, Carlos
shrank even more. The man had lost seven family members. He
was hardly able to speak, simply skipping words now and then.
He spoke of those who were left behind — himself, Grandma,
uncles, aunts, some nephews and nieces. Carlos felt like a traitor,
an interloper, someone with every reason to choose a seat at the
back. He didn't want to listen to the man for another minute,
but still stayed seated, as standing up and walking away would
only attract more attention. The man's children lit candles. The
pianist and singer played and sang an Ave Maria. The CEO
of KLM. All of the speakers mentioned the staircase. A spiral
that reached up into eternity but was abruptly broken off. The
US ambassador. He mentioned Dorothy Kelly, a surviving
stewardess, here today. He didn't say this as a statement, but
questioningly, looking at the audience for a moment. No one
raised their hand. The Dutch minister of transport and water
management. A Limburger, a young guy still. The president of
the Canary Islands. The national anthems were announced, people stood up. Carlos had no choice but to stand up too. Spain.
The USA. The Netherlands. The speakers pushed the music into
the auditorium like a wall of sound. Sitting and standing just
in front of him were some photographers. They offered some
protection. The Spanish and American anthems weren't his, and

left him cold. When the Dutch national anthem started playing he had to sit down. And he stayed seated while the auditorium slowly emptied. People took the exits on the sides. He looked up at the ceiling. Now that he could see more than just the tops of heads, he didn't feel any urge to study faces. Only when everyone was gone did he stand up.

Slowly he made his way back to the botanical gardens. The bulldozers and diggers were motionless. He sat down on the same bench and lit a cigarette. He wiped the sweat from his forehead and loosened his tie. It had warmed up a little. The sun was still shining just as brightly and the breeze was still blowing. He sucked the smoke into his lungs and blew it out forcefully. At one stage the angel touched the prototype mother's cheek. "'There's a leak," she pronounced. "I told you you were trying to put too much into this model." "It's not a leak," said the Lord. "It's a tear." "What's it for?'" the angel asked, and God answered, "'It's for joy, sadness, disappointment, pain, loneliness, and pride.'" The angel told God that He was a genius, but 'the Lord looked sombre. "I didn't put it there.'" Carlos really had listened carefully to the American who had lost her mother. That afternoon he skipped the unveiling of the monument. But he didn't go to work either. He pulled on old clothes and his hiking boots, put Pablo in the car, and drove to El Teide.

A volcano! That was what he had thought the first time he came here and Lobo went crazy running around in dusty circles. A lunar landscape. He still found it beautiful, but he'd never again felt the euphoria of that very first time. That must have something to do with growing older. When you get older, things become normal. You should actually go in search of new things to give yourself a chance of feeling euphoria like that once again. But as you grow older and see the things around you as normal, settling into a new life, the possibility of turning back becomes more and more remote. The crowns of those heads this morning. The crowns of all those heads arrayed before him. All people with their own lives. In America, in Holland, here on the island. He walked and walked, and Pablo stayed close. There was nobody else. It was windier here than on the coast. There's something moving about it, about the crown of a head. Such a guileless part of a person, a part of your body you never see directly. He'd seen thousands and thousands of them in his lifetime. And he was also the one who showed the customers theirs. Slowly moving the mirror from one side of the back of the head to the other. 'Satisfied?' Only rarely had someone answered no, and when they did it was a man who could see a bald spot emerging. He walked and walked. Pablo barked at something, then came bouncing back. He gave him a treat. The third dog, he thought. I've already been here three dogs. How old was Pablo now? Six? Seven?

On the way home he drove past Mesa Mota. It was deserted, twilight. He looked at the staircase, he looked at the wreaths, he looked around. In the distance he could see the runway of the old airport, now only used for flights between the islands. Pablo snuffled at the flowers and sneezed loudly. '¡*Salud!*' said Carlos.

He took the next day off as well, drove to Martín's, and picked up Gustava. 'Loro Parque?' asked Martín.

'Yes,' said Carlos. 'We'll go and see the orcas.'

'Poor things,' said Martín's wife.

In just under half an hour they drove to Puerto de la Cruz. Gustava looked around with interest. Carlos wondered how things were going for them at home. Martín and his wife were quite elderly now. The daughters-in-law probably helped. When he looked to the side, he saw that Gustava was getting old too. Mentally she had always stayed a child, but this child was also getting wrinkles and grey hair. Her teeth were pretty bad. She was probably more or less his age, and his hair had long stopped being blond too, of course. Pedestrians at traffic lights would think that they were an ageing couple on their way somewhere in the car. The idea made him smile. Gustava saw it and said, 'Beeuhuhu.'

They had sat too close to the pool. Carlos should have known. Gustava found the orcas' dancing, to the rhythmic clapping of the audience, the most beautiful. She crowed with delight. Carlos couldn't understand where the staff found the courage to swim with these enormous animals. He stared at the ocean, which was behind the pool — the vast body of water the orcas were supposed to be swimming in. Gustava nudged him. Yes, it's fantastic how they leap out of the water, in exchange for a bucket of fish. During one of the last rounds that the orca with the crooked dorsal fin swam, it slapped the water with its enormous tail, splashing them. When they went to get ice cream afterwards, Carlos's trouser legs were still dripping. Gustava looked at him, ice-cream on her cheeks and the tip of her nose and her hair stuck to her forehead. 'Hmmm,' she said. She's actually not that different from a pet dog, Carlos thought. You take them somewhere and they're contented, you give them something to eat and they're happy, and later they'll go to sleep and you'll have no idea what's going on in their heads.

On Thursday Carlos was back. He went downstairs early, wanting to be the first one there so he could have the coffee ready when

Santiago walked through the door. Santiago would ask him how it had gone. He unlocked the door and stepped out onto the street. Pablo bumped into his legs, heading for the tree on the other side of the road. The dog raised his leg and started pissing while already being distracted by something else. A smell, the stray cats, a noise. Never taking the time to piss properly. Carlos went over to the tree too and looked back at the hairdressing salon. In the corner of his eye he saw Pablo about to walk off. 'Stay!' he said.

Peluquería Carlos W. In the corner of his other eye he saw his oldest employee approaching.

'Are you admiring your own shop?' Santiago called.

'Why not?'

'Yeah,' said Santiago, pushing the dog away, 'yeah, why not actually?'

'But I'm also thinking about whether I should trade you in for someone younger.'

Santiago looked at him with astonishment. *'¡Hijo de puta!'* he shouted.

'Come on, let's drink some coffee.'

'And talk,' said Santiago.

'Yes, that too.'

That night, Pablo got a scolding for having dirty paws. He had to lie on his cushion. Instead he lay down on the still damp coat that Carlos had thrown on the floor the day before. He curled up and stuck his black muzzle between his white front paws. On that coat, with what looked like a deeply contented dog on top of it. Carlos looked on from the couch. For some reason he found it an unpleasant sight. 'Here, boy,' he said after a while, patting the couch invitingly. The dog tried to ignore him, but couldn't help but prick up his ears. 'Here!' The dog groaned. Carlos kept staring at him. It's as if I'm not here, he thought. As if Pablo is seeking comfort from an item of clothing with my scent on it. Why won't that animal come and lie down next to me on the couch when I've called him?

29.

Simon is sitting in the chair in front of the window. He can tell from the clothes people are wearing how warm it is. They've left their coats at home. Earlier in the morning it was still chilly, and when he went back outside after his swim he saw that it was no longer narcissuses in the bed, but tulips. Red tulips. There wasn't a red-headed man standing next to him smoking when he noticed it. He hasn't seen him since. The merry, merry month of May, he thinks. He's feeling a bit listless, like always after swimming, and sits in the chair to stare out of the window. It'll be a while before the first customer arrives. As often in the shop, at least when it's empty, it feels like time is standing still. A barber's shop without customers, a swimming pool without swimmers, a school corridor during the holidays. The corridor occurred to him recently when he went to look at the small pool after swimming. He doesn't remember why, but once he had to go to the hairdressing school at the start of summer. To pick up something or drop something off, it doesn't matter what. The total abandonment. As if he'd stepped into another world. That red-headed guy, who had apparently only come to the pool that once. Why? Or did he happen to go in the morning that day, but otherwise goes in the evening or afternoon? And more importantly, would I be OK with it if I bumped into him again? Simon picks his phone up off the windowsill and types in his mother's number.

'Weiman?'

'It's me.'

'Good morning.'

'Yes, good morning. Hey, shall I take Igor for a haircut Saturday?'

'Um, yeah. Fine. I'll pass it on. You'll probably have to take him back to the home yourself when you're finished.'

'I can do that.'

'Would you like me to come with you?'

'No, why would I?'

'No,' she repeats. 'Why would you?' She's quiet for a moment. 'You can handle him. Everything fine otherwise?'

'Yep. With you too?'

'All good here. Do you have customers today?'

'Absolutely. Four of them.'

'You're not working too hard?'

'I take good care of myself, don't worry about that. What are you up to?'

'I'm on the balcony. I've already been to the garden centre this morning. Shouldn't you have a couple of nice planters next to the door?'

'Planters?'

'Yes, with flowering plants.'

'In the Jordaan? I don't think plants like that would survive long round here.'

'Maybe it would attract some extra customers.'

Simon sighs. 'Plus, it's a public pavement and quite narrow

too. There's probably a by-law against it. I'll see you Saturday.'

'See you then.'

Around five he's at his grandfather's. Two glasses of Rutte Oude are waiting on the table along with some sliced sausage on a wooden board. The door to the garden is open. Classical music is playing on the radio. Simon stands in the doorway and looks out at the garden. Some of the shrubs are flowering. 'My mother wants me to put some planters next to the door,' he says.

'It's not allowed,' says Jan.

'I suspected as much. She thinks flowering plants would entice more customers.'

'I didn't think you wanted any more customers.'

'Nah. Not really. I'm not that bothered.'

'Here. Genever!'

Simon accepts the glass carefully and sips the meniscus. Incredible that the man was able to carry the genever glass across the room without spilling it.

'I requested them from the council once,' Jan says. 'The pavement's too narrow there. Nobody on that side has planters.' He's already half-emptied his glass. 'Still, that must be getting on for thirty years ago now. Bit of sausage?'

'Yes. Thanks. Shall we sit here by the door?'

'Fine by me.'

Simon drags two chairs over to the door and puts a side table between them. 'Well, that's good. Or at least it's one less thing to worry about.'

'Were you worried about it? I didn't get that impression.'

'In a manner of speaking.' He picks up the ash tray and the board with sausage.

Jan sits down. 'Phew,' he says. 'It's like summer.' He looks out.

'Have you seen that the rhododendrons are about to flower?'

'Which ones are they?'

'Those ones over there with the red buds.' He points. 'Then you always know that it's really May.' Other doors are open too. A quiet murmuring is filling the garden. 'How's your mother?'

'Fine. She's always busy with something or other.'

'I could never work out why she never managed to find another guy. Such a beautiful woman.'

'Ask her.'

'When do I see your mother?'

'I can invite you both over to dinner sometime,' Simon says. He sips his genever. 'Doesn't it bother you that Chez Jean isn't as busy now as it used to be in the old days?'

'Not at all. It's nothing to do with me. The old days are gone. It's your business. You're not running at a loss, are you?'

'No. Maybe it's different if you're doing it by yourself. There were always more of you, then it's not as intense. If I've had four customers, well, I'm …'

'Your father was like that too. He couldn't take too much. He'd get moody. I never asked him directly, but I had the idea he never really wanted to become a hairdresser.'

'No?'

'No, or a hairdresser without me. That's possible too. That he just couldn't stand having me as his boss.'

'It can't have been that bad, surely? You're a nice-enough guy.'

'You'd think so. I don't know. These women here think I'm extremely nice.'

'I'd like to talk to one of them one day.'

'Why?'

'Because I think those stories of yours might be just a tad exaggerated.'

Jan stands up to get the bottle of Rutte Oude. He refills both glasses and takes a piece of sausage from the board before sitting down again. 'There. How's it going with that writer?'

'Well, I think.'

'Yes, I'm sure. I mean, is he making progress with his book? The book we're in?'

'That's not how it works, at least I don't think so. He's done research. He talked to you, but that doesn't mean right away that you're going to be in the book.'

'No?'

'Not at all. It's going to be a novel.'

'Pity.'

'The last time I spoke to him, he said he was writing about my father.'

'What? He doesn't know anything about that at all.'

'Yes, it seems strange to me too. I think you were right when you said that writers always milk something for all it's worth.'

'And can he just do that? Are you allowed to just write about anyone?'

'No idea. I think so.'

'Have you looked up more stuff on your computer too?'

'Yes.'

'And?'

'You know what it is with things like this, they're almost addictive. You dig deeper and deeper, and it takes you further and further. The other day I found out something about a Martinair pilot who was involved with both Tenerife and the Faro disaster. First he tried to expose the air-traffic controllers at Los Rodeos for watching a football match, then later he refused to give the families of the victims of the Faro disaster access to Martinair's findings.'

'Self-interest both times.'

'Yes. Or else KLM steered his investigation in a certain

direction. But where does it get you?'

'Nowhere. Probably.'

Simon takes a sip of his genever. Somewhere in a neighbouring flat a TV turns on. He sees that his grandfather's glass is empty, and pours him a third. 'And there's something else strange. The more I find, the more I get the feeling I have to go and look for him.'

Jan looks at him as if he's gone mad. 'You mean that you want to find out more about him?'

'No. Or, well, that too, but I mean *really* look for him.'

'Look for him? But son, he's dead, right?'

'That's the thing. When I'm digging for information like this, I forget.'

'Maybe you need to ease off a little. You're losing your grip.'

'Oh, it's not that bad, but I am starting to understand how someone can turn into a conspiracy theorist, and that's a bit worrying.'

Jan takes a sip of his third genever. 'We have to close the door,' he says. 'The cold's rising.' After his grandson has closed the door, he lights a cigarette. 'That Israeli plane, that was bad too. I remember I was watching Studio Sport, Annette van Trigt was the presenter at the time, and something got interrupted, probably the report of a football match, and then she suddenly appeared on screen with a very shocked look on her face.'

'Yes,' Simon says. 'I remember that too, but especially because my mother—'

'Succumbed,' says Jan.

Simon's surprised to hear his grandfather use that word too. Maybe he sat next to Henny on some of those birthdays. Then an enormous noise blares through the corridor. It's the foghorn he recently heard in the distance on the phone.

'Dinner!' cries Jan. He knocks back his old-style genever and stubs out his cigarette. 'And you know what's funny?' he asks.

'No,' Simon says.

'A couple of those women are a bit senile and they don't understand the sound of that foghorn so very well, but they think this is a ship and I'm the captain, and they all want to sit at my table!'

'I really have to see that one day,' Simon says.

'Another time,' Jan counters. 'I have to announce it in advance, otherwise they'll get totally confused.'

30.

Back home he gets a pizza out of the freezer. After all that genever he has no desire to cook. He's not even very hungry. He opens a bottle of white, puts the pizza in the oven, sits down at the kitchen table, and opens his laptop. In no time the links have led him to a documentary about dealing with loss. About grieving. With an interviewer who asks people who have lost a child, spouse, sister, or brother what it's like. The documentary is called *Surviving Relatives* and was made in 2017. Simon has to keep fast-forwarding because the interviews have been intercut in the edit. The only one he's interested in is with a youngish-looking guy in a pink polo shirt. He was nine when he came into the kitchen on the morning of Monday, 28 March to find a whole group of people sitting there — his grandmother and his grandfather, who had come to look after him and his brother for a week, plus a bunch of his father's employees. His father and mother had driven off the day before in a brand-new Mercedes that had only recently been delivered from Germany. It was their first long trip in the new car. They'd waved goodbye, and his father had called out cheerfully that they'd be back in a week.

And now the whole kitchen was full. People were crying. That made it quite a disturbing sight. Then a friend of his parents came in, a policeman. He took the two boys into the living room and sat them on his knees. He told them that he had bad news: their mummy and daddy would never be coming back. The boy was angry with the policeman. What kind of nonsense was this? The policeman was someone he knew well. 'I didn't actually believe it,' says the man in the pink polo shirt.

The following Sunday, 3 April, the nine-year-old boy spent the whole day sitting on the low wall that separated the front garden from the street, waiting for the return of his father and mother. After all, he hadn't believed the policeman. His anger had subsided, he'd remembered his father's promise, and that was why he was sitting there, like a faithful dog trusting to instinct and waiting. Every car he heard could be the brand-new Mercedes. Towards the end of the day, his grandfather came out. 'Come inside,' he said. 'Come on now. They're not coming back.' They didn't talk about it much. The boy did judo, and the sport was an outlet for his sorrow and aggression. Every night, Grandma made three signs of the cross over the boys' beds. And if they were sad at bedtime, Grandma said, 'Just say three Hail Marys, then everything will be fine again in the morning.' Grandma and Grandpa moved in with them. Grandma and Grandpa became their father and mother. They did kind of help, those Hail Marys. Because Grandma said they would. Life went on. He never saw the new Mercedes again.

Many years later the nine-year-old, who of course stopped being nine long ago, but in a certain way never has, goes in search of help. 'So,' the interviewer asks, 'is it still an open wound? Even now, after forty years?' Yes, now he stops to think about it, he can only agree. 'Sometimes I feel completely alone,' the man says. 'I feel like Remi in *Nobody's Boy*.' And: 'I'd work the rest of my life for free if I could talk to them for just five minutes.' This is partly fed by the attention that 'modern next of kin' seem to get, as if all the overwhelming displays of grief, sometimes even national, have finally made him realise what he went through himself. The conversations with someone he trusts have given him some breathing space. He's learnt to stop wearing himself out every day at work to make sure he's so exhausted he won't think about things at night.

'So work was your escape?' the interviewer asks.

'Oh, yes,' he says. 'I had tremendous escape behaviour.'

There's a photo from New Year's Eve 1976 of the boy pressed against his father's side, and he'll always remember his father telling him that 1977 was going to be a tremendous year. 'I've never forgotten that.' Of all those interviewed, this man is the only one who doesn't express some kind of resignation, who doesn't say that the grief has been overshadowed by everyday things, little things, who hasn't been able, to use an ugly cliché, to come to terms with it. 'I wish I could stuff it into a backpack and hang it up somewhere,' he says. He's the only one who breaks down, takes off his glasses, and dries his eyes. He doesn't say 'Sorry', the way many people do when they cry in public.

And then he talks about his son. At the hospital, after the baby has been washed and dressed, when things have calmed down a little and his wife has fallen asleep, he goes over to the window with the baby. It's an enormous window, at least two-and-a-half by three metres. Outside a lot of sky is visible, a lot more sky than buildings, trees, or bushes. You could call that sky the firmament. Or the heavens. He lifts the baby up a little and shows him to his parents. The little boy's name is a composite of three names, his grandparents' and his father's. The man feels like he has to do something symbolic, and this is what he chooses. He doesn't say anything while holding up the baby, he doesn't want it to get ridiculous, but now, faced with the interviewer, he simply says it: 'I was holding him in my arms, and I showed him to my mother and father in heaven, and then I felt very small and sad that those people never got to see their grandson.'

Those people, Simon thinks. He closes the laptop. Something stinks. God, the pizza! The oven light has been broken for ages — he can't judge the damage straightaway, but once he's opened the door and pulled out the rack, he sees that he won't be eating pizza tonight. He hears his grandfather saying that he's losing it. Or was it his grip he was losing? He slides the charred pizza into the bin, and in that instant he sees the similarity between this man and one of the speakers on the video of the international commemoration in 2007, on Tenerife itself. That man, the chair of the surviving relatives' association, was scarcely able to talk. Thirty years later. Both men kept choking up. Because it wasn't finished. But he finds the man in the pink polo shirt much nicer. Really, a very sweet guy. Not the other one, though he can't work out why exactly. Maybe because the man's children played a large role in the commemoration. As if it was a kind of family reunion. Which probably wasn't the idea when they rented an opera theatre with room for the relatives of all 583 victims.

He cuts himself a piece of cheese, eats a handful of salty crackers, and tips half a glass of white wine down the sink. Then he brushes his teeth. In bed a little later, he sees the new Mercedes in the car park at Schiphol. A dated-looking car park. All kinds of other cars drive in and then leave again a little later, constantly changing the composition of the car park, but the Mercedes stays in the same spot. Forgotten. Planes land or take off overhead, vehicles drive in and out, around an expensive car that is losing its shine. The writer's book has been lying on the bedside cabinet aimlessly for a while now; he's stopped reading it. It has already accumulated a very thin layer of dust. Still somehow magic, he

thinks. Closed is closed, but if you open it, you open a whole
world. And that world is now lying there untouched and gathering dust.

31.

It was something he'd been planning on doing for quite a while, so now he does it. On Saturday morning. He opens a Twitter account, and it's a lot less hassle than he'd expected. Name: Simon Weiman. Bio: Barber. But what about the profile photo? He thinks for a moment, then goes downstairs. He looks around the shop. A chair and a mirror? He backs up a good distance and takes a selfie, and then, to be on the safe side, five more. He goes back upstairs and adds the profile photo. It turns out they show it very small, so that's even better. Then he makes an espresso and sits down again. 0 Following, 0 Followers. How does something like this work? If nobody follows him, nobody will see what he posts. He stares out of the window at the tree in the garden. Maybe it will all reveal itself? He types in the writer's name. Ah, OK, your Twitter name is your name with an @ in front of it. He's @simonweiman; apparently there are no other Simon Weimans. There's a possibility to click FOLLOW. He does it. There, now he's on the page. The writer has 1,998 followers. Is that a lot? Simon thinks it's a tremendous number, especially after he's gone back to his own profile, which now says 1 Following, 0 Followers. If he types in something now, the writer will probably see it, and then he'll follow him. Then he'll have one follower at least. Otherwise he'll stay in a kind of vacuum. On it, but without anybody knowing. He thinks for a moment. 'Bum tit screw fucking's good for you.' When it's too late, after he's sent the tweet off into the world, he sees that he should have used a comma, maybe more than one. He makes and drinks another espresso, and eats a banana. Then he packs his swimming bag and leaves the house. It's only on the way, in the car, that he wonders what he's going to use Twitter for.

'Planters aren't allowed.'

'What?'

'Planters on the pavement. Grandpa's already asked about it.'

'Yeah, thirty years ago! Maybe it's changed.'

'I doubt it.'

They're sitting next to each other on the steps, up to their chests in the water. In the pool, the usual scenes. Melissa and Frits swimming laps. Jelka and Buari whispering in a corner, where Jelka keeps going underwater and Buari keeps pulling her back up. Igor is flipping the rubber raft over and over again, and Sam and Johan never get tired of climbing back onto it.

'The girl that's in the corner with Jelka,' Simon says. 'What's her name actually?'

'Who,' says his mother.

'What?'

'The girl *who* is in the corner. Bella.'

'Gosh,' says Simon.

'Have you noticed how much calmer it is?'

'Compared to what?'

'The first couple of times you were here, they were restless.

They crave certainty. They really hate change.'

'Sam and Johan haven't changed much.'

'No, but they're just like that. They were born that way.'

It's raining outside, and the light in the hall is greyish.

The fluorescent lights are on in the showers.

'Are you on Twitter?'

'Of course. Everyone's on Twitter these days.'

'I've only been on it since this morning. How many followers do you have?'

'About three hundred.'

'Really? How can you have that many?'

His mother looks at him. 'What are you suggesting now? Is it so hard to imagine your mother having something to say?'

'Sorry, I didn't mean it like that.'

'But I follow more people. I'm a follower.'

'I follow one person.'

'Yes, for now, but that will change. Have you already posted something?'

'Bumtitscrewfuckingsgoodforyou.'

'No!'

'Yes.'

'Are you five years old? Why, for Christ's sake?'

'I was feeling a bit rebellious, I think. It's a test tweet. Nobody follows me.'

'You're not right in the head.'

'That'll be it.'

'Simon!' Sam screeches.

'What do you want?' asks Simon.

'Bumtitscrew!' shouts Johan.

'Now you've done it,' Anja says.

Sam and Johan start yelling at the tops of their voices, trying to outdo each other. Igor stands next to them and forgets to flip

the raft. Buari, or Bella, screams 'Bumbumbum!' from her corner.
Strange, Simon thinks. Unable to pronounce her own name, but
a word like bum is no problem. Anja looks at the clock, then
hurries over to Bella and Jelka's corner, where Jelka has been
underwater for quite a while. 'Come on,' she tells the two girls.
'It's time. We're getting out.'

'Igor,' she says, taking him by the shoulders and looking him in
the eye. 'You're going with Simon. Simon is a hairdresser. He's
going to give you a haircut.'

The boy looks back vacantly.

'Snip, snip, snip,' she says and gestures.

'Snnn,' says Igor.

'Yes! Simon will take you in his car and then drive you back
home afterwards. Would you like that?'

Simon looks on. They'd both get the fright of their lives if
the boy suddenly said, 'Yes, I'd like that very much.' There's still
nothing going on. It's still possible that in a little while what
happens will be what everyone thinks is going to happen. That
Igor comes home with a neat haircut and probably a nice scent
to go with it.

'A haircut?' Johan shouts indignantly. 'Are you a hairdresser?'

'Yes, Johan, I'm a hairdresser.'

'Yeah!' shouts Sam. 'Why not us?'

'We want haircuts too!'

'Bumbumbum!' shouts Bella.

Jelka starts to cry.

'Just go,' Anja says. 'It's making them all too restless.'

'OK,' Simon says. 'We're going.'

The boy watches the windscreen wipers as if in a trance. He doesn't see anything of the street. Marnixkade, Rozengracht, the narrow streets of the Jordaan, some of them even narrower because of illegal pavement gardens. Simon's in luck — there's a parking space not far from Chez Jean. He gets out on the street side and walks around to open the passenger door. He unbuckles Igor's seatbelt. 'Come on,' he says. To his surprise the boy simply gets out, as if he knows what 'Come on' means. As they're walking to the door a plastic bag blows past, then catches on the pedal of a bicycle a little further along. He unlocks the door and pushes Igor in. The boy looks up. 'Yes,' Simon says. 'That's the doorbell. Look.' He points it out. Either Igor's not interested or he doesn't know the meaning of a pointing arm. He's got his swimming bag on. Just now he was sitting in the car with that same swimming bag pushing him forward like a soft hunch on his back. Simon gently removes it. 'Glass of Coke?' he asks. He peels off the boy's coat too and leads him to the chair in front of the window. 'Sit down.' Then he hurries upstairs and fills a plastic cup. Before going back down, he scans the living room. It's exactly as he left it earlier in the morning. Nothing's changed. Igor glugs the Coke down in one go. Then burps loudly. Simon locks the door and checks that the sign is turned so that FERMÉ is facing out. Music, he then thinks. I have to put on some music, that will be sure to calm him down. Not that Igor is restless now, but later, when he's cutting his hair, that could change. He turns on the radio and looks for a station playing dated, nondescript music. Golden oldies. Without any wound-up DJs. 'So,' he tells the boy. 'We're going to start.'

Scissors chirping through thick black hair. What a fabulous sound that is. Simon goes to a lot of trouble, using clips, layering.

He notices that his gestures are more flamboyant than usual, as if he's trying to show Igor what he's doing. As if he's acting out a caricature of a hairdresser. Meanwhile he brushes the boy's neck and shoulders. He hasn't washed Igor's hair. It was still damp from swimming, and he imagined the boy wouldn't enjoy leaning back over the sink. There are completely normal customers who don't like cracking their spine, who can't or won't entrust their neck to the curved opening designed to hold it. It's been a long time since Igor had a professional haircut, that's very clear. The boy looks at himself with apparent interest, his hands calm in his lap under the hairdressing cape. He's motionless except for his feet, which never stop jiggling. 'Eye of the Tiger' is playing on the radio. Every now and then Simon presses Igor's head to one side very carefully. At other moments he pulls it towards him. He feels an ear, a cheek, his fingers go in search of the pulse in his neck. A couple of times he sprays his hair to make it a little damper. He bends his knees to look at Igor in the mirror. 'OK?' he asks.

'Hnnn,' says the boy.

Simon leaves the hair long enough to tuck it behind his ears so that, if somebody wanted to, they could still make a very small ponytail. Then Igor would look like a modern guy who knows how to put his best foot forward. He doesn't have much of a beard yet, just a vague moustache. 'Come On Eileen' is playing on the radio. Simon thinks really hard. He knows this number, but he doesn't have a clue who's performing it. A car drives past, much too fast. Igor looks to the side. Simon calmly turns his head forward again, but when he lets go, Igor shakes his head hard, flinging his hair around so that it ends up in front of his eyes. A clip comes loose, hitting the mirror with a sharp click that sets off a kind of panic reaction. Igor raises his hands and tries to brush his hair to one side, but can't do it properly because he's still wearing the hairdressing cape. Simon presses the hands back down, then pulls the hair to the side and tucks it behind his ears. 'Look,' he tries to explain, despite knowing better, 'like this.' Igor looks at himself in the mirror, less calm now. OK, Simon thinks. I'll have to do it differently after all. He had already imagined Igor with short hair sometimes, Popov hair. He doesn't actually have a clue how the boy relates to his hair, usually he only ever sees it wet, stuck to his forehead and cheeks in magnificent strands. It will be simpler for everyone if it's a bit shorter. Popov short. It won't be difficult to do. It's thick enough, and Simon has to cut it so it won't need any gel.

He starts again. But first he picks the plastic cup up off the windowsill and holds it next to Igor's head. The boy nods. Another Coke. Simon runs upstairs, half fills the cup and runs back down again. Igor is still sitting there as if he lives in the barber's chair. Again the boy drains the cup in one gulp, and again that's followed by a hearty belch. Simon takes the scissors and starts cutting off centimetres. The radio plays two numbers by two men who are dead: 'Purple Rain' and 'Heal the World'. Simon hums along, Igor makes a quiet sound every now and then. In the street it's still raining. So many people are already dead, Simon thinks. Kurt Cobain. Amy Winehouse. Donna Summer. Whitney Houston. As if the devil's reading his mind, 'Heal the World' is followed by 'One Moment in Time'. Simon pushes Igor's head forward a little and uses the clippers to shave the back of his neck up to his hair. 'Huungg,' says Igor. It's a satisfied sound. Simon runs his hand over Igor's neck and, seeing as his hand is already there, over his throat as well.

He bends his legs a little, puts his hands on Igor's shoulders, and looks at the boy in the mirror. Igor doesn't look back, he's looking at himself. At his new haircut. 'Classic,' some people would say. Popov, thinks Simon. I've cut myself my own Popov. He runs his fingers through the hair — that's allowed, it's the barber's prerogative. Hair, ears, neck, throat. The hair falls back into position perfectly. Isn't it a little long still? Then Igor does look at Simon, as if he's suddenly worked out how a mirror works and that Simon's face is somehow real. Is that a searching look? What's wrong with this boy? What's gone wrong inside his head? Why doesn't he burst out of that shell? 'Finished,' Simon says, just to have something to say. He undoes the hairdressing cape, takes Igor by one arm, and puts him back in the chair in front of the window. On the way from one chair to the other, the boy makes no attempt to grab him like he did in the swimming pool. Simon takes the broom and starts sweeping. Rarely has he swept up such an enormous quantity of hair. When he looks at the boy now and then, he sees him calmly staring out at the street. Sometimes he follows a passing cyclist, sometimes it's like he doesn't even see the pedestrians or cars. Simon sweeps slowly and meticulously. He's dragging it out. He's unsure. He's getting cold feet. On the radio, Madonna's singing 'Don't Cry for Me Argentina'.

Three quarters of an hour later, he parks the car in exactly the same spot. The parking space is still free, the rain's kept up, the plastic bag on the pedal is still flapping in the wind. He goes into the shop. It's empty and quiet, the clock is ticking softly. Everything neatly tidied up, no trace of the boy. No, that's not true, there's a plastic cup on the wide shelf under the mirror with a minuscule amount of Coke in it, next to the ashtray that's used exclusively by Jan. His grandfather, who's growing older as if there's nothing to it, as if death's a tall story told by others.

32.

In the kitchen he mixes yoghurt and little bit of muesli in a bowl, and sweetens it with a generous scoop of raspberry jam. He puts the bowl on the table and goes over to the window. The trees are dripping. On the other side of the gardens, someone is rummaging around at a sink, then disappears out of sight. A bit further along, somebody opens the curtains. That's possible too, of course, just getting up now, when he's already put in half a day. Then he hears a strange sound. He turns around. Was that his phone? On the screen the push notifications are coming in one after the other. Twitter. That was why he didn't know the sound. *On the nail. This newcomer could prove entertaining.* That's the writer's reply to his tweet. Under that, someone else has written: *Can't wait for the next poem.* The heart and the number 15 under it are red. Hang on, do fifteen people like this? He taps his profile photo. 1 Following, 21 Followers. There's a blue 1 on the envelope icon. He taps it. *When?* The writer. Hang on, who can see this? Just him? Or all twenty-one of his new followers. He types *Joker* as an answer and sends it back with the arrow. Then he eats his yoghurt, and waits.

you know that this is called a DM and nobody else can see it?
Now I do.
welcome. It's fun here
Really?
yes you going to answer
All these people who are following me now, are they your followers?
yes they see things I've liked, and then they can react or like them
too
Do I have to follow them back?
nope only if you want to
Why don't you use full stops?
it stops anyway and some people think full stops are passive
aggressive
The answer is no.
beer tonight then?
Sure.
Queen's Head
OK.

He types @ followed by his mother's name. She has 299 followers. He makes it 300. Then he thinks about a new tweet, but after his *Bum tit screw fucking's good for you* he has no idea what to say next. Is Twitter really meant for people like him? He has to remember to ask the writer tonight how to remove a tweet. If that's even possible.

Even now, on a Saturday night, The Queen's Head is almost empty. It is still early, that's true, but Simon doesn't get the idea the place will be thronging with warm, surging bodies two or three hours from now. It's like the top of Zeedijk is something from the old days, when young guys smelt of patchouli and wore

Afghan tops that were too small for them. When Waterlooplein still existed. An era he associates more with his father than himself. There are a few men sitting at the bar, a couple of them speaking Swedish. Like last time, they sit at the back. One of the doors is open. At the end of the afternoon the sun broke through, and now spring is asserting itself in the air above the motionless water and on the street-light-lit branches of the blossoming elms.

'Ah, the turtle doves are back again,' Oscar says, putting two beers down on their table.

'Christ Almighty,' the writer says. 'I'm slowly starting to understand why this place is always so deserted.'

'Aren't you a ray of sunshine?' Oscar is a real Amsterdammer.

'No, seriously.'

'Come on, they're all at home watching Netflix. Snuggled up on the couch with just the two of them. With drinks and nibbles.'

'And you're stuck with people who order öl.'

'They're two very friendly tourists, and they've already got through quite a lot of öl.'

'Earl?' Simon asks.

'Beer,' says Oscar.

'Do the drag queens still come?' the writer asks.

'Nah,' Oscar says stoically. 'They're all obsessed with some TV show or other, and of course that's much more important than performing in a grimy bar somewhere.'

'They're absolutely right about that.'

'Should I close the door?'

'No,' Simon says. 'I like it like this.'

'Två öl!' calls one of the Swedes.

'Oh, now they're getting impatient. We can't have that. I just suggested a Tuborg, and they looked at me as if I'd turned into an elk. Seems it's Danish.' Oscar walks back to the bar.

'You're an Amsterdammer, aren't you?' the writer asks.

'Born and bred,' says Simon. 'But I've betrayed my birthright by suffering from a dearth of humour.' He thinks for a moment, then adds, 'I'm pretty sure I've never used the word "dearth" before.'

'Willeke Alberti.'

'Damn,' says Simon, and they sing her most famous song together, quietly at first, feeling their way. *Every time, I get it in my head, that I'll find paradise, all those things he said. Every time, all the blues turn grey, and I'm outside again, on a rainy day. But every time, I think someone will come, who will see my worth, and embrace my love, someone who will fill this dearth. Love forever, every time.*

Even though it's very short, Oscar turns the music down so the last lines can be heard through the whole bar. The two Swedes clap and raise their beers, and from the front, the Zeedijk side, they hear whoops of appreciation. Oscar pulls two beers and brings them over. 'On the house,' he says. 'This way we don't need any drag queens.'

An hour later, the door's shut. The cold was rising from the water. It may be spring, but it hasn't made it inside just yet. The place hasn't got any busier. The Swedes have gone, Oscar's leaning over the bar, probably eavesdropping. He's just let the customers who are left hear how Willeke sang it, then he put his usual clichéd music back on.

'Of course you can delete a tweet,' the writer says. 'But not other people's reactions.'

'Well, I'll think about it,' Simon says. He looks at his phone. 'There you go,' he says, 'I now have twenty-seven followers, and one of them is my mother. That can't be the idea, surely, your mother following you?'

'You can block her.'

'You obviously don't know my mother.'

'What was behind it, actually, this morning?'

'I was a bit wound up.'

'Why?'

Simon sighs. He takes a swig of beer. He hears his grandfather exclaiming, *They'll milk it for all it's worth!* 'You know how I swim with the mentally handicapped every Saturday. Or, at least, walk around in the pool with them. There's one, a boy of about eighteen, with black hair, who's always grabbing hold of me. This morning I took him home with me to cut his hair. But—'

'Whoa. Did you do it?'

Simon looks at the writer. He could ask 'What?' for the form. He could also leave it. 'No.'

'Why not?'

'Because I'm not Sam and Johan. They're Mongs, and they're always pulling Igor's trunks down, that's the boy with black hair. They're pretty wild and uninhibited.'

'And?'

'Yeah.'

'You know you're not allowed to call them Mongs.'

'It's just the two of us and—'

'Three!' shouts Oscar.

'I'd think long and hard about it if I were you.' He winks.

'Are you winking at me?' Simon asks.

'Did I do that? I must have something in my eye.'

'Oscar!' Simon calls. 'Have you got a couple more beers for us?'

'Of course,' Oscar says. 'Something to eat too? I've got nuts.'

'OK.'

Oscar comes over with a tray. On it are three glasses of beer and a bowl of mixed nuts. He puts the bowl and two glasses down in

front of Simon and the writer, and the third on the side of the
table for himself, then slides a stool over and puts the tray on the
floor. After taking a big swig of beer, he wipes his mouth with
the back of his hand. 'I was once,' he says, 'in Iran. It's somewhere
I'd always wanted to go, the men are so beautiful there. A lot of
hassle, a visa, a permit, reason for visiting. It was terrible and it
was fantastic. I was a good bit younger than I am now, that's
important. It was terrible because within three days I'd been
robbed of almost all my money, and on the fourth day— I was
there with a friend, not *my* friend, *a* friend — we got caught up
in a revolt. For us, it came out of nowhere, thousands of people
pushing forward. Soldiers, rifles, teargas, yelling. Of course, we
didn't understand the yelling. I've never experienced anything as
frightening before or since. I was a nervous wreck. Completely
at the mercy of that strange world.' He looks at the writer. 'We
fled into a bookshop. There were a few people there who were
acting like what was going on outside was nothing special. A
safe haven. Surrounded by books. Every evening we visited the
same coffee shop. Not an Amsterdam coffee shop, but one where
they really do drink coffee. On Hijab Street. There were two
young guys, the son of the owner and one who worked there.'
He takes a sip of beer and munches his way through a handful
of nuts. 'Those guys found me very interesting. Sometimes being
foreign's enough. I started teaching them English from a phrase
book that was floating around the coffee shop. We were sitting
on a couch with me in the middle. They enjoyed it, and acted like
I was another Iranian. Men there are very affectionate with each
other. It's a kind of affection we Westerners don't understand
properly. That we misinterpret. I fell madly in love with the
employee. Or maybe I should say "in lust with". Maybe it's the
same thing. He slept in a small dark room above the coffee shop,
you had to use a stepladder to get up to it. Sometimes during

the English lessons he'd point up, and I'd realise he wanted to show me his room. But the son was there too. The two of them. And I couldn't read the situation. I was scared. I wanted to go home. I wanted to get back to a world I understood. In the daytime we walked the streets of Tehran, magnificent streets with concrete gutters and old plane trees. Lots of people walking around with bandaged noses. It was October, and thirty-two degrees every day. I knew they hanged men and boys if they caught them at it. But those evenings in the coffee shop were so innocent. A moment came when I couldn't hold back any longer, the night before the day we were due to fly home. Maybe he really only wanted to show me how he lived in that room above the shop. I left my friend down below with the owner's son and climbed up the ladder. Mirsad was his name, and he closed the hatch. My God, he was so good looking. Or maybe I should say sexy. Maybe it comes down to the same thing. I did it because the robbery and the uprising had left me like a hunk of raw meat in a completely foreign world. I was defenceless. I was scared. I was so removed from my normal life that the fear of execution became subordinate. Plus I told myself that they surely wouldn't do something like that to a foreigner. My friend, I'm exaggerating a little, but not very much, they almost had to drag me onto the plane. I was crying. I was crying when I left Iran.' Oscar drains his glass.

It's quiet for a moment. Then the writer says, 'Gosh, Oscar.'

'Yeah, sure,' says Oscar. 'Knock yourself out. I can elaborate if necessary. Otherwise it was a pretty ugly country, to tell the truth. Bare. Dry. Dusty. A very weird variety of grass in the parks.' He thinks about it. 'Thick and leathery, kind of like a succulent. One park was called Laleh Park. That means tulip.'

Simon sits there quietly. He has the uncomfortable feeling he's been given a lesson. But what in?

'Two more for the road?'

'Please,' says Simon. 'Make mine a head butt.'

As the barman's walking away, the writer whispers, 'Oscar's single.'

'Oh, yeah,' Simon says. 'There's something else I wanted to ask you. How do you do it when you want to write about sex in your books?'

'I don't. And, believe me, I've tried. In Oscar's story just now, when he said the guy's name, he just said, "and he closed the hatch". That's how you do it. Oscar could be a writer. If you wrote down what he just said, you'd follow it with a blank line. Blank lines are brilliant, and badly underrated by a lot of writers. And readers, in general, are far from stupid.'

'And if it's really long sex, you do two blank lines.'

'Haha. Or end the chapter. Often that says a lot more than words.'

They stare out through the window. Simon knocks back his genever. He's quite tipsy, maybe drunk. On the bridge somebody falls off his bike, the sound of metal on cobblestones crossing the water and echoing off the Queen's Head windows.

'Ouch,' says Simon.

'Yes,' says the writer, and it sounds rather final. 'Blank lines. I love 'em.'

'OK,' says Simon. He burps.

'You have to go home. You've had enough.'

There's still something Simon wants to ask. 'How's it going with your book?'

'Fine.'

'Still about my father?'

'Yes.'

'Is that allowed?'

'Your father seems like a fictional character to me,' the writer says. 'And I think you'll be satisfied when I'm finished.'

33.

Simon can't remember ever having had a headache this bad before. He has to stay in bed a long time with his head completely motionless on the pillow. It's raining again. Now that spring has really arrived, the sunny days from two months ago have given way to rain. He can't see it, the orange curtains are closed. He can hear it. It sounds cosy and safe. Just stay in bed a little longer. He doesn't feel like anything. Not coffee, not food, not even water. He lets his mind wander. In a while he'll watch the *Air Crash Investigation* episode. He's been saving it. Because it's dramatised. Fictionalised, in a way. Will they ever make a movie of it? That story of Oscar's. Until last night, Oscar was a barman, someone you see and forget. Now he's become someone. What possesses someone to go to such a difficult country? Simon himself has never been to a difficult country. North Korea, that's another closed country, one you can get into if you really want to. Perish the thought. But of course that's also because he won't fly. Is that what writers do and want, writing a story, turning it into a book, so they can become someone? The writer didn't make any effort at all to get him to go home with him. That was fine by Simon, he was glad, but on the other hand it stung a little. Doesn't he want him anymore? And if not, why not? The rain taps on the window ledge and the roof of the dormer window. A plane flies over. A seagull shrieks. Cormorant, he thinks, almost as a Pavlovian reflex. He dreams regularly of a flight on a plane. It never goes wrong, but it's menacing. The plane always flies horribly close to the ground. The planes in his dreams have sofas, not regular seats, and everything is covered with deep-pile carpet. Chairs, walls, floor. And there's also an awful lot of view, much more, he suspects, than you'd get through those tiny portholes. There are also no, or very few, other passengers. Does that mean something, his mostly being the sole passenger? Oscar. Simon really looked at him for the first time when his story turned him into someone. Quite a striking guy really, with lines and wrinkles, bright eyes, good hands. Oscar single, the writer single, him single, his mother single, even Jason and Martine single now, and Jan, but he doesn't really count, he's a widower. But his mother is a widow, although she could have easily remarried. No, she's single of her own accord. All loners. Ow, stay still. He presses the back of his head down on the pillow. Simon had unconsciously seen Igor on that bench in the coffee house. On the bench, in the room upstairs, the shall-I-shan't-I. There is something Persian about Igor. Maybe he is an Iranian. He doesn't know anything at all about the boy. Not a thing. Yes, he now knows his hair. Why hadn't he popped in for a moment yesterday when he dropped him off? Why does what he should have done only occur to him now? It's always the same. There was a swimmer once, nicknamed The Albatross. Or was that Michael Phelps? Couldn't Popov be called The Cormorant? I'll google his nickname in a bit. He sits up, turns onto all fours, then slowly puts his feet on the floor. 'Owwww,' he mumbles. He stands up straight and shuffles over to the stairs as cautiously as possible. Fortunately he doesn't have anything he needs to do today.

Two paracetamols and a long hot shower do him good. He still has a nagging pain in his head, but he can move freely again. Two espressos do him even more good, and an hour after that he's able to eat something too. The windows at the back of the house are wet. This afternoon, which is already almost here, he can turn on the TV. Sport. There's nothing you can close your eyes to as pleasantly as sport. He should also do some bookkeeping, and he should top up his supply of hair lotion, which means ordering it on the French manufacturer's website. But first he meets two new stewardesses. He can't remember encountering their names earlier. Joan Jackson and Suzanne Donovan. They're sitting alongside each other in a very cosy-looking cabin. Wooden walls, a full bookcase, some shrubs and trees visible in the window. They could be sisters. Both with typically American, short, snappy hairstyles. They both seem far too young. And look, here's Bragg again, now in Tenerife. He feels like an old friend. Dead in the meantime, as it happens, in 2017. Before watching any more, Simon slides the programme ahead to the titles. *MMVI DISCOVERY COMMUNICATIONS, INC.* 2006. And back again. It is a very incomplete, almost grotesque documentary. A narrator talks about Von Shanten and Claus Murs, and there are three actors playing the Dutch crew. Simon doesn't understand a word they say, it sounds like Swedish. They all have blond hair and blue eyes. Still he hears something new, not just from Bragg, but from Donovan and Jackson too. No emergency services came. They were the ones who dragged the passengers away from the plane as best they could, and promised them that help was on its way. It wasn't. The KLM plane was closest to the control tower.

All the emergency services deployed there. The firemen probably didn't even know there was another plane a few hundred metres further along. Right at the end, Suzanne Donovan talks about something that happened on the flight back to the US. Not wearing her uniform, she asked a stewardess if she could sit in one of two free seats next to an emergency exit. The stewardess asked her jokingly if she was capable of assisting in the event of an evacuation.

'Oh, yes,' she answered.

'So you can open the emergency exit and lead people out?'

'Oh, yes,' Donovan said again. 'I did it just the other day.'

Both women smiled as the picture faded to black.

Typing the name Suzanne Donovan on Google takes him to a website that lists every survivor, photo and all. *Peter's Tenerife Crash Page*. She turns out to be called Suzanne Carol Donovan in full, and in 1977 she was twenty-eight. She and Joan Jackson didn't break their ankles or legs because they were in the front section of the plane, which detached from the hull and then tipped over. A jump of some five feet. What always happens happens again: he reads everything. He can't help it. When he has a bag of wine gums they always disappear in one sitting too, and then he curses the manufacturers: they clearly put something in the mix that makes it impossible to eat just two or three. All those old, grainy photos, mostly of people who are dead by now because they were already fairly old in 1977. The Trumbulls, the Tartikoffs, the story of the man who saw another man dangling from the wing by the seat of his pants and pulled him loose, the story of the other man who describes how the first one freed him. Lots of couples. Then he sees that this page sums up not only the survivors but also the dead, and he makes the mistake of clicking on the icon for victims. He sees a photo of Francoise Colbert de Beaulieu, the purser who swapped places with Dorothy Kelly because she was embarrassed (it turns out that her full name includes Greenbaum, as she was married to Marc Greenbaum), sees a photo of a good-looking young guy, Miguel Ángel Torrech, who brought that same Dorothy Kelly a coffee just before the *Rhine* came racing towards them. The Goedharts, Robert and Beverly. The husband was the son of Gerritt, born in Holland. Maybe he spoke Dutch.

Wait, Eve Meyer! It turns out she wasn't travelling alone. She was sitting next to Martha Elaine McPartland, 'a worldwide traveller and amateur photographer'. Married with three children. On her way to 'a Greek cruise'. There is a photocopy of an article from *The Atlanta Constitution* of 18 May 1959 headlined 'Who is Eve?' and published on the occasion of the release of the movie *Operation Dames*. It's a rather sarcastic, local-girl-made-good piece. The reporter phones Eve's mother, who says she's very proud of her daughter, who she almost never sees as she lives in Hollywood. Her sister doesn't seem to know a thing, and describes Eve as an actress and fashion model; they communicate by mail. The mother, who is just home from hospital, also says she probably won't get to see the picture because of her health. Simon reads that Eve devoured books, sometimes as many as five a week. *Gone with the Wind* was her favourite. She'd already read it about five times. According to the movie's press book, Eve's ideal night out was to see a movie starring Clark Gable or Claudette Colbert, then 'to Piedmont Park and top the whole evening off with a snack at the Yellow Jacket Drive-In'.

Why isn't there a site like this for the Dutch victims? And why has he been sitting here for hours now reading about side issues?

Because it *has* become hours, there's no longer any point in turning on the TV for *Studio Sport*. And they remain side issues, even if it feels like immersing himself in someone like Eve Meyer brings him closer to his father. Nonsense. They were two separate planes, the Americans and Dutch were two different worlds, completely ignorant of each other, except in the cockpits, where they swore and complained about each other, with Spanish air-traffic control as the go-between. In a way it's not complete nonsense. Miguel Ángel Torrech died at more or less the same time as his father. They're linked forever. When he closes the laptop it's like leaving a cinema after watching a movie. For a moment everything around him seems unreal. Simon is the kind of person who, long ago, after seeing *Jurassic Park*, wouldn't have been surprised to see velociraptors running down the street.

Simon makes himself something to eat. Cutting up the vegetables, he notices that it's still not dark outside. It really is spring. The birds are still singing. Get up, he thinks. Work. Eat. Drink coffee. Cook again, watch TV. Sleep. Get together with someone now and then. And meanwhile winter turns to spring. And autumn to winter. A short summer in between. He pours himself a glass of white wine. And in a few years he'll be fifty. A half a century. He puts his plate and the glass of wine on the coffee table in the living room, and turns on the TV. *Studio Sport*. Fifty! That's always been ancient. Beards, grandchildren, sagging bellies, a game of billiards, a glass of bock beer, unisex coats on E-bikes. There's a football match on. When Simon watches football he never pays any attention to the ball. He looks at the footballers' hair. No idea what the score of Heracles — FC Groningen is, but you can bet that not one of the twenty-two players needs a haircut, and you can't say that of the coaches.

Later that evening he arranges a dinner date with his mother and grandfather. That way he's completed at least one task today. Once — strange how you remember things, fairly unimportant things more often than not — he heard someone say that. That a day isn't a failure if you complete at least one task, no matter how small, 'even if it's just cleaning the cat tray'. He can't resist asking his mother if she's noticed that he's showing some initiative.

'Not indolent,' he says.

'Aha,' she says. 'You've remembered.'

'Yes, that's not something you forget. Your own mother saying something like that about you.'

'It's all positive. In this case to promote heightened self-aware-ness. Friday?'

'Yes, Friday. Grandpa couldn't come any earlier. He's stuck in the routine of the old folks' home, of course.'

His mother sighs. 'I sometimes wonder which era you live in. Old folks' home? Anyway, nice. I'll bring some wine.'

An hour later he's rummaging around the bedroom. He pulls out the rolled-up posters, then puts Mark Spitz and Matt Biondi back again. He's brought a damp cloth with him, and wipes off one of the frames. He knocks a nail into the fresh white wall. There's Popov, hung up again. He missed him. It was much too bare in here. Strange that neither his mother nor his grandfather said a word about the date of the dinner.

34.

Someone has written *we want more* under his first and as yet only tweet. Someone. Now that he's followed back all of the people who have followed him, he's seeing a lot more on his timeline. It's all very busy. Politics. Inclusivity. Diversity. Save the trees. People get enormously wound up about things, and there's even one follower who's melodramatically announced his imminent departure from Twitter, because *this isn't what I signed up for.* Off you go then, thinks Simon, I'm not stopping you. But then he reads all the reactions, and realises that people post things like that so that others can beg them to stay. He thinks about a second tweet. *I'm a bear called Jeremy, teddy with a big bear dick, I can push it in and out, knock the girls up with my spout.* No idea which forgotten corner of his brain that's come from, but there it is. Within a couple of seconds, the heart has already turned red.

Simon makes an espresso and a mettwurst sandwich, and pours himself a glass of orange juice. It's the third morning in a row he's swum. His upper arms feel warm and heavy, his scalp itchy. Tomorrow he'll swim again. Each time he's thought about what to cook for his mother and grandfather, and he still hasn't decided. Fortunately, Anja gave up being vegetarian a couple of years ago. He doesn't just think about food while swimming, he also thinks back on races he swam in. It's all a long time ago, but they made an impression on him, and apparently things that make an impression stick. He feels the nerves, the expectation, even this morning, there, in the swimming pool. An hour ago that feeling turned him into a twelve-year-old who's been driven to the pool by his mother. A seventeen-year-old who's cycled to the pool himself, with weak knees, as if on his way to the dentist. The swimming itself and the boys' bodies around him. A kind of vague feeling centred in his chest. Not unpleasant, nice really, so nice he considers getting a permit again and putting his name down for masters' competitions. Maybe he's changed. It's going well, he has the idea his swimming has got stronger. Maybe faster too. But before he knows it, he's thinking about steak or salmon again, asparagus. This is why he keeps swimming. This detachment; the concentration that leads to distraction. He eats his sandwich and drinks his orange juice.

ok there with your big bear dick
yeah fine. You?
I haven't got a big bear dick. you busy sublimating
don't use such difficult words
you know very well what I mean
no
... anyway do you know this one: canaryislandscrash.com
no
have a look

There aren't a lot of photos from just after the crash. A few. A couple. Five were supposed to have been taken by David

Alexander, a twenty-nine-year-old American who, after emerging unscathed from the *Clipper Victor*, realised he had a camera hanging around his neck. It was his own camera, of course; he'd just taken a photo through the window of the planes parked on the runway in front of the *Clipper Victor*. He took a couple of photos and only then did his legs buckle beneath him as the realisation that he'd jumped out of an exploding plane sank in. 'I wanted to take some photos of the KLM plane too,' he said in an interview with the *Noordhollands Dagblad*, 'but it was too far away.' Evidently he, unlike almost everyone else, including the airport fire brigade, did realise that two planes were involved. The number five is given in the interview. Simon clicks on Peter's Tenerife Crash Site, which he's saved on his reading list. He can't find this man, and yet he vaguely remembers reading something about photos, and what's more it's a complete list, so he must be on it. Finally — another half hour has passed unnoticed — he finds him. He's listed as David Wiley. 'Wiley, a microwave technician and amateur photographer, said he took two colour pictures of the wrecked jetliner … he gave them to a reporter for an Amsterdam newspaper …' 'It seems he changed his name to David (Yeager) Alexander.' Apparently three more photos have been added over the course of time.

Alexander never received any recognition for the iconic photos, and that's due to Hans Hofman, former leader of the Dutch Free Sex Party and a press photographer, who worked for *Nieuwe Revu* and other publications. The son of a Vietnam activist and a herring vendor, his sister was shot dead in her own home in 1981 by a policeman because she'd threatened him with a paring knife. Hofman was a yob, the kind of guy who raced around Amsterdam on a moped and listened to the police radio to be the first at the scene of a fire or accident. He was called a 'street photographer', probably an old-fashioned word for paparazzi. He approached

David Wiley at his hotel on 29 March. He didn't have anything, and needed something — a good shot, not a photo of two ash-grey wrecks. Wiley was in shock, as it's called, and didn't realise what was happening when the two of them delivered the roll of film to the hotel photo service. He saw Hofman write his own name on the envelope the film was slipped into. He saw it and let it happen. 'I wish I'd been stronger back then,' he told the journalist from the *Noordhollands Dagblad* dozens of years later. He returned to America and saw his photos in all kinds of magazines and newspapers. © Hans Hofman. In 2015 he brought a book out under the name David Yeager Alexander: *Never Wait for the Firetruck.* The website includes this blurb: 'Please remember this. If you are on an airplane on the ground and you see smoke in the cabin, whip off that seatbelt, get up and move. Don't wait for instructions, head for the nearest exit, if it is a safe one, or find a new one like I did. But most of all, never wait for the firetruck.' There's also a photo on the website of Alexander next to his sail-boat *Jamaica 3* on San Francisco Bay. 'The sailboat is my home on weekends.' Lucky him, thinks Simon. Lucky him. Is that it? Researching all these stories so you can think, 'Lucky him'?

did microwaves already exist in 1977?? what on earth is a microwave technician??

they've existed since 1947. great title
never wait for the firetruck
did you see you've already got thirteen likes
weird
you've struck a new chord. keep it up
I'm sick of it already
you've made your bed
something else: so you're writing about my father but tenerife too
sure am

I only just realised. I'm starting to get very curious
patience

Downstairs the doorbell rings. It's almost the first time that's happened to him. When a customer arrives, he's always ready and waiting like the keen service provider he is. 'Coffee?' he calls down the stairwell. 'Yes, please!' Jason calls back. He's been coming often lately. A lot more often than when he was going out with Martine. That undoubtedly means something or other, but for now Simon is still preoccupied with the street photographer's sister. Shot dead. A paring knife. Thirty-three years old. Surely you could shoot someone like that in the leg? He puts a cup in the espresso machine and looks out into the garden. Magnificent spring weather, glaring. His chest opens, vague images of earlier springs flash by, along with a feeling he could almost call happiness. Simon always experiences happiness, if that's what it is, as an enormous draught of healthy air, which makes his chest expand more than usual. 'Take a seat!' he calls towards the stairwell. A quick beard now. Tomorrow, swim again. Friday, make dinner. And then don't drink too much, because Saturday ... Yeah, Saturday. Jason says something he doesn't quite catch. He takes the espresso cup out of the machine and goes downstairs.

No, he thinks, while shaving Jason's neck, it doesn't have anything to do with 'lucky him' or 'lucky her'. It's more like people who at a certain moment go in search of their biological father or mother. Who have just lived life as it was for years and years, but have reached a stage, inevitably, when they want to know, see, feel, and maybe even smell who they're really descended from. And more often than not, that's when they're getting older themselves, almost when it's too late. The big difference for him, of course, is that there'll never be any seeing, feeling, or smelling.

'Lovely,' says Jason.

Lovely, thinks Simon.

'We'll see if it helps.'

'With what? Or against what?'

'The ladies. You know.'

35.

He's settled on asparagus. With potatoes, expensive ham, eggs, and melted butter with finely chopped chives. White wine. German white wine.

'I thought I was going to bring the wine?' his mother says.

'I'll put it in the cupboard for later.'

'It happens to be my favourite wine.'

'I didn't bring anything,' his grandfather says.

'That doesn't matter. No need at all. Do you even do any shopping these days?'

'No. Cigarettes. Rutte Oude. M&M's.'

They're in the living room. Simon has bought a bottle of Rutte Oude too. His mother is drinking the white, which she finds 'a little tart'. He's put a bowl of smoked almonds on the table. The windows are open on both sides, and now and then a breeze blows through the house. Jan calls it a 'draught'.

'Windows shut?' Simon asks.

'No, no, it's a good draught. Nice. It feels like summer.'

'It is almost summer,' Anja says.

'I do have to be careful, of course. I'm an old man, and old men have to die of something, even if it's just a cold.'

That's a remark that's best ignored. 'Any news?' Simon asks.

His mother understands immediately. 'They're still moving from house to house, and now they're somewhere up north. Swimming pool and all. The owners are back in the UK. They didn't want to have to live with all the renovation mess.'

'Who?' Jan asks.

'Henny. And her new flame.'

'Ah, Henny. I'm very fond of Henny.'

'And with her there playing the tourist, Simon's now helping me swim with the mentally challenged.'

'Is that any good?'

'What do you mean?'

'Does it help those kids?'

'Youth,' says Simon.

'They enjoy it,' Anja says. 'I think that's enough.'

'And it keeps you two off the street,' Jan adds.

'How did Igor like the haircut?'

'Fine,' Simon says. 'He seemed pretty happy. I put on some music. I cut a good bit off. But it should actually be even shorter. I can do that tomorrow.'

'As long as they know where he is. And you take him home again afterwards.'

'Of course.'

Anja grabs a handful of almonds out of the bowl. Jan lights a cigarette. The lighter quivers slightly in his hand.

'I have to cook,' Simon says.

'I'm not going to help,' Anja says. 'I'm just going to put my feet up. Maybe I'll cadge a smoke off my father-in-law.'

'Help yourself,' says Jan.

While peeling the asparagus, Simon hears them talking about Twitter. About *him* on Twitter. About Jeremy the Bear. Anja says it's like her son is someone else when he's on it. She really is smoking. Simon finds it very impressive of her: she never gets hooked. She can light one up now and then, on very rare occasions actually, and still not get addicted. Evidently the way she feels about it isn't important enough to discuss in his presence. He only needs to hear it in passing. He reads her tweets too, of course. She gets agitated about nitrogen and how unreliable politicians are, and provides free book recommendations to all and sundry. Jan has to laugh at 'big bear dick'. And he says that his grandson's probably not taking it too seriously. Simon puts the potatoes on the hob. The eggs have already boiled for six minutes — asparagus eggs have to be hard-boiled. He pours himself a first glass of wine and walks over to the other side of the room to top up his mother and grandfather. They're now talking about prohibited planters. And he doesn't have to worry about how much they drink, because the dinner includes the taxi fare. He'd invited his mother to stay the night so they could drive to the swimming pool together tomorrow, but she wouldn't even consider it. 'I'm an old woman,' she said. 'I want to sleep in my own bed.'

He puts a small saucepan on the gas with the butter in it, and uses kitchen scissors to cut the chives into small pieces. In various kitchens on the other side of the back gardens, other people are cooking too. Other windows and balcony doors are open too. On the street, dogs are barking. Jan gets up to look out of the front window. Sometimes Simon forgets that his grandfather looked out of the window here for years, that he and Grandma ate and slept here. In those days the living room was quite dark, and when he visited them they mostly sat in the kitchen. His mother comes up and looks in the saucepan.

'Butter,' he says, then calls out 'Dinner!' to Jan, who is leaning out of the window with his forearms on the ledge, like a true son of the Jordaan.

'That's actually what I miss most,' he says, sitting down at the kitchen table. 'Just leaning out of the window for no reason. You can't do that in the rest home. Well, you can, but nothing ever happens there anyway.'

'Would you like a glass of wine now too?' Simon asks.

'It would be ridiculous anyway, seeing I live on the ground floor. Yes, nice.'

When everyone's seated, Simon puts the plates on the table. 'Plate service,' he says in English.

'What's that mean?' Jan asks.

'That I dish it up in the kitchen and serve it on the plates,' Simon says. 'Like in a restaurant.'

'This is my first asparagus of the year,' his mother says. 'Even though they've been in the shops for a while.'

'We only get asparagus soup,' Jan says. 'And I doubt it's fresh.'

'Well, you're in luck tonight,' Simon says. They eat and drink.

'As far as I'm concerned you can close that window now,' Jan says after Simon's dished him up some seconds.

'First I thought it was a bit sour,' says Anja, 'but now, with the food, it's perfect.'

'Can I top you up again?'

Simon gets the bottle out of the fridge and closes the window. He lights a couple of candles and sits down again. Jan is the only one who's still eating. 'Of course, this isn't just any Friday night,' Simon says.

'No,' Anja says. 'It's the birthday of the man who got your mother pregnant.'

'Is it?' Jan asks with his mouth full.

'Don't you know that? Your own son?'

'No,' Jan is forced to admit. 'I didn't realise.' He washes the last mouthful down with a big glug of wine. 'Why do you call Cornelis the man who got his mother pregnant?'

'Because Simon makes such a big thing of it.'

'That's his right, isn't it? Cornelis is his father.'

'Is somebody your father if you're born five months after their death?'

'Of course,' Simon says. 'Coffee?'

They'd both like a coffee, but not espresso. That's no problem — Simon's machine can make ordinary coffee too, and even heats and froths milk. He shakes a packet of Albert Heijn truffles out on a saucer.

'Look,' Jan says. 'All three of us have lost someone in our own way. A son, a husband, and a father.'

'He never knew him! And you've even forgotten his birthday.'

'Does that matter?'

'I think so.'

'Why should I remember somebody's birthday if they never celebrate it?'

Anja sips her wine. 'You do have a point there.'

'And what's the flipping point of us having a who's-suffered-the-most contest?'

Simon puts two cups of white coffee on the table with the truffles, then turns back to make himself an espresso. The light is starting to fade, the candles are no longer merely decorative. The window on the living room side is still open.

'Why, now we're talking about it, did you never move on?'

'Jan, please,' says Anja.

'I'm genuinely curious. You're a beautiful woman, not uninteresting …'

'Not uninteresting? What kind of way to describe someone is that?'

'Yes, sorry, that was a little thoughtless of me.'

'I have absolutely no desire to justify myself.'

'Justify, justify. It's just a question. I was talking to Simon about it the other day.'

'Oh, really?'

That's not smart of his grandfather. Simon sits there quietly, eating truffle after truffle, listening as the taciturn third person. He can't remember when and where the three of them were last together. Normally he plays the role of go-between. Now they're sitting across from each other, and Jan shouldn't be saying things like this, because his mother tends to feel superfluous anyway.

'Yes,' Jan says innocently.

'Let's just say I never felt the urge.'

'Fine. That's an answer.'

'Thank you. Do you ever ask Simon why he's single?'

Jan looks at Simon, and thinks for a moment. 'No, now you mention it.'

'Always why, why, why,' Simon says to head off the question. 'Why does somebody become a tiler? Because he thinks it's nice? That's not an answer, of course, and apparently you're not allowed to use the word nice anymore either. Why go on holiday to the Maldives and not Sri Lanka? Because the Maldives are more beautiful? That's not an answer, of course. People just do things. Things happen. Done.'

'So,' says Anja. 'We've learnt something new.'

'And the Maldives, as I heard recently, are no fun at all. There's nothing there. Not even animals.'

'What are you talking about all of sudden?' Jan asks.

'The why of things,' Simon says.

'How much wine have you had?' Anja asks.

'Less than you.'

Jan slides his empty coffee cup to one side. 'I could manage another genever. Before we call it a night.'

'Anyway,' Simon says, after he's cleared the table and poured drinks all round, 'today is my father's birthday. I wanted to celebrate it.'

'Thanks for the invitation,' Jan says. 'The meal was delicious, and it was an enjoyable evening. Maybe we can make a habit of it?'

'I'd have to give that some thought,' says Anja.

'More to the point,' Jan says. 'We should have done this much sooner, when Grandma was still here. We're family. And next year I turn ninety.'

'Hey,' Simon says, 'nowadays everyone lives to a hundred at least. We can do it ten more times.'

Anja is quiet. Then she says, 'You're family. I'm an in-law. You're called Weiman. I'm a Wiegers.'

'You're not an in-law to me,' Simon says. 'I'm your son.'

Twenty minutes later, they're gone. Each in their own taxi, because the rest home isn't on the way to South Amsterdam, where Anja lives. Simon loads the dishwasher. He's opened the window on the kitchen side again to let out the smoky air. After dinner, Anja smoked a second cigarette with Jan. The last time he aired it here because of a smoker it was the guy with red hair.

36.

'Us too!' Sam and Johan shout.

Igor's hair makes it look like he's wearing a helmet. That's why, Simon tells himself, he has to take a little more off. 'What for?' he asks Johan and Sam. 'Your hair could hardly be any shorter.'

'Not fair!' shouts Sam.

'Yeah!' Johan yells. 'Igor's your pet!'

'No, he's not,' Simon says. 'Of all the people here in the swimming pool, I love you two the most.'

'Really?' Sam asks.

'Of course.'

'Even more than …' Johan gestures at Anja, who is sliding a water wing up Jelka's arm, '… more than her?'

'Well, that's hardly possible, is it? She is my mother, after all.'

'What?'

'Are you his mother?' screams an indignant Sam.

'You know that, Sam.'

'No! Why didn't we know?!'

'Because you're both a bit forgetful,' Simon says.

'Oh, yeah,' says Sam.

It's still peculiar to see how impassive the others remain during a row. Igor is standing in the same spot with that wet splash of black hair still stuck to his forehead. Frits and Melissa are swimming laps. Jelka and Buari — no, Bella — are whispering in each other's ears as if they're the only girls in the whole world. They can all flip in a second, but don't notice when others are agitated, yelling, getting angry. Or they choose not to notice. Simon still finds it completely baffling.

'It's fine like this, surely?' Anja asks.

'No. Look at the way it hangs when it's this wet.'

'It's not like he's going to complain.'

'I think I need to use the clippers.'

'Igor!' Anja calls. 'Ball?'

Igor comes out of his corner and grabs the luminescent yellow ball that's floating in the middle of the pool. He tosses it to Anja. Bella shouts something. Is that 'bum' she's saying? Has she remembered that from last time? Sam and Johan can't bear Anja and Igor throwing the ball back and forth, and start hitting Igor with their noodles. They don't dare hit Anja. Frits smacks Simon on the side with one hand. 'Sorry,' Simon says, mainly to himself. 'I'm in the way.' Strange, when he started, Igor couldn't leave Melissa alone, constantly grabbing her legs when she was trying to swim. That hasn't happened for a while now. Is it because Frits has joined them? Has he disrupted the dynamics of it all? Anja warns Sam and Johan to stop it and let them play with the ball. 'Ask Simon if he'll teach you how to swim properly,' she says.

'Will you teach us how to swim?' Johan asks.

'Sure. Then we'll put on water wings first.'

'No!' Sam screams. 'That's for babies!'

'OK, no lesson then,' says Simon, staring at Igor's back muscles, which appear at every throw. Igor isn't really much more than a body.

'By the way,' Anja says, 'I thought it was fun yesterday. And you cooked really well.'

'Thanks.'

'We can do it more often. I like Jan.'

'OK,' says Simon. 'Your place next time?'

'Fine by me.'

'Brreuhh!' says Igor.

'Yeah, sorry, Igor. Here comes the ball.'

Half an hour later, the boy is sitting next to him as if they've already done this drive together dozens of times. No rain this Saturday, but the sun's not shining either. One of those still, grey days that could be mid-October as easily as early June. It's quiet in the city, you get that sometimes on a Saturday morning, as if everyone has slept in and had a late breakfast and is only now thinking about how to spend the rest of the day. Sam and Johan just got on the minibus. Very reluctantly, almost needing to be pushed. Simon happened to drive the car up just when they were boarding. 'No!' he heard Sam yell. 'Us too!' shouted Johan. Anja was standing at the entrance to the swimming pool. She waved goodbye to the minibus and Simon and Igor, and stayed behind by herself. She'd surprised him by mentioning the dinner, but Simon hadn't forgotten her final remark before leaving. All those things, all those feelings he'd never thought about that obliged him late last night, in bed, to see himself in alliance with his grandfather, an alliance that apparently excluded his mother, at least in her eyes. And because he was lying there thinking about things, he unavoidably reached the point where there was no longer any trace of his father — well, apart from the name on the passenger list, there *was* that, but had anyone even seen his remains? And where was his name at Westgaarde? Why couldn't he, Simon Weiman, go to a place where he could stand still and contemplate the name Cornelis Weiman, his father's name? Just because his mother, for whatever reason, hadn't considered it necessary? He slept in very late, also the fault of the dinner. No matter how you look at it, something like that is a cause of tension. Fortunately he managed to show some restraint when it came to alcohol. And it's because of last night that the way his mother was standing there just now struck him. Alone at the entrance to the swimming pool, waving goodbye to her son and a group of mentally handicapped youths. 'Ghhhh,' says Igor, watching the tram that just passed them at the traffic lights. Does he realise he doesn't have anyone either? Simon wonders. He looks over his left shoulder, turns into the Jordaan, and starts, as usual, on the circuitous route he has to take to get back home because half the streets in the Jordaan happen to be one-way.

There's a free parking space. Igor starts tugging on his seatbelt, but makes no attempt to try to find the button. Simon presses it, and the belt shoots free. Now they're both loose and they can get out of the car. There is no wind to speak of, no plastic bags blowing along the street. It is exactly one week later. What would happen if I just stayed sitting here in the car? Simon wonders. Nothing, probably, maybe until Igor starts to get bored. Can this boy get bored? Or do sitting in a stationary car for no reason and pacing around a swimming pool for three-quarters of an hour amount to the same thing? A body on the passenger's seat, and later that same body in the hairdressing chair, and then …

Simon starts moving. He gets Igor out of the car, and together they walk to the door of Chez Jean. The bell. The boy looks up. 'Yes,' Simon says. 'That's the doorbell. Look.' He points it out. Either Igor's not interested or he doesn't know the meaning of a pointing arm. He's got his swimming bag on. Just now he was sitting in the car with that same swimming bag pushing him forward like a soft hunch on his back. Simon gently removes it. 'Glass of Coke?' he asks. He peels off the boy's coat too and leads him to the chair in front of the window. 'Sit down.' Then he hurries upstairs and fills a plastic cup. Before going back down, he scans the living room. It's exactly as he left it earlier in the morning. Nothing's changed. Igor glugs the Coke down in one go. Then burps loudly. Simon locks the door and checks that the sign is turned so that FERMÉ is facing out. Music, he then thinks. I have to put on some music, that calms him down. Not that Igor is restless now, but it seemed to work well last time. He turns on the radio and looks for a station playing dated, nondescript music. Golden oldies. Without any wound-up DJs.

Thus far, an almost literal repetition of what happened the previous week. But now Simon wants an espresso. He could have made one just now while he was pouring the glass of Coke, but he already knew then that he would want to go back upstairs again to take his time listening to the buzz of the expensive Siemens machine and look around the living room once more. It remains strange, the almost imperceptible change in atmosphere when you've been away from home for a long or short period, as if the time spent in the swimming pool has given all the familiar objects a slight nudge. Last week he must have seen it like this too. Or does the weather play a role as well? The kind of light from outside? He picks the cup up out of the machine and takes it downstairs. Igor is sitting in the chair in front of the window. 'Coffee!' Simon says, to have something to say. The boy looks up. 'Come and sit here. Exactly where you sat last week.' Igor gets up and sits down again. Simon takes a sip from his tiny cup, then pushes Igor's hair up from his forehead with his hand while watching him in the mirror. 'We're going to make it shorter, OK?' Igor doesn't say anything. Simon lets his hand rest on the boy's head for a moment. 'But this time we're going to use something that makes a bit of noise.' He puts a light-blue hairdressing cape on the boy. The radio is playing Yazoo's 'Only You'. 'First a bit with the scissors.' He takes a comb and a pair of scissors, and cuts off about a centimetre, regularly touching the boy's head, and now and then brushing the hair off his lap, which naturally involves touching his thighs. Then he slides out a drawer in the wall unit and takes out the clippers. Igor keeps a sharp eye on the hand with the device in it. Simon turns on the clippers and holds them in Igor's field of vision for a moment.

'Clippers,' he says. He starts on top with not too low a number. What comes off can never go back on, but what's too long can always be cut shorter. Igor is making a quiet noise, almost like it's arising by itself in his chest from the vibration of the clippers against his head. The radio is now playing 'Stairway to Heaven'. I have to think in floors, thinks Simon. Now we're here, later in the kitchen — Coke — and finally we have to make it up to the second floor. Well, 'we' — *I* have to get *him* up there — there's not always a 'we'. He brushes the hair off Igor's crown and puts a one-and-a-half guard on the clippers. Starting at the neck he shaves upwards, steadily advancing his spread fingers further up the back of the boy's head. And when it's necessary, but also when it's not necessary, he brushes away the hair. He takes hold of an ear and folds it double. The radio has been here for centuries, a relic from Jan. There are always some customers, not many, who like to have it on. For himself, Simon would never choose it. He loves the quiet in the shop, the sound of cars and cyclists going past the big window. Street noise in general. Igor has started humming along, but Simon can't tell whether he's following the melody or rhythm of 'Du'. German, thinks Simon, that's a rarity. Apparently they never really made many golden oldies. Or does it have something to do with the war? He folds the other ear double. Igor stays calm and lets him do it. As if he realises this is part of getting his hair cut. He keeps staring at himself in the mirror. Peter Maffay sings, 'You, only you can understand me.' What goes on in that head, thinks Simon. Who does he see? What does he see? The clippers go off. Simon takes the nape razor and scrapes Igor's neck smooth. When he's finished, he flutters the fine hairs away with the soft brush and puts some oil on his hands. Slowly he rubs it into the back of Igor's neck and his throat. The neck, the throat.

'Finished,' he says, and pulls off the hairdressing cape with an exaggerated gesture.

Of course, Igor doesn't say anything. What can he say?

'Come on,' Simon says. 'We're going to have another Coke. Upstairs.'

Igor is sitting on a kitchen chair, and once again pours the glass of Coke down his throat in one go. He burps: a coarse sound from a sculptured head. *Crew cut*, an English name, and for the first time Simon realises that it must have been the haircut the crew got. Which crew? Of an American warship? Brush cut, he then thinks, and that term reminds him of the writer and with him, for the first time in quite a while, the word *cormorant*. Cormorant, seagulls. He seems to remember him even talking about walruses at some stage during that haircut, but what they have to do with anything escapes him. Igor burps again, without any sign of embarrassment. Simon has an empty espresso cup in front of him. Empty. He wonders whether to fill the boy's plastic cup with yet more Coke. From the garden comes the sound of at

least two pigeons fighting. Igor looks to the side for a moment.
Slow, thoughtful, not startled. Maybe he recognises the sound of
fighting pigeons. Simon has had an idea, and the idea he's had
makes his excitement grow. 'Come on,' he says. He stands up, the
boy gets up too. He walks over to the landing in front of him. He
pushes the boy onto the staircase that leads up to the bedroom.
'Go on,' he says, pushing him a little harder. Igor doesn't resist.
He himself goes into the bathroom, where a damp towel and
damp swimming trunks are lying on the floor. He gets undressed
and worms himself into the trunks. He shivers. When he emerges
from the bathroom, he sees that the staircase is empty. The boy
has gone upstairs. He did what he was told. He was able to do
what he was told. He understood.

Igor is standing in the middle of the room facing the dormer
window. The T-shirt he's wearing falls from his shoulders without
touching his back, the bottom edge resting on the curve of his
arse. Simon swallows. He gets a hard-on, or rather, the one he
got just now when he pulled on his trunks now stretches them
even more. He swallows again, and then he coughs. Igor turns
slowly towards him. Now the most beautiful thing would be if
what had already happened several times in the swimming pool
happened here. Without any further prompting. If the boy did
it himself. But he just stands there, and because it's light behind
him, Simon can't see his expression. So he himself takes a few
steps forward until he's so close to the boy he can feel his breath
on his face. The boy's arms rise up. Simon feels a tingling in his
chest. But together with his arms, his hands rise up too, and he
puts those hands on Simon's chest and pushes him back and uses
just enough force to make him lose his balance. Simon stumbles
back a step, bumps into the side of the bed, and falls over.

'No,' Igor says.

His voice is neither high nor deep. A little flat. Uninterested. Not aggressive. As he's a good bit closer than he was a few seconds ago, Simon can now see his expression.

No, he said. Loud and clear. His swollen cock in the damp trunks. He thanks his lucky stars he's not a flabby forty-something, with a hairy belly and tits instead of a chest. All kinds of things flash through his mind. Including this: no blank lines. He'd fantasised as little as possible out of self-protection, but this was a development he could never have anticipated. He also thinks: I must really take after my father, I have to, because if I took after my mother I would now definitely succumb on a massive scale. This flashes through his mind too: a moment in the swimming pool, months ago now. Months or weeks. Igor looking at him, just after his mother had snapped at him. The boy looked him straight in the eye. In that instant it was like there was somebody else in that magnificent Popov body. He looked right through him, not skewed but shrewd, as if the roles had been reversed. Now the roles had definitely been reversed. Simon hadn't really understood what he'd said, he'd heard the word no, but it hadn't got through to him because it was as if a dog had suddenly started talking; then you'd be sure to miss the first words too in your absolute astonishment. And then his cheeks start blazing with embarrassment, not even about the position he's got himself into, but at the thought of his recently opened Twitter account. 'Bum tit screw fucking's good for you.' 'I'm a bear called Jeremy, teddy with a big bear dick, I can push it in and out, knock the girls up with my spout.' God almighty, he thinks. Strutting his stuff on Twitter. If only he could make it all undone. It's like being nauseous, to the point of puking: you're doing your utmost to think of nice fresh things, but your mind keeps returning to greasy fried eggs or Pisang Ambon.

But those blank lines? The blank lines in which he'd wanted to hold Igor tight, use him, abuse him, pushing his arse up while the boy growls, growling without any embarrassment, the way he burps without any embarrassment, letting go, letting go of everything, only being aware of flesh and sweat, smells, things he's summoned up so many times, his forehead on white swimming-pool-changing-room tiles or pressed into soft pillows, and the boy not resisting but going along with it all, or letting himself be led, the weight of that magnificent body on top of his, and now, now, the boy really is standing over him as if he's the one who's intellectually challenged and he can see through him, he's already seen through him. Or actually there's nothing to see through. Kissing, something Simon really loves and can do for hours, he sometimes calls it 'vanilla sex', is the only thing he could never imagine. As if kissing is something for 'normal' people, people who can also talk. He hadn't thought Igor capable of it. God no, don't think of 'vanilla sex' now, what a term. He blushes even more. And look at Igor standing there now with a curl of something playing on his lips. Contempt? Compassion? A word that starts with C anyway. He's now sitting on the side of the bed. Wait, thinks Simon, this whole bit, the whole bit from the moment I decided to put on my swimming trunks to confront him with something familiar, to get him back into the atmosphere of the swimming pool, to get him to molest me the way he does in the pool, casually and shamelessly, this whole bit has to become a blank line. Because then you can, as the writer says, leave it to a reader or whoever to imagine it all, but in fact it won't say anything at all. You can always fall back on that: it doesn't say anything. It's fantasy.

•

'What's going on here?' he asks through the thick, viscous shame in an attempt to get things back to normal, maybe even as a way to save face.

Igor gestures at the wall. 'Hoo?'

Hoo? Is that Dutch *hoe* and he's asking how? Or is it English and *who*? 'Aleksandr Popov.'

The boy moves his arms as if swimming, and taps himself on the chest with his index and middle fingers.

'Yes.'

Igor looks at him. For a moment it's as if he's about to say more or do something. That shrewd look in his eyes. Then he walks to the door. Just before disappearing downstairs, he swings his arm.

The sun has more or less broken through, a milky light is draped over the city. The streets are still more or less deserted, as if all the people who slept in still haven't decided what to do. It's quiet in the car. Igor buckled the belt himself and is staring straight ahead with a gruff expression. Once only he points to the right. Simon obeys and turns right earlier than last time. Just before he parks the car, Igor says, 'Huuughhh.' Simon understands that he has to get out to open the passenger door and release the boy from the seatbelt. He walks him to the door. This time he doesn't have the slightest inclination to go in through the automatic glass door with him. He really doesn't want to know what it's like in there. He doesn't watch Igor disappear inside either. He turns and, half sitting on the bonnet of his car, looks back at the building. On the first floor Sam and Johan are standing at a large window. They've both put their thumbs in their ears, and they're fluttering their fingers. Sticking their tongues out at the same time. It looks like they're making a noise too, but of course he can't hear that. Simon stares at them for a moment, but when Igor comes up behind them, he pushes off from the bonnet with his bum and crawls in behind the wheel of the car.

Later he sweeps up Igor's hair. First with the broom, then with the brush and pan. He sees the boy's swimming bag on the floor next to the chair in front of the window. The radio is still on. 'Bloed, zweet en tranen' by André Hazes. Street noise, cyclists passing the window, someone unloading something, maybe kegs at the bar on the corner. A helicopter flies overhead: the police hunting a bag snatcher or a Vespa rider who's caused a crash. That sticks in his thoughts for a moment. He wishes it was possible to shake off shame like water. But, and this is something he realises as he lets the tufts of pitch-black hair slide into the bin, the shame is his alone, a shame nobody need ever know about and most likely never will.

Former cormorant, former Popov doppelgänger. No, he's still that, but Simon won't see it anymore. This morning he helped his mother in the swimming pool for the last time. He looks at the swimming bag. He'll have to think about what to do with it.

37.

'We don't need those drag queens round here anymore,' Oscar says. 'We've already got a drama queen.'

The writer is on his second beer and has just delivered a miserable rant about little libraries. How nowadays everyone's got a little library in their front garden or on their street or in their village. And how he can't resist looking in them, and every time he's terrified he's going to find one of his own books in it. And not only that, the bloody things had now made it onto the staircases of his own building. The writer lives in a large apartment building with multiple exits and entrances, and everywhere there were cardboard boxes full of old books. HELP YOURSELF! FREE! And there's a fair chance of one of his books showing up in one of those boxes between trashy books like *Windows 10 for Dummies* or *The Clan of the Cave Bear.*

'What's more,' says Oscar, 'Jean M. Auel's books are far from trashy.'

'Really?'

'Really.'

'But you get my point, right? It's embarrassing.'

'Embarrassing for some,' Oscar says diplomatically.

They're sitting at the open door. Across the canal from them is Major Bosshardt. If they do their best, they can see her bronze Salvation Army cap, her shoulders, an arm on the back of the bench she's sitting on. The small ripples on Oudezijds Voorburgwal are catching the sunlight, the elms are nice and full. As Oscar just explained to the writer, it's because they hardly blossomed. A tree like that can only concentrate on one thing per year: reproduction or thick foliage all summer long. The writer only seemed slightly interested. The front door is open too, the smell of flat beer drifts sedately through the bar without disappearing completely. It's Tuesday, bingo day. Tonight Miss Windy Mills will be returning once only to call the bingo. Oscar's got his hopes up. Their Tuesday evenings with Miss Windy Mills were legendary, at home and abroad. But that's still hours away. It's now a quarter past six. There's a new barman, a young guy the writer has never seen before.

'Egan,' Oscar says. He pronounces it Eh-gun.

'Where's he from?'

'Colombia.'

'Hm.' The writer's distracted.

'How's your book coming along?' Oscar asks.

'Well, I think. I'm up to the last chapter. As usual, I've managed to slip your name into it.'

'Thanks. I guess.'

'Don't worry, it's a very minor role. You could even call the character insignificant. I did spell it with a K. A Dutch Oscar with a C is a little too pretentious to my taste.'

'Now, now.'

'The funny thing is, and it's a feeling you probably don't know, but one day you think it's masterful, and the next you want to throw it all away.'

'No, I don't know that feeling. I'm satisfied with myself every day of the week.'

'Egan,' the writer calls, 'could we have a bitter lemon and another beer over here?'

'¿Qué?' Egan calls back.

'You'll have to teach him Dutch. Bit slow otherwise.'

Oscar gestures at the two glasses on the table in front of them, and a little later Egan arrives with their drinks. *Alstobleif,*' he says.

'He looks like someone,' the writer says as Egan walks back to the bar.

'Everyone looks like someone.'

The writer hardly hears it. He, like Oscar, is very satisfied with himself, if not every day. Writers are often like that when they're approaching the end of a book. Self-satisfied and full of themselves. 'Did you know that only one in ten plane crashes are caused by the weather?'

'No, why should I know that?'

'You might have been curious.'

'Hardly. Why were you? You're scared to death of flying.'

'The rest are from technical failings and human error. More than eight out of ten crash during take-off or landing.'

'I know someone, someone who comes here sometimes, who was on that Turkish Airlines plane that ended up in a field on the side of the A9.'

'Really?'

'Why would I make up something like that? She still has neck problems, and regularly dreams of landing gear smashing up through the floor of the cockpit.'

'I've been writing about that air disaster on Tenerife.'

Oscar's not interested. Or rather, he is interested, but also annoyed by the writer's self-obsession, the way he ignores or hijacks every subject he, Oscar, raises. He watches a sloop full of drunk students go by. They've all taken off their shirts, and they're waving green bottles of beer and singing. Flabby little boys. Unattractive. Arrogant for no reason. Students used to be guys you'd like to go to bed with, now there was no point to them except to annoy you. The sloop waddled into the shade under the next bridge. Oscar is a couple of years older than the writer. Sometimes lately he's found himself wondering what it was like to be in love, how it felt to be faint with lust. He also wonders sometimes, and has for a while, why he and the writer never got together. They liked each other, they were able to laugh together, they could imagine going to bed with each other, yet there was still something missing. Incompatible, as they say. Love is a strange thing. It's not in your brain, as far as Oscar can tell, but not in your heart either. It's somewhere else. But where? Maybe in your soul, another intangible concept. And of course explaining one intangible with another won't get you anywhere. Still, he settles on the soul rather than body parts you can grab hold of, or organs you can hear and feel when you press your head against someone's chest. He looks over to Egan, points at the writer's empty beer glass, and lays his hand on top of his own glass. Someone who can drink more than two bitter lemons in a row isn't right in the head, thinks Oscar. The writer hasn't noticed, too busy watching the raucous students, and he's surprised when Egan comes over with a beer for him. 'Thank you, Igor,' he says.

'He's called Egan,' says Oscar.

'Yes, of course,' he says, then adds in English, 'Egan, can you please bring me, or us, a double portion of bitter balls?'

'Sí, por supuesto,' says Egan.

'That night, you know, when you were here with your barber, did you end up going to bed with him?'

The writer looks at him with a slightly glassy expression. Egan has just put the *bitterballen* on the table. 'No,' he says. 'I wanted to, but that guy is way too good-looking for me, and although he'd had a lot to drink, and me too, I didn't want to run the risk of being rejected. That hurts with men who are as old as us.'

'Goes without saying,' Oscar says.

'I imagined it. Something else men our age know all about.'

'Better just speak for yourself.'

The writer dips one of the bitterballen in the mustard, then burns his tongue and the top of his mouth on it. That cheers Oscar up. He doesn't touch them himself. He's got vegetarian lasagne in the microwave, and will have a good healthy meal before starting his shift.

'But the most beautiful thing about writing,' the writer says, as if Oscar has asked him about it, 'is still the way anything goes. Anything! No matter how crazy it is, as long as you write it so it's believable, it's all right. Did I ever tell you about that reading in Edam?'

'Not that I remember.'

'Well, I was giving a reading in Edam. You know how one of my books is set around there' — Oscar doesn't say a word. He's read one and a half of the writer's books. Affectation, as far as he's concerned. Instead he'd rather reread *The Land of Painted Caves*, the sixth book in *Earth's Children*, because he's only read that one once — 'there was a decent audience, and I launched into my story. I always just wing it. It's not as if those people know what a reading's supposed to be like. But then someone held up a rather urgent finger, wanting to know if I knew there wasn't a branch of Hornbach in Edam at all. "Yes, of course, I know that," I said. "But then you're just deliberately spreading lies!" somebody else shouted. The whole audience was in an uproar. It was like they'd planned it in advance. And then I said, "But dear people, this is what writing is. If I, or in this case, my main character, needs a Hornbach to purchase a particular tool, then there *is* a Hornbach in Edam!'"

'I think Hornbach make really brilliant ads,' Oscar says.

'Yes, but that's not what we're talking about here. Those people were furious.'

'Look,' Oscar says, 'I'm going to go eat. I'm on the bar with Egan from about seven or so. I'm expecting a crowd, even if you never know for sure these days. Maybe all the people who know Miss Windy Mills have already moved into that pink nursing home in the Jordaan.'

The writer drinks another beer. After the two serves of bitterballen, he's not hungry anymore. Plus the beer, which can also satisfy your hunger. He's now the only person sitting by the door. The water has grown smoother. Today's wind turns out to have been a day-wind. Day-winds die down towards evening. Every now and then a small boat passes. Apparently tour boats don't go through here, maybe Oudezijds Kolk is too narrow. He feels like staying for a while longer. He's on the last chapter, so he's procrastinating. He's delaying his reward. This too and that too, and then it's finished. But within that this-too-and-that-too, small variations can occur, late inspiration, maybe even the word 'day-wind' that's just occurred to him. He has the goal of using at least one new word in each book, one he's thought of himself. In the corner by the window there are four Italians. Fortunately no French. He feels completely at ease, this is where he's meant to be. Satisfied and full of himself, it's no surprise he doesn't feel in the least bit awkward about sitting here alone. The young Colombian brings him another beer. He hasn't asked for anything. 'Gracias, Egan,' he says, and rests his hand on one of the boy's hamstrings for a moment. Egan is less than appreciative and seizes the writer's hand with surprising strength before guiding it back to the tabletop. To hide his discomfort, the writer immediately grabs the fresh beer with that same painful hand and takes a slug. He watches the boy head back to the bar. No, he then realises, I'm on the last chapter but one. It's always like that. You think you're finished, that you've got it all laid out, but then something extra imposes itself on you after all. A short chapter. The Italians are buzzing, and all four of them are doing things on each other's phones. A solitary seagull shrieks down over the water. Across the canal a living person has sat down next to the bronze Major Bosshardt. Yes, he thinks, I'll stay here and see how Miss Windy Mills handles the Tuesday evening bingo. And daydream a little. Maybe about that short chapter. There's also something else he wants to tell Oscar.

38.

Simon is swimming. He was the first one in the pool. Gradually more and more others have joined him. He swims. Backstroke, breaststroke, crawl. He skips butterfly — that would be too disruptive in the pool. He should have started with it before anyone else arrived, but starting with butterfly is tough. It's a stroke for when your body is already warmed up and tired, when you're feeling the burn in your arms and legs. Ten minutes. Another ten minutes. The water moves over his body, he breathes when he can or has to. He practises his turns. Someone at the side of the pool is coaching a boy. When Simon surfaces he hears snatches of instructions. Another ten minutes. He hangs off the side for a moment. The swimming coach comes up to him. 'Did you swim?' the man asks.

'Yes,' Simon says. 'A long time ago.'

'But you've always kept it up.'

'Yes.'

'Do you do masters' races?'

'No.'

'Why not?'

'Ah …' says Simon.

'Your registration's lapsed, I suppose.'

'Yes.'

'I'd think about it if I were you. It looks good. Very good.'

'I will. Thanks.' And he goes back to swimming. Another ten minutes. Turns, breaststroke, the water flows around him, he displaces it, and he imagines being in a race. It's not so very different from swimming like this. And he'd be on a rankings list again, no matter how low. National, international. Instead of websites about the survivors of a plane crash, the circumstances of a plane crash, he'd search for international ranking lists and follow the KNZB and FINA websites. Races in Hungary, France, Germany. The masters' competition is a world in itself.

In the showers, the man with red hair suddenly appears. Where's he come from? Was he in the pool too this last hour? They nod to each other, but don't say anything. As Simon is stepping out from under the shower, the other man shakes the shampoo out of his hair.

'Hey, watch it,' Simon says.

'Sorry,' says the man with red hair.

Doesn't matter, thinks Simon — if we're playing the game properly, that's what I say now. But he doesn't say anything, and he knows that either way they'll meet each other in front of the building in a few minutes. He dries himself off and gets his things out of the locker. He gets dressed. Then he walks into the corridor that leads to the second pool. A physiotherapist is in it with a client, a young woman. He's lowered a kind of walking frame into the pool. Refracted in the splashing water, Simon sees the woman's legs making walking movements. The physio looks up for a moment. 'You're not actually allowed in here,' he tells Simon.

'I'll be gone in a sec.'

It's a different world here now. As if it's a different pool in a different swimming centre in a different city. He looks through the enormous windows at the park. Trees in full leaf, joggers, people with dogs or strollers, little kids in the playground. The young woman in the pool is breathing heavily, the exercises are taking a lot of out of her. He turns and heads for the exit.

'Do you remember that there were narcissuses here?' he asks.

'Sure,' says the man with red hair. 'A few of them were broken. People like to take shortcuts.'

There are now roses flowering in the bed in front of the swimming pool. First it was yellow, then red, and now white. They're those bushy council roses, small but prolific. There are no more desire paths visible. Apparently people are less inclined to cut through a rose bed.

'Have you got a cigarette for me too?' Simon asks.

'I thought you didn't smoke.'

'There always has to be a first.' He pulls a cigarette out of the proffered pack and sucks on it when the man holds the lighter to the end.

'After swimming, a cigarette always tastes of ammonia,' the man says. 'Because of all the chlorine in the pool.'

'This really is very filthy,' Simon says. He tosses the burning cigarette down between the roses, then spits a couple of times.

'You'll never be a smoker,' the man says.

They stand there for a moment, the man still has to finish his cigarette.

'Of course, you're not called Jean at all, are you?' he says.

'No,' Simon says. 'Simon.'

'Oskar.' His cigarette still isn't finished.

Simon looks to the side, inspecting the hair on the nape of his neck.

'Anything happen lately?' Oskar asks.

Simon thinks for a moment. He spits into the rose bed once again. You could say that quite a lot has happened, but he wonders if you should share everything that happens to you with others, especially virtual strangers. 'Nothing special,' he says.

They walk to their bikes, which turn out be parked closely together. 'I'm curious,' Simon says, as he wraps the chain around the seat post, 'how you can just come with me on an ordinary weekday.'

'I've got money,' the man with red hair says. 'A lot of money.'

'Nice,' says Simon.

'Yes, I think so too.'

As they ride away from the pool, Simon thinks about the swimming coach's remarks. He swam well today, relaxed and unconstrained, giving his all. He saw the small pool as a rehab centre. He no longer has anything to do with other things that may or may not happen in it. Even if his mother doesn't know that yet. And now he's decided, you can bet Henny will come back next week, or soon at least. Summer is all around him, he can smell and see it, and the man with red hair is there too, in the corner of his eye. Finally he feels some respite. A breath of fresh air. 'Left here,' he says as a warning.

'Yes,' says the man with red hair. 'I remember.'

39.

The evening has gone just as Oscar hoped. It was busy. Miss
Windy Mills really did lure customers back. It was almost like
old times, and there wasn't a single moment when Egan, who
is still learning the ropes, wasn't able to keep up with demand.
He stayed calm, stoically accepted all the admiration from the
customers, and simply ignored the men — many far over sixty —
who got too pushy. The writer stayed sitting where he was. Oscar
kept an eye on him. He got into a brief conversation with the
group of Italians who had been there since early in the evening,
drank steadily, and seemed to largely ignore the bingo. He was
already fairly tipsy at seven; he must be blind drunk by now. Why
hasn't he gone home?

Egan is rinsing and drying glasses. It's strangely empty, as
always after a busy night. The doors on the canal side are still
open. Every now and then there's yelling from a boat on the
water. More students, probably.

'Come here!' the writer shouts.

Oscar sighs. Why didn't he leave with everyone else when
they turned on the fluorescent lights? The fluorescent lights

always work a treat. The customers get the fright of their lives from each other's old faces, and can't get away fast enough.

'Let Igor pull one last beer. And a whisky for yourself.'

Oscar looks at Egan, then pulls the beer himself. He pours a whisky, the most expensive one they have, then walks over to the table by the open door.

'Cosy,' says the writer.

Oscar decides to not make too much of a point of it. He's not ready for bed yet, and after a long night on lemon mineral water he can do with a whisky. 'His name is Egan,' he says. 'Can't you get that into your head?'

'Pfff.'

'How'd you like it?'

'She was in top form, our Miss Windy, but I didn't really take it in.' He takes a slug of beer. Oscar doesn't know many people who can put away this much beer.

'Why's that?'

'I was thinking about the last chapter, of course. That doesn't stop. Strangely enough, you think about it most when all kinds of other things are happening around you.' Full of beer and still full of himself. 'Are you capable of listening to me now?'

Oscar sips his whisky and doesn't answer.

'Look, that Dutch plane had never been through anything. It just flew thousands and thousands of kilometres to and fro, full of holidaymakers. It had 21,195 flying hours on the clock and—'

'How do you know that so exactly?'

'Research, man. What else? All that research. And most of it just goes out the window once the book's finished, you can count on my editor to make sure of that. But it's like this, listen, that American plane was, simply because it *was* an American plane, like that pilot who docked his plane in the Hudson, you know, in that film with Tom Hanks, he—'

'Sully.'

'Yes, damn it, that's the one. Strange title, by the way.'

'The captain was called Sullenburger.'

'See, something else you know. You weren't born yesterday either. But the *Clipper Victor*, right, first of all, that was the first 747 to ever fly anywhere, christened by Pat Nixon in 1971, or was it 1970? Fine, and this is the point, later that year — I think it was 1970 — it was hijacked.' The writer empties his glass and holds it up to Egan. Egan sees it, but doesn't react and calmly continues drying the bar.

Oscar gets up, walks over to the bar, and pours the very last beer. 'Close it down,' he tells Egan. He comes back and sits down again. 'I'm exhausted,' he says.

'Allow me this. It's going to get the chop. I'll resist, but I already know.' He falls silent, swallows.

Is he going to start crying? Oscar looks at him attentively.

'Always just giving in and resisting, giving in and resisting! Your whole life is letting go and holding tight, both at once. But listen now.' He swallows again and only then takes a mouthful of beer. 'Nobody knows this. Listen. It was flying from Kennedy Airport to Puorto Rico, but—'

'Puerto Rico.'

'What?'

'The island's called Puerto Rico.'

'Jesus, man, let me tell the story! There was a hijacker on board. He showed a stewardess — I've forgotten her name for the moment, but I've got it written down somewhere — a pistol, and said he wanted to go to Cuba. The stewardess thought it was a joke! She told him he'd be better off flying to Rio because it was a nicer at that time of year — it was August. So anyway, it turned out not to be a joke, and she took him to the cockpit. The pilot thought it was a prank too, but he also thought the guy was a bit crazy, "kooky" he said, so he flew to Havana.'

'My whisky's almost finished,' says Oscar.

'Yes, yes. And do you know who's waiting at the airport? As if it was all arranged in advance? Fidel Castro! Watkins, that was the pilot, and the hijacker get out, and Castro gets a tour. Outside, right, around the plane. Castro has all kinds of questions, and the pilot answers them. And then, here it comes, he asks Castro if he wants to look inside too. "No," says Castro, "I'd scare the passengers." They're just sitting in their seats, they don't have a clue what's going on. And the hijacker, he asks the pilot if he can have his suitcase, because he's reached his destination. That wasn't possible, of course, so the pilot promises to send the suitcase back after they've arrived at Puorto Rico. And then they take off again and arrive seven hours late.'

It's quiet for a moment.

'No, wait! They had another stop in Miami to refuel, and in Miami the pilot's wife, who was also on board, got off to walk their two dogs. They must have been in the hold.'

It's quiet again. 'You really need to go home,' says Oscar.

'Yes, no doubt,' says the writer. 'But hang on, isn't Miami going back? I mean, isn't it the wrong direction?'

Oscar stands up and pulls him up off the chair. Often people who drink enormous amounts don't have a problem as long as they stay seated. It only goes wrong once they're up on their feet. The writer gives himself a shake, like a dog. Then he takes a step. He manages. He walks to the door under his own steam. 'You're a real friend!' he shouts before stepping out onto Zeedijk. The door closes behind him. Oscar sees him walk past the window and then stumble. Suddenly he's out of sight. Then a hollow-sounding 'Let go!' echoes through the old, narrow street.

40.

On his birthday he lost Pablo. Not that it made any difference, he'd obviously never celebrated his birthday, but he noticed it himself. The dog was sick, probably bone cancer. A day came when it couldn't go on any longer, so Carlos lifted him into the car and drove to the *veterinario*, who had her practice on the edge of La Laguna. She started with an extensive examination, then phoned a colleague who had also treated Pablo a few times. This annoyed Carlos, as it made him feel like the vet took him for the kind of person who would have his dog put down for no reason, just because it was getting in the way or had become too much bother to look after. The vet sighed and said, 'Está terminado.' Just before she administered the sedative, Pablo lifted his head to look at his owner. Carlos felt like turning away, but thought, no, watch. He couldn't make out anything in those eyes: no fear, no sadness, no hope, no recrimination. The black muzzle on the white paws stretched out on his legs, tongue lolling. Carlos had sat down on the floor, the vet had left the surgery. He stroked the dog, whispered a completely superfluous 'Tranquilo', and kept repeating it until the vet came back. Then she gave Pablo the final injection, and within twenty seconds he was gone. *Terminado*, Carlos thought, and started to cry. He couldn't get back up onto his feet, so the vet gave him a hand, with Pablo sliding onto the floor in the process like a bag of meat and disconnected bones. He left the dog behind — the salon didn't have a garden, just a tiled courtyard. When he — still snivelling — returned to the peluquería alone, Nilda and Conchita started crying as well, and a little later, after Nilda had told the woman who was getting a water wave what was going on, even the customer joined in. Such a faithful beast, a fixture in and in front of the salon for years.

Nilda and Conchita were no longer charming girls, but nudging middle age. Martín was dead, Felipe was dead, Gustava was dead. Carlos had seen the loading platform of the forklift go up and down countless times. Santiago was ancient and in an old people's home. There were some islanders, often men, who seemed indestructible. Weathered faces, sharp noses, canes, or walkers, but still serenely eating breakfast every morning, coffee after coffee, and a hot meal with wine every lunchtime. Santiago had never given up smoking, but had cut back heavily now that he had to drag himself into the garden for it. And he still had a good head of hair that the home's hairdresser wasn't allowed to touch. Carlos had to cut it, once a month. He had permission to bring Pepe with him, as the nurses had noticed that the mood in the dining room was noticeably better with the little dog running around. A plain, sandy-coloured animal with a pointy muzzle. Santiago called him Lobo, Pablo, and Oro by turns. Never Pepe. As usual, Felipe had arranged Pepe. Carlos, also as usual, hadn't paid anything or asked any questions. Two days later, Felipe died. Carlos drove a car he had bought himself. Santiago couldn't wangle anything from the old people's home.

He had taken on a new hairdresser. A young guy, Javi. He came from Lanzarote, and saw Tenerife as the great leap forwards. Madrid or Barcelona didn't seem to have occurred to him — big cities in a distant country. Nilda and Conchita found him incredibly handsome, and that wasn't surprising because Conchita was convinced that 'Those of Lanzarote, they have that.' And Nilda added, 'It's like they're a different species.'

'Is it all right, with the new guy?' Santiago asked.

'Excellent lad. Always punctual. He attracts a younger clientele. That's a nice change for Conchita and Nilda, and for me too.'

They were outside, sitting under a tree because the scorching summer sun was merciless. Carlos had bought a bottle of red wine at the bar in the old people's home. Pepe was asleep after his customary circuit past all the legs in the dining room. And the kitchen, of course. Santiago put in the effort to lift one foot off the ground and give the dog a good-natured poke in the side. 'So, Oro,' he said, 'life's hard, isn't it?'

'Pepe,' Carlos said.

'What?'

'The dog's called Pepe.'

'Never. Have you got sunstroke?'

'Santiago, do you remember Alanza?'

'Of course. Your former future wife. At least, that's what Felipe thought.'

'She's dead. Her husband too. Car crash.'

'Oh. Did she still come to the shop?'

'Yes.'

'And that new lad?' Santiago asked again, maybe because he

wanted to hear more about him, possibly because he'd forgotten his earlier question.

'He's called Javi. He does wear unusual clothes.'

'Is he one of them?'

'Yes, I think so.'

'Oh, well, there are many rooms in God's mansion.'

This was the first time in — Carlos counted back — forty years that he'd heard Santiago refer to his religion. Apart from all the times he'd sworn, of course.

'He wants to set up a *coffee corner*. That's what he calls it. In English.'

'A *coffee corner*? What's that supposed to be?'

'One of the salon chairs out, a few chairs next to each other, a small table, glass case with cakes, an expensive espresso machine.'

'Why, for Christ's sake?'

'To make it more entertaining, he says.'

'Isn't it already entertaining enough? It was always *muy entretenido*?'

'I think so too. But we're old men.'

Santiago grunted and poked Pepe in the side again. 'With you there definitely, Lobo. It was always very cosy and homey.'

They lit cigarettes and blew the smoke towards the ocean. Quiet together.

'He rides a bike,' Carlos said.

'To work?'

'No, for fun. As sport. A racing bike.'

'Rather him than me.'

'Maybe I should see him the way Manuel once saw me,' Carlos then said.

'Hm. How old are you actually?'

'Other men my age have already retired.'

'And when did I stop cutting hair?'

'Before you dropped.'

Santiago has to laugh. They weren't the only ones in the beautifully laid out garden. Some of the old people were alone, others had visitors. It was quiet, Santiago's laughter echoed between the pines lower on the hill. It might have been because of the landscape architects' inventiveness, but it was the kind of place that radiates a sense of unchangeability, as if everything here will always stay the same, partly because of the bluish-green ocean far below and the gorgeous, fairly mild summer weather. The kind of place that even pulls the wool over the eyes of the people who sit slumped in the garden or shuffle through it. An eternal holiday.

'But still,' Carlos said.

'But still,' Santiago said. Leaning on the grips of his walker, he pushed himself up onto his feet. It was time for him to lie down for a while in his air-conditioned room. Slowly they followed the central path to the building.

'Do you think,' Carlos asked when they'd almost reached Santiago's room, 'that someone will come into the salon one day and ask, "Who's Carlos W?", and none of the hairdressers working there will have the faintest idea?'

Santiago got it. 'Just like we didn't know who Juan Flórez was.'

'Exactly! Boy, those brains of yours.'

'Still working fine.' He pushed open the door of his room. He was the kind of person who would shrug off a helping hand in annoyance. Pepe tried to go in too. There was always something to eat in there. 'No, Pablito, you're going home. Scat.'

After the dog had jumped into the back of the car and Carlos had closed the door, he realised that Santiago hadn't answered him. The question was much too difficult, of course.

•

Pepe was the first of his dogs to jump up on his lap. Perhaps the other three were too big for it. Pepe was also the first to occasionally growl at him at night, for no obvious reason. He'd be lying there contentedly under a stroking hand, and the next moment his lips would be curled back and the tip of his tongue would be showing. Never in the daytime. Carlos decided that the dog got touchy when he was tired, and decided to leave him in peace at night, which was almost impossible because Pepe jumped onto his lap of his own accord. And still that weird growling. 'What do you want?' he had to ask very often. Pepe would stare back at him, showing a lot of white in his eyes. Otherwise he was a good-natured dog, friendly to customers and other people, tolerant of other dogs. Carlos drove over the whole island with him but, unlike before, now left the walking largely to the dog. Pepe was happy on El Teide, on the beach, at the coast, in the streets of La Laguna. Although Carlos still had the stubborn idea that dogs enjoy being in new surroundings, he knew deep in his heart that they don't mind walking the same circuit every day. They're creatures of habit. Like Lobo and Ora, Pablo had become a framed photo, but now the photos were no longer on the old sideboard but on a real side table, more or less forced on him by Conchita. He had been here four dogs now, and he sometimes wondered if Pepe would be the last. And why people always looked after him so much. As if they felt like he couldn't manage on his own. As if he couldn't buy one of those long, narrow tables himself. Though he had to agree with Conchita when she remarked that it made his living room a lot more modern. And now he stopped to think about it, when he took on Conchita and Nilda he was already an older man in their eyes; they were approaching fifty themselves, he had gradually become elderly.

One day he asked Javi if he'd already been on El Teide. Of course he'd already been on El Teide. On his bike. 'But we have volcanoes too,' he said.

'Of course you do. But no El Teide. Have you already walked around it? Or only cycled?'

'I've never walked there. I'm not as much of a walker as you.' As always, he'd used the polite form.

'Can we drop the *usted*?'

'Fine. Though I do find it difficult.'

They took the backroads to the south-west in Carlos's car. Javi was wearing a snappy cap and fluorescent runners. It was a Sunday. Carlos had asked him because he thought Javi could use a distraction. When you're new to the island it takes a while to make friends and get to know people. The windows were down, Pepe was panting in the back, and every time Carlos slowed down for a bend, he started whimpering because he thought they'd arrived somewhere.

'Everything OK?' Carlos asked.

'Sure,' said Javi.

'No regrets?'

'About what?'

Carlos gave a group of bike riders a wide berth as he overtook them. 'Yeah, what could you regret?'

'It's fine. I feel at home. Nilda and Conchita are sweet, in a different way from my mother.'

Now a group of cyclists was coming from the other direction. Carlos kept well over to the right. They were all wearing the same clothes. 'What is this?' he asked. 'You never used to see bikes here.'

'They're Dutch,' said Javi. He'd turned to watch the riders.

'See, they're wearing JUMBO. That's a Dutch supermarket. Jumbo-Visma, actually, but I don't know what Visma is. At home we used to have a lot of triathletes.'

'Yeah?'

'Not anymore. I don't know what happened to them. And now all these cycling teams have discovered Tenerife. They're doing high-altitude training.'

'How do you know all that?'

'I like to watch bike racing on TV. I follow it a bit.'

'Do you have a favourite?'

'Yes, Primož Roglič. I couldn't see properly, but there's a good chance he was riding in that group just now. I follow him on Instagram and Twitter, and yesterday he posted a photo.'

'And he's good?'

'Really good. And very good-looking.'

'A-ha. Do you want to take the Teleférico?'

'How high does it go?'

'Three-and-a-half thousand metres?'

'Ooh, that's quite high.'

'It just carries you up.'

'Hm.'

He probably felt like turning back now and slowly driving past the riders.

Carlos parked the car at the base station. Pepe immediately started yelping. Javi got out and opened the back. Then he looked up along the line of masts, not even needing to put his hand over his forehead because of the bill of his cap. The moment he heard Pepe yelping, Carlos knew they wouldn't be going up. When you're out and about so often with a dog, you sometimes forget that it's a dog, an animal that's not admitted everywhere. He had no idea why dogs weren't allowed on the cable car. Dangerous for other passengers? Hygiene? 'We're not allowed,' he said.

'I don't mind,' Javi said. '3,500 metres, you can hardly breathe up there, surely?'

'We can do a circuit here. This is already 2,400 anyway.'

'Really?'

Pepe sniffed a miniature schnauzer. 'Is that a male?' the small woman holding its lead asked.

'Yes,' said Carlos.

She dragged the schnauzer away before Carlos had time to tell her his dog was castrated.

They walked out of the car park. It was windy up here, and at least five degrees colder than at La Laguna. The path in front of them was punctuated with small tufts of people. Javi pulled a tennis ball out of his coat pocket and threw it. Pepe raced after it. They walked like that for a while: Carlos taking it easy, Javi throwing the ball, Pepe fetching it. There were moments when they couldn't see anyone else, and Carlos remembered those times dozens of years ago when he felt like he was walking on Mars or the moon. He watched his youngest employee, his dog, and the bright-yellow tennis ball. He raised a hand to some kids in a cable car who were waving at them frantically. He thought about things.

'Quick smoke?' he asked.

They used a boulder as a windbreak, and Javi lit one up too.

'I find that so impressive of you,' Carlos said.

'What?'

'You smoking a cigarette with me now, probably to be friendly, and then not smoking at all for however long. I started once because a … well, you could say a girlfriend of mine smoked, and I've been smoking ever since.'

'Yeah,' says Javi wisely.

'Look …' Carlos said, 'now we've stopped for a moment …'

'Yes?'

'I'm not the youngest anymore—'

'No,' Javi said.

'What do you mean, no?'

'Hairdressers don't retire, and I don't want to think about it yet.'

'But you've already thought about it, otherwise you wouldn't have interrupted me.'

Javi looked at him. 'I'm sorry, that was rude of me, but I mean it. How can I decide what I want now? Where I'll be ten years from now? How long have I been here anyway, fifteen months?' He blew out the smoke, spat, threw the cigarette down, and twisted it into the dusty ground with the toe of his fluorescent sports shoe. 'Can we talk about it some other time?'

'Sure. If you like.'

'And why not Nilda or Conchita?'

'They have husbands, children. They've got jobs, they go to work somewhere.'

Javi looked back at him. 'And I don't have any of that. And I'm a hairdresser.'

It was all taking too long for Pepe, who started whimpering.

'Maybe I'll want to go to Barcelona one day.'

'Out into the world.'

'Something like that. All right, Pepe, give me the ball.'

They walked back in the same constellation. As they approached the car park, Javi turned and tossed the tennis ball back in the other direction. 'Wait!' he shouted, and started running towards the car. Carlos put his foot on the ball and watched him. He was throwing up a trail of dust. Pepe jumped up against him.

'What's got into *him* all of a sudden?' he asked the dog. Calmly he followed Javi, kicking the tennis ball along in front of him. Bending was getting more and more difficult.

When he arrived at the car park he saw a group of cyclists riding off, followed by a car in the same colours as their black-and-yellow jerseys. Javi was coming back towards him, looking like a bunch of schoolkids had just sung his number on TV during El Gordo. 'Look at this!' he shouted, waving a piece of paper. Carlos took it. It was a kind of postcard with a picture of Primož Roglič, a young guy with a remarkably pointy nose, black hair, and dark-green eyes. He turned it over: FOR JAVI, WHO SAYS HE IS A BIG FAN OF MINE.

'Primož Roglič's signature, ¡qué guay!' Pepe was jumping around him like a wild thing, as if he'd worked out there was something to be enthusiastic about.

It was only after a second glass of beer in the cafeteria that Javi calmed down a little. 'Primož Roglič,' he whispered, staring into space while fingering the postcard. 'Maybe he'll win the Tour this year.'

It's a Thursday. The back door is open to let a breeze blow through the salon. Pepe is lying outside on the pavement with his head in the doorway, because he likes to keep tabs on what's happening inside. Javi said earlier in the day that they really could do with some air conditioning, whereupon Conchita said that she'd heard that it only made people sick, all those sudden swings of temperature. And 'Plus it's not forty degrees here like in Madrid.' During the coffee break, Nilda asks Javi if he's not lonely. When someone says something, it's with their mouth full: Conchita's baked an almond cake for the birth of her first grandchild. Pepe walks from plate to plate.

'Lonely? I've got you, haven't I?'

'Ha-ha,' says Nilda.

'No, really, Nilda. I've got Grindr.'

'What have you got?'

'Grindr. A dating app.'

'I hear what you're saying, I just don't know what it is.'

'It's very simple. Everyone who has that app can see where potential dates are.'

'Yeah?' Nilda almost chokes on a mouthful of cake. Conchita hasn't added enough butter.

'Imagine I turn it on now. Then I can see if somebody's walking down the street or sitting in the bar around the corner.'

'Somebody.'

'Yes, a potential date.'

'A man.'

'Yes, otherwise you have to go on Tinder.'

'Tinder?'

'Look,' Javi says, 'I'll show you.'

'Nilda …' Carlos warns her.

'Why? He started talking about it himself?'

Javi pulls out his iPhone 11 Pro, opens Grindr, and turns the screen towards Nilda.

'No, no, no, I don't want to see things like that at all,' Nilda shouts, clapping a hand over her eyes.

'Guys,' Carlos says. 'Customers.'

It's still Thursday. Ten minutes later. Conchita, Nilda, and Carlos are all busy with a customer. In general, Peluquería Carlos W. works by appointment. Conchita is dyeing, Nilda is putting in curlers, and Carlos is shaving a somewhat older man. The spot next to Nilda — the chair by the window, opposite Carlos's mirror — is still free. Javi is washing the plates and coffee cups; Pepe looks on expectantly. The front and back doors are still open, and nobody is complaining about the draught. The tree across from the salon is blossoming as if it doesn't care that Pablo pissed on it every day for years.

'But' — despite her customer, Nilda can't restrain her curiosity — 'what kind of photo do you have?'

'Nothing special,' Javi says. 'Head and shoulders.'

'Thank goodness.'

'¿Qué?' asks Nilda's customer.

'Nada,' says Nilda.

A woman comes in wearing a colourful dress that is much too young for her. She has a hairstyle that should be short and snappy but won't really be short and snappy until later, after Javi has cut it. 'Buenos días,' she says. Conchita looks over her shoulder for a moment and answers her greeting. Carlos catches a glimpse of her in his mirror. Javi puts the last coffee cup away and walks over to the woman. He gestures towards the chair in front of the window. As Carlos puts the razor back on his customer's throat, he remembers — where has this come from? — the arrogant dredger who strode in with long, confident steps and announced in Dutch, 'You're the one I'm looking for!' A guy from Bodegraven, that too comes to mind. He'd thought from the woman's good morning that she might be Dutch, and now he's listening to her instructions for Javi, he's sure of it. Her Spanish is reasonable and, just like him, once, she's learnt to say *Cómo se dice* if she's at a loss for a moment, and via the two mirrors he sees that she also has a hand movement to go with it.

'Are you paying attention?' asks his customer, a man called Pasquale. He's not Carlos's favourite customer.

'Absolutely. Do you have a different impression?'

'You seem a little distracted.'

'Don't worry, I won't cut your throat.'
'No, that's the last thing I need.'

Now and then, when Javi and Carlos step aside in opposite directions, he catches the woman's eye. Briefly. He turns away and she turns away. Pasquale has closed his eyes, pretending he's not here. In the meantime, the memory of the dredger from Bodegraven has brought back the feeling he had then too. Apprehension. The fear of being caught out, but, both then and now, caught out at what? It's not as if he's done anything wrong. He hasn't murdered anyone. The woman tells Javi that she and her boyfriend are staying in holiday homes that belong to Brits. That her boyfriend does renovations for them. And that she has a different hairdresser almost every month. She doesn't have a loud voice. The colourful, overly youthful dress doesn't mean she's vulgar. He's finished with Pasquale, who, without any sign of being satisfied, runs a hand over his beard and pulls his wallet out of his back pocket. He extracts the exact amount and hands the notes to Carlos.

'Thanks again,' he says.

'You're welcome,' Carlos replies.

Pepe barks at him. Pepe has an impeccable sense of which customers to bark at.

Carlos walks over to the cash register and puts the money in it. He thinks for a moment. He looks at the clock. He still has the taste of almond in his mouth. In a few minutes his next customer will arrive. He ponders and sighs. It's buzzing in the salon. Conchita, Nilda, Javi, and the clientele are exchanging hairdressing chat. And then he sits down on the chair Pasquale just left — the seat is still warm, and the armrest feels almost damp. He looks at himself in the mirror. He rotates the chair a half-turn by pushing off on the floor with his feet and can now look at the woman through one less mirror. She looks back at him. 'That W,' she says in Dutch. 'Is that for Weiman perhaps?' It could sound like an accusation, but the question comes with disbelief, almost bewilderment.

'¿Qué?' Javi asks.

'Sorry, son, I'm not talking to you,' the woman says.

'Henny,' Carlos says. 'I …' Yes, what actually? He is suddenly extremely tired, the bitterness of the taste of almond is increasing.

Everyone has fallen silent. Conchita looks to the side, Nilda has turned, and Javi is staring at Henny. Even the woman under the dryer and the woman with silver foil in her hair — who has been talking constantly — are now holding their tongues. 'What's going on?' asks Javi.

'The woman whose hair you're cutting is called Henny,' Carlos says. 'I know her from before.'

'The man behind me is called Cornelis,' Henny tells Javi, while watching Carlos in the mirror. 'He's dead.' *Está muerto.* She's even got the O right.

Pepe, who has gone back to lie out the front again, barks at a passer-by in the otherwise silent street. It sounds hollow, as if Pepe is barking at no one in particular.

And still it is Thursday. Cornelis is stretched out on his couch. Pepe is lying on top of him. 'We don't live in Greenland, of course,' he tells the dog. 'Or the Kalahari.' Pepe groans. All of a sudden he knows so much. It's like the last forty years have homed in on him like a whizz-bang, whistling and all, to explode at his feet. Simon, his son is called. His father's still alive. Anja never remarried. Simon. Who's taken over the shop. Three generations of hairdresser, or four or five really, because Jan's father was one too, but he's forgotten how it went before that. He's buried under a kind of millstone in a cemetery in the west of Amsterdam, 'the nastiest cemetery you can imagine,' Henny had said. 'I wouldn't be seen dead there. But,' Henny babbled on as if she was drinking a glass of wine with a girlfriend she hadn't seen for a couple of weeks, 'you're not really buried there, because your name's not listed anywhere.' Is that because she's an Amsterdammer? he wonders. These wry, deadpan jokes?

What was I thinking all these years? he thinks while stroking Pepe's sandy, wiry coat. Not Patagonia, not the Gobi Desert, but Tenerife. How many Dutch people come to the Canary Islands every year? How was this able to go on like this for so many years? Well, hardly anyone who comes here on holiday goes to the hairdresser. They go to bars and cafés, to restaurants, to the beach, to shops when their swimming costume splits. But they also go to El Teide. Yes, Henny had babbled on, but she'd also cried and looked at him as if he was a ghost. The babbling was undoubtedly a reaction. He didn't remember her as the kind of person who never stops talking. 'I don't know anymore, Pepito,' he says. Pepe groans with contentment. It's all the same to him, and tonight's better than usual, because it's not that often his master lies down on the couch. 'Do I have to think about whether I want to see Simon now?' But that boy, that man, doesn't mean anything to me, he thinks. He was a tadpole when I left, an invisible little tadpole. Cornelis has been drinking, and not holding back either. No, Pepe's coat is not wiry at all. It's only wiry if you rub it the wrong way. In the right direction it's soft and warm. He presses his nose against the dog's neck. Pepe starts to growl and bares his teeth. 'Why, Pepe? Tell me why you do that? What's the matter? It's me.' He reaches out to the coffee table, which has a glass of whisky on it. The movement calms the dog, maybe because he thinks it's over now. But if so, *what* is over? he thinks as he takes a big sip. Does he feel threatened by me? 'Why?' he asks. Pepe growls. But the idiotic animal doesn't budge, he doesn't make any attempt to extricate himself from his master's grip, so it can't be that bad. 'What now?' Henny had asked when she was saying goodbye as she, despite telephone contact in the meantime, urgently needed to get back to a man called Ko, 'because before you know it,' she said, 'he'll start thinking I've bumped into someone.'

Somehow Cornelis has never been able to really imagine that — how far is it? Three thousand kilometres away? — there are people, people he knows, knows well in fact, like his father, who are alive and doing things. *Able?* Willing? Brave enough? No, he doesn't want to think about it anymore. Did he just want to get away for a week forty years ago, or was it a springboard? Would — come on, what was that guy's name again? — Jacob … that's it … have flown home alone, no matter what? He doesn't know anymore. Tomorrow is Friday, the planner is fairly full. Conchita's got the day off; Nilda, Javi, and he will be busy all day. And the looks that Javi and Nilda will give him tomorrow morning. 'Hush now, Pepe,' he says. 'Do we need to go to the veterinario tomorrow? Do you want an injection?' The dog curls his lips back even further. The tip of his tongue appears, quivering and all. Cornelis is sick of it, he brushes the dog off his body. 'Get!' he says. Pepe lands on his feet and walks over to his cushion as if he's just come in from outside, as if he's just been for a long walk, fetching a tennis ball a hundred times. Cornelis is never really angry with the dog, there must be something causing that growling. It's not aggression. There's something bothering him, something he can't do anything about, and that's why Cornelis only ever feels sorry for Pepe. He sits up and looks out of the window, which is fairly pointless because it's pitch-black out there, although there is a light on in a window across the road. He takes another sip of whisky. 'I don't know either,' he'd told Henny. 'First, nothing at all.' When she didn't reply, he asked, 'OK?' She started crying again and then she said, 'OK.' Pepe stands up again. And now what often happens happens. The dog acts like there hasn't been any kind of disruption at all, and comes over to the couch. He raises a paw and scratches Cornelis's knee. Cornelis lifts him up with one hand holding him by the scruff of the neck and the other under his chest, and puts him on the couch, where the dog does a little circle, then rolls up. When Cornelis scratches him behind the ears, he groans with contentment again. Jacob, yes, that was the guy's name. Cobby even, that was what he told Cornelis in business class, and that he didn't mind it at all when his parents or brother or sister called him that.

Yes, Pepe is a strange dog. Probably his last one. In any case, the dog he'll spend the most time with, simply because the people have fallen to the wayside. He tries to imagine the salon without a dog, and in the process he sees alternatively, or successively, Lobo, Oro, Pablo, and Pepe too lying in front of the door, then nothing for a moment, just sand blowing over the empty pavement on one of those cold winds that can rise up out of nowhere in early spring. The image makes him shudder. Don't think about it. Pepe will last a while yet. No point worrying about the future. Another sip of whisky. 'Hey, Pepe,' he says. The dog bares his teeth. Cornelis lowers himself back down again and closes his eyes. First, nothing at all, he thinks.